Acclaim
Transgender Erotica. Trans Figures

"Transgender people have been seen for too long as people without a sexuality, as if their status as transgender has separated them forever from the world of intimacy and passion. This book dispels that myth, revealing transexuality as fervently passionate and transbodies as delightfully compelling.

The voices of both transmen and transwomen are evident in this book, though after reading a few stories you will forget all about the binary of sexes and revel instead in this enchanted world where bodies are a mystery to be explored, and where one sometimes, often, finds more than one expected.

Transgender Erotica does what all erotic books should do—offers the reader pleasure in a yet unchartered world. It also dispels a myth and uncovers a little known secret: trans people are HOT, not despite their different bodies, but rather because of them. Having traveled a long distance to create a body that feels right to live in, trans people are masters in knowing how to pleasure those bodies, and in this book, they share exactly how they do that."

—Arlene Istar Lev, LCSW
Author of *Transgender Emergence*
and *The Complete Lesbian and Gay Parenting Guide;*
Board Member of the Family Pride Coalition

"Over the past few years, the world of book publishing has come a long way in its nonsensational recognition of the transsexual, the transgendered, and the intersexed. Through literary novels like Jeffrey Eugenides' Pulitzer Prize–winning *Middlesex* and T Cooper's *Some of the Parts,* and lovely, entertaining memoirs such as Jennifer Finney Boylan's *She's Not There,* mainstream readers have begun to be exposed to the fact that *trans* can also stand for transcendent, that we can find emotional connections with folks who have historically been alienated from society. *Trans Figures* now daringly invites us to make erotic connections as well, an invitation that this rich and imaginative anthology makes well worth accepting."

—Jim Gladstone
Editor of *SKIN & INK: Gay Men's Erotica;*
Author of *The Big Book of Misunderstanding*

"Kudos to M. Christian for conceiving, and Haworth Press for publishing, this expansive, passionate, incisive, and—yes—*important* marriage of short fiction and non. To strictly categorize *Transgender Erotica: Trans Figures* as erotica, however, would be a disservice to its intent. For if knowledge equates power, then this collection most assuredly empowers. You want specifics? You got 'em! Are specifics necessary? Absolutely, considering that the collection's numerous sexually explicit passages are among its most revelatory, if better understanding our species is a goal worth striving toward.

In smashing the binary perception of sexuality our God-fearing society so reverentially clings to, *Trans Figures'* twenty-four brave contributors, deftly coaxed by M. Christian's editorial baton, utilize sex to illuminate the multifarious variables that comprise the long-overdue redefinition of gender, and in so doing, clarify, once and for all, the discrepancy between the two.

I am not only a more informed (albeit militant) human being, having read *Transgender Erotica: Trans Figures,* but a more compassionate one as well."

—Michael Huxley
Editorial Director of STARbooks Press;
Editor of *Wet Nightmares, Wet Dreams*

"It doesn't matter if your personal bits are original, factory rebuilt, or in progress, this book will touch you. *Transgender Erotica: Trans Figures,* edited by the inestimable M. Christian, is, first and foremost, a book about people in transition. Unsatisfied and unhappy for a variety of reasons, mental and physical, they strive to change themselves and the perceptions of those around them until reality matches desire. And, because everyone in this book is also human, the results are endlessly fascinating.

You'll read about full-blown changes and casual crossing, elegance and brutality, long-term commitments and one-night stands, love and sex and death and friendship. You'll read about men and women and everything in between, including those for whom any gender at all is needlessly restrictive. And you'll recognize more of yourself here than you might expect."

—Chris Bridges
HootIsland.com

"It's one thing to desire both genders, but quite another to be both. *Transgender Erotica* accomplishes what no textbook, talk show, or documentary ever could: with astounding maturity, it explores the confusion and elucidates the clarity that transgendered people feel. These writers show us how lust morphs and blossoms as sexual boundaries disintegrate. You cannot possibly read this book without learning something about sexual identity, longing, and self-respect."

—Sage Vivant
Owner, Custom Erotica Source;
Co-editor of *The Best of Both Worlds: Bisexual Erotica*

"Transgender is an unpredictable category, an almost inexplicable state of being that encompasses the simultaneous attraction and mystery of the unknown. This collection of stories gives some trans authors their own unique erotic voice, and also lets non-trans authors tell us what they find erotic about transgendered people. From the irresistible inconsistencies of Coven, Kaldera, and St. Aubin, to Califia's crossing multiple boundaries with permission, to Jones', Williams', and Wharton's various explorations of forbidden territories, and Sheppard's hot intellectualizing, this collection surely has something for everyone. Roche's 'The Waters of Al Adra' and Dean's 'Tango' in particular are enticing and surprising. Levin's 'Shoes' is a wonderful expression of compulsion. Each contributor brings us his or her own sense of urgency, inviting each reader to connect with a previously unimaginable new reality."

—Jamison Green, MFA
Author of *Becoming a Visible Man*

Transgender Erotica
Trans Figures

HARRINGTON PARK PRESS®
Southern Tier Editions™
Gay Men's Fiction

The Man Pilot by James W. Ridout IV

Shadows of the Night: Queer Tales of the Uncanny and Unusual edited by Greg Herren

Van Allen's Ecstasy by Jim Tushinski

Beyond the Wind by Rob N. Hood

The Handsomest Man in the World by David Leddick

The Song of a Manchild by Durrell Owens

The Ice Sculptures: A Novel of Hollywood by Michael D. Craig

Between the Palms: A Collection of Gay Travel Erotica edited by Michael T. Luongo

Aura by Gary Glickman

Love Under Foot: An Erotic Celebration of Feet edited by Greg Wharton
and M. Christian

The Tenth Man by E. William Podojil

Upon a Midnight Clear: Queer Christmas Tales edited by Greg Herren

Dryland's End by Felice Picano

Whose Eye Is on Which Sparrow? by Robert Taylor

Deep Water: A Sailor's Passage by E. M. Kahn

The Boys in the Brownstone by Kevin Scott

The Best of Both Worlds: Bisexual Erotica edited by Sage Vivant and M. Christian

Tales From the Levee by Martha Miller

Some Dance to Remember: A Memoir-Novel of San Francisco, 1970-1982 by Jack Fritscher

Confessions of a Male Nurse by Richard S. Ferri

The Millionaire of Love by David Leddick

Transgender Erotica: Trans Figures edited by M. Christian

Skip Macalester by J. E. Robinson

Chemistry by Lewis DeSimone

Friends, Lovers, and Roses by Vernon Clay

Beyond Machu by William Maltese

Virginia Bedfellows by Gavin Morris

Independent Queer Cinema: Reviews and Interviews by Gary M. Kramer

Planting Eli by Jeff Black

Seventy Times Seven by Salvatore Sapienza

Going Down in La-La Land by Andy Zeffer

Transgender Erotica
Trans Figures

M. Christian
Editor

Southern Tier Editions™
Harrington Park Press®
An Imprint of The Haworth Press, Inc.
New York • London • Oxford

For more information on this book or to order, visit
http://www.haworthpress.com/store/product.asp?sku=5508

or call 1-800-HAWORTH (800-429-6784) in the United States and Canada
or (607) 722-5857 outside the United States and Canada

or contact orders@HaworthPress.com

Published by

Southern Tier Editions™, Harrington Park Press®, an imprint of The Haworth Press, Inc.,
10 Alice Street, Binghamton, NY 13904-1580.

PUBLISHER'S NOTE
The development, preparation, and publication of this work has been undertaken with great care.
However, the Publisher, employees, editors, and agents of The Haworth Press are not responsible
for any errors contained herein or for consequences that may ensue from use of materials or information contained in this work. The Haworth Press is committed to the dissemination of ideas and
information according to the highest standards of intellectual freedom and the free exchange of
ideas. Statements made and opinions expressed in this publication do not necessarily reflect the
views of the Publisher, Directors, management, or staff of The Haworth Press, Inc., or an
endorsement by them.

This is a work of fiction. Names, characters, places, and incidents either are the products of the
author's imagination or are used fictitiously, and any resemblance to actual persons, living or
dead, business establishments, events, or locales is entirely coincidental.

Copyright acknowledgments can be found on page 245.

Cover design by Jennifer M. Gaska.

Library of Congress Cataloging-in-Publication Data

Transgender erotica : trans figures / M. Christian, editor.
        p. cm.
    ISBN-13: 978-1-56023-491-3 (pbk. : alk. paper)
    ISBN-10: 1-56023-491-1 (pbk. : alk. paper)
    1. Erotic stories, American. 2. Transsexuals—Fiction. 3. Transsexuals. I. Christian, M.
(Muncy)

PS648.E7T73 2005
813'.01083538'0866—dc22

                                                                                2005015847

This is for all of us:
men, women, both, and/or neither—
and those we love.

CONTENTS

Preface

I may have had more than an average person's experience with friends who've revealed themselves, caterpillar to butterfly, as what they knew they were, not what gender they happened to be born with; all those Roberts now Renees, Justins now Juliettes. Some look in the mirror and do not see themselves or, in the case of other friends, alter their beings for a night, and with a pair of heels and hose become the belle of the ball, or with a flannel shirt and a pair of jeans become the stud among the muffins.

That's where this book comes in. It will hopefully shed light on what it must be like to be the flesh of one sex, the mind of another; spend every day knowing that you and your body don't belong together, that a major part of your life is simply *wrong*.

The goal of this book is to help readers understand the pain as well as the allure of being transgendered. It will explain and communicate, through the language of eroticism, what being transgendered and/or transsexual are like.

Some of the stories are of frustration, flesh not reflecting soul, and others are transformative, surgery or simply fashion, making flesh reflect soul. Others are different. Some stories relate that male and female are not the only options, that gender is in the mind, and that the body can be anything we want it to be. Male? Female? Their gender is all, or a blank slate waiting to be painted, or just *trans*.

I applaud these writers, not just because they know how to put one word in front of another, but because they have exposed themselves, played with gender and sex, identity and orientation, and shown that gender isn't written in flesh. With excitement and revelation, these writers have demonstrated that we can become what we want to be.

Defying Normal
Raven Kaldera

I always wanted a same-sex relationship. It just took me some time to figure out what sex I was.

I'm on top of him, my body pressing him down. I always worry that I'm going to crush him, skinny as he is, even though he's taller than me. He reassures me that he likes it, though, that he likes my big furry belly, my layers of burly muscle and fat. I didn't come out to be the man I'd secretly wanted to be—less like a squat bearded biker and more like an action figure—but it doesn't matter. I look in the mirror and I see myself, more than ever before.

He's wriggling under me, his pierced tongue clicking against my teeth as I suck it into my mouth. I grab the piercing with my incisors, growl and worry it like a puppy, then let it go as he gasps and bucks against me. His tongue retreats momentarily into his mouth, and then he thrusts it back to me, half trustingly, half challengingly. I suck on it like a cock with a really big ampallang. I want to suck his other cock, lower down, but right now we're still wrestling with mouths and teeth.

He's boy to my man physically—his beard is just a fringe along his jaw, his body hair is softer and lighter, just a brown-gold haze along his belly and chest. It rubs against my sweat-matted pelt, the sort of way-too-much hairiness that has so many guys waxing their chests so that straight women and fagboys won't see them as too animal look-ing. I've worked too hard to get this pelt to ever do anything like that. I straddle him, feeling his pubic mound press up between the cheeks of my ass. Some positions, it's hard to tell who's got the advantage, who's going to end up fucking who. His fur rubs against mine, tangles together, creates friction. No woman could ever know what it's like when two moustaches tangle together, two flat hairy chests grind against each other, a closer embrace than anyone with breasts to get in the way could ever possibly know.

No man could ever understand what it's like to put a hand down between your boyfriend's legs and stick your fingers into his hot wet cunt, and feel his hand similarly searching its way into yours. It's a subtle competition; one of us is going to have to let go and roll over, to give in to the white noise building up in our cocks. I think this time it's going to be me. Almost reluctantly I pull out of him and arch up, giving him more leeway into me. Two fingers, then three, then four, then he's in past the knuckles and out from under me, and I'm screaming my way through a driving fuck. His hands are tiny, with long skinny fingers, a legacy of when he was a girl. My cunt is tighter than his, even though I've given birth, but it was twenty years ago and I didn't let too many single-gendered people fuck me very often.

The shrinks who are our gatekeepers traditionally encouraged us to avoid dating each other, because having a lover who was a "real" man or woman was the ultimate test of your own "realness." We're members of the only sexual minority that isn't supposed to look for partners in our own demographic. We're supposed to pretend that we're just like everyone else.

Somehow this never made sense to me. It's not just the joy of not having to explain yourself, your gender, your anomalies, your pain to some clueless person who will never really understand. It's also that I've just always been hot for trans bodies—their smell, their multitude of shapes, their smorgasbord of male and female cues. I'm as much a tranny chaser as I am a tranny. They are my kind, my people, my species, and something deep in my brain knows it. Having sex with men or women is rather like doing it with aliens . . . fun and exotic, but requiring costly and problematic translators, and you never know when some local custom will offend them.

Allow me to sing a hymn, a paean, a madrigal of lust for trannyboy genitalia. Let me sing it with my hands and my mouth and anything else I can get hold of. Gay male porn seems to be filled with praises sung to cock and balls, counting every blue vein in the shaft, and lots of leaping and thrusting. Lesbian porn is flooded with poetic references to "delicate folds" and "pink caves" and "tender buds," and metaphors of fruit and oceans. It's about time somebody said something pretty cool about our equipment, because we need to hear it bad. We need to hear how good we really are, because we so often have a hard time believing it of ourselves.

Let me praise the cunt swollen and flushed with testosterone, its clit chemically grown into that perfect thumb-sized phallus with its foreskin that blends so beautifully into those winglike inner labia. Let me tell you how your eyes are riveted to it, how it seems to dwarf the cunt that it crowns. Let me wax rapturous about how perfectly that cock fits into your mouth, how it seems made for sucking on, how its length and girth grows as you pull it further in. Inch, inch and a quarter, inch and a half, and then its head is nestled perfectly into the hollow spot in the roof of your palate while your lips and tongue work on its shaft with lazy, minute motions . . . and the trannyboy attached to it rolls his eyes back into his head and moans.

Let me talk about having your pick of holes to slide your fingers into while you suck that cock—the wet cunt or the tight asshole cradled between furred cheeks. Let me talk about fucking each other roughly in both or either holes, because we gave up gentle when we left female. Our hands are men's hands, hair crawled up the backs and blue veins standing out on the corded muscle, and we fuck each other like we were using a punching bag, because we're not interested in gentle. We're interested in impact.

Sometimes we bleed, after a particularly rough fuck, because the chemical counteraction of estrogen has made our cunts more fragile, like a postmenopausal woman, but it's an entirely different thing than when we were living as women and we bled every month. Then it was a brutally painful reminder of organs we wished we didn't have. Now it's a scarlet badge of pride in endurance and toughness, like the scrapes that boys show off after roughhousing. Little girls rarely masturbate themselves raw and bloody, but nearly every boy that I slept with admitted to it at least once. There's something about the testosterone experience that makes you want to push your flesh sexually, to see how far it will go. I notice that the majority of the heavy players in the body modification community, the ones who do drastic things and proudly display the photos on the Internet, they're men. There's a reason for that.

Let me talk about the smell of mancunt . . . less fishy than womancunt, more meaty smelling, with an odd hint of something vaguely resembling chlorine bleach. No better or worse than girlcunt, just entirely different. Let me talk about the way I feel when I realize that this person smells like me, feels like me, and knows exactly what it felt like for me to get the way that I am. For years I wondered about all the things that gay men and lesbians said about how wonderful and validating it was to be with someone of the same sex . . . because it didn't feel that way to me with women, and now after transition it doesn't feel that way with men. It wasn't until I climbed into bed with another FTM that I understood that awesome feeling of mirrored-self, mirrored-body, of deep physical understanding.

The problem isn't who you're having sex with. It's the worship of that terrible, cold, hard God named Normal. He is a jealous god who will try to prevent you from having any individuality at all. Normal tells you that this is the way X or Y is supposed to be, and anything else must be destroyed or changed to fit the mold. Normal says that all men have penises between five and twelve inches long, with closed scrotums and two testicles apiece. Normal says that fag sex happens between two men who are both similarly equipped in this way. Normal says that if there is a phallus larger than two inches in the room with a cunt, and they're on two different bodies, the one with the cunt is the girl, and the one with the phallus is the boy, and the phallus should be somehow fitted into the cunt regardless of what the two individuals holding that anatomy would like.

(Normal has only one thing to say about those bodies with both phalluses and cunts: Kill it.)

But in our bed, Normal has no place. We don't even let him over the door of our threshold. When he shows up at the end of the driveway, we get the shotgun and drive him off. In our bed, it isn't even that one or both of the fags have cunts, but we love them anyway in spite of their shortcomings. It's that, in our bed, Fags Have Cunts. (And the lady of the house has bodacious tits and a Really Big Clit.)

In the arms of my transgendered lovers, I have found sanctuary . . . not from the terrible pain of body dysphoria, which never permanently leaves us, but from the scourge of Normal. In the arms of my own kind, I've learned that my body is really desirable. I've learned it by desiring them, wholeheartedly and without reservation.

Of course, once you've created your own definition of normal, other people's definitions start to seem pretty strange. My boyfriend and I have both agreed sheepishly that after years of sucking transman diclit, ordinary girl genitalia can be a bit of a shock. One's first thought is, "Where's the cock?" The second one is, "Oh yeah, there's a clit in there someplace. I'd better go look for it." To have to hunt for the erogenous point is something we've forgotten how to do; we're spoiled by the erect fingerlike shaft thrusting forward, begging to be grabbed and stroked. Girlcunt is jarring to us, and it takes a while to get used to it again. We guiltily admit to each other that at first glance, it seems somehow underdeveloped, immature; like the hairless bodies that have yet to sprout fur, the thin arms that don't yet ripple with muscle.

It's especially difficult to refrain from having that pattern set into your brain when you've loved a trannyboy through transition. It's a different situation from a bisexual who simply looks at a female body after coming from a male body and is slightly jarred by the differences, or vice versa in the opposite direction. Loving a body while it slowly shapeshifts is the kind of spiritual privilege that few people have in this lifetime. Watching the fat distribute from hips to belly, the ass flatten out, the narrow waist fill in with sheets of muscle, the biceps and deltoids slowly rise, the shoulders broadening, the neck thickening and the voice deepening, the hair sprouting (if you're dealing with someone whose genetics allow it), and the smell of their sweat changing to male . . . these things fool your brain into believing that it's normal for a female-bodied person to mature into a male-bodied one. (And vice versa, of course.) You'll never look at a girl-body again without idly imagining in your mind what she'd look like if she went through that slow, bumpy metamorphosis.

I have a button that I like to wear in public, just for the looks that I get. I invented it. It says, "I'm cross-dressing you with my eyes." People need to be shaken up in that way. It's good for them.

Of course, it's beautiful in a different way to love a body through the opposite transformation. The path from male to female is harder on the body, more like a jolting ride over a bumpy path than the turbojet blast of testosterone. Estrogen is more delicate, more subtle, less of a match for the formerly testosterone-stained flesh. Still, the changes come . . . the silky-soft skin, softer even than a biogirl, is the one I notice first and most. The scent lightens, maybe even vanishes entirely. The breasts grow, the nipples become larger and more responsive. Playing with them often gets you a chance to see that open-mouthed, gasping, wide-eyed, entirely feminine response of surrender, complete with starfishing limbs and tossing hair.

Then there's the day that you find yourself lying on top of her, and suddenly you want more than anything to just knock her up, shoot your seed into her as if she was the fertile ground. You tell her, and you find out that she wants the same thing . . . to spread herself wide and have you fill her with babies . . . and you both have to shove those misprogrammed atavistic instincts back into the dark corners of your brain, because it's never going to happen, for either of you, even if some piece of your wiring is convinced that it could work, somehow, if you both just tried hard enough. . .

As more and more of us decide that the ban on dating our own kind is ridiculous, the percentage of FTM/MTF couples (generally referred to as "reverse couples" or "cross couples" in transgender circles) grows every year. We're told that it's straight, but it feels pretty queer to my wife and myself. The only dark side to this coupling is the issue of libido. MTFs all report a definite drop in libido from the high doses of estrogen used to counter their native testosterone, and then usually another drop when the source of that testosterone is surgically removed. Some drop so far that they become nearly sexless except for that awfully feminine reason for having sex: intimacy and bonding with your partner. At the same time, FTMs find their sex drives skyrocketing, and sex becoming less and less about love and more about just scratching the itch before it drives you mad.

Maybe I'm just projecting that this is a uniquely cross-couple phenomenon. Maybe it's integral to the basic energy of all heterosexual relationships. Maybe this disparity is just what happens when you push hormone levels in opposite directions as far as they'll go. Whatever it means, I thank all the gods that we're polyamorous, or I'd be climbing the walls.

Let me sing of the euphoria of lying between your two very different lovers at night, reaching a hand out in each direction and touching silky skin and long hair, touching furry butt and lean, muscled leg. Running your hand up to the smooth chest with small breasts and nipples, touching the furred pecs with their large nipples pegged through with piercings. Sliding up further, to the electrolysis-smooth throat with the Adam's apple, and the bearded one without it. Sliding your hands down, then . . . all the way down . . . this is far beyond bisexuality. This is a place where the lines blur and become irrelevant. Roll one way into the touch of delicious opposition, roll the other way into the arms of the mirror . . . and then touch myself and know, beyond a shadow of a doubt, that in this country the duality has become meaningless.

Sex, in the country with no dualities, has few gender roles. So does house-work, and everything else you can think of; in our house, people do what jobs they're good at, and split the rest evenly, and there are no gendered assumptions about who does what. There is no struggling about that, either; without clearly socialized gender, those assumptions all trickle away like dirty bathwater. In a way, it's the early feminist goals made manifest, strangely enough . . . a place where each person is valued not for the configuration of his or her body but for the utility of his or her mind. Unlike merely same-sex space, where unques-tioned early gender socialization may unconsciously permeate the entire atmo-sphere, third-gender space mixes and matches those programmings in ways that don't divide people into two distinct groups. It's still a terrible irony to me that we are such pariahs in the feminist community, when we have managed to cre-ate, at least in our small fishbowls, what they have still failed to manifest. Yes, it's at a steep cost, but surely there's something to be learned from our creation?

We may play with gender roles during sex, though, because they turn us on. There's power in those roles, especially the ones that are the closest to the extreme biological sexual responses, the monkey responses. There's heat in those arche-types, those stereotypes. Their cultural permeability means that they can stir sexual responses in us as well, used in the right way and the right combination. The difference is that we choose to use them, and we discard them as soon as we get up and go to the kitchen for a sandwich. Sometimes we may even swap them back and forth. Pass the strap-on and spread your legs. Oh, honey, give it to me. Take it, slut. By fucking this way, we expose them for the sex toys that they actually are.

That's right, you heard it, the sex toys that they actually are. We've discov-ered the dirty little secret that underlies the entire monstrosity of sexism, the an-swer that everyone is looking for and no one dares to actually see. It must have happened a long time ago in our species, when we lost the trusty estrus system that fuels the mating habits of all our closest relatives. The gentle waves of the ocean took that from us, and left us with . . . what? What's there to stimulate the cock to rise, the cunt to open? What's there to make sure that the human race goes on? Somehow, we learned to fetishize gender differences, and the more dif-ferent the genders were perceived to be, the more the fetish worked. The cultural cues as to what was masculine or feminine might change from culture to culture, but the base fetish remained . . . the sexes being as different, as oppositionally opposed, as possible. Sexism was what kept us procreating when we lost those chemical triggers. That's right, heterosexuality is just a fetish, like rubber or bootlicking or trashy lingerie. It's just the majority fetish.

That's why it's so hard to eradicate, of course. When every heterosexual un-consciously fears (knows?) that a society with no gender roles is a society where they may never get hard or wet again, or at least where they'll have to work a lot harder mentally to find their fetish, something deep and primal in their brains rebels. To eradicate sexism and gender roles, we have to work against the libido, and that's a tough one. Working against the cock-mind, the cunt-mind, that almost never works. We have to figure out how to accomodate the heterosexual fetish in all of this, or it will never work. And that means being honest about it.

There's something critically important about showing mixed-gender people as sexually attractive in a way that isn't simply freakish or exotic. It's a necessity that I can't stress enough, making us a normal alternative to how human bodies are configured . . . and that's not just because it will get us laid more often. To have acknowledged beauty in mixed gender cues, even when it's not someone's sexual preference, softens the hard edges of the rigidly divided heterosexual gaze. It also trains their eyes, used to being immersed in a permeating sea of their fetish, to look for the right cues to turn them on in the mixture. Queers are used to searching for their fetish, and they know that even if the process is a struggle, it does work in the end. Straight people are used to being lazy about it, and they need to learn to work for it, and be reassured that it will still be effective. It'll do them good. It'll do the transgendered community some good as well.

Of course, this is also the community where "admirer" is a dirty word. It conjures up clueless drooling fetishizers who want "chicks with dicks," who want to fuck you in ways that don't validate your gender identity while raving about how great it is to be with a real androgyne, and then get your pronoun wrong on the way out the door. Clueless jerks aside, it's hard for anyone, even another transperson, to communicate to someone how beautiful their dissonant bodies are, especially when they may hate that dissonance and wish for nothing more than to be normal, boring, garden-variety single-gendered people. It's a tightrope that I walk whenever I touch a new transperson. Will this one be able to enjoy my preference, at least on every other Tuesday? If I find beautiful the transposition of his or her bearded chin over his or her sensuous girlish lips; or the curve of a newly grown breast next to the curve of a bulging bicep, will I be able to communicate that without triggering self-hatred for the 50 percent of that equation that they wish they didn't have?

We seesaw back and forth between pride and dysphoria. I'm hardly immune from it, either. One day I'm reveling in being a sacred genderfuck deity in all my sexual glory, and the next I'm curled up saying, "Don't touch me!" It happens with all of us, and there's nothing to be done with that special pain except to wait it out, and let it make us stronger. There's pain on the back side of every part of glory. The one is just as true as the other. We are mistakes, not quite right, misprogrammed and broken and mismatched creatures . . . and we are sacred third-gender beings who are perfect exactly the way we are. Both are true, simultaneously. To comprehend this is to comprehend our mystery, and to understand our power.

To touch the body of a sacred androgyne with both lust and reverence is an act of worship and magic, a spell of healing for our culture. Go ye forth and beg for the privilege. We will teach you more about yourself than you ever knew existed, and you will be forever changed in the process. It's our gift, being the catalyst. In our ambivalent bodies lies the gateway to the future.

Coming Soon to a Theatre Near Me

Bree Coven

My boyfriend was a lesbian porn star. She used to be a lesbian. Sometimes he still is. I met him on butch-femme.com. I know. But having plowed through most of the butches in New York like a dyke dervish on a quest for the holy clit, I needed something new. So I imported. Answered an ad specifically on the West Coast. A sex ad. "Transgender butch boi seeks slippery submissive femme for surreptitious sex and/or spankings." Alliteration makes me wet. So do spankings. I fired off an immediate response, safe in the knowledge that since Mr. Tranny Butch Boi was so far away, nothing was likely to come of it. So I wasn't intimidated. It was easy to be utterly honest. And bold. He said he was always packing, so I asked if he traveled. "If you're ever in New York," I taunted, "let me know, and I'll meet you in a nice dark alley somewhere."

When I first saw his picture, I recognized him immediately. There was no mistaking the cool blue gaze, shoulders too broad to be a girl's, lips too lush to belong to a boy. The gentle slope of nose, a stark, breathtaking contrast to the strong, angular jaw. The sexy blond wave of hair screaming "stroke me." I knew his face well, though we'd never met. I'd been watching him for years, had jerked off to him furtively all through college.

"Um, forgive me," my e-mail began politely. "I don't mean to be impudent, but you look really familiar. Is it possible, by any chance, have you, um, starred in any lesbian porn? I'm thinking *Go, Dyke, Go 2, 3,* and *4*—my personal favorite series—the scene where the pregnant femme is picnicking with her girlfriend and out of nowhere this big butch stud comes in with a toolbox, fucks her sweetly up the ass, and then leaves?" I'd said too much. Or just enough.

I stared at the screen, barely blinking until the reply came. Checking and rechecking. Five full minutes, then finally it appeared. Subject header: "Yes." I clicked on the message, holding my breath.

"Yes, that's me."

My wet dream come true.

We talked on the phone that night for the first time. I immediately confessed to blowing off my college graduation party to cram into a crowded dorm room with four femme friends, one of whom had secretly borrowed the video from an older cousin, to watch and rewind and watch that scene over and over again. We'd convinced the only girl on campus with a VCR to let us take over her room. She was a religion major. When we popped in the movie, she murmured, "Oh my God."

I knew that whole scene by heart, and the other ones, too—the threesome, the shaving scene. I used my graduation money to buy my own VCR and order my own copy. I proudly displayed the glossy cardboard box in my room as a centerpiece and catalyst for countless conversations. The cover featured the blond beefcake butch towering above his costars, staring straight ahead with that cocky gaze a silent, relentless dare. A ripped man's work shirt hung open, revealing the impossibly smooth expanse of skin beneath. Tight abs and completely flat chest—he looked like a boy even then. For years, I continued to watch my favorite blond porn star over my girlfriend's shoulder as she fucked me, my eyes intent on my pet porn stud's ass, perfectly framed by the leather harness, thrusting over and over again. I fantasized about being on the receiving end of that equation. I dreamed about my own private audition for *Go, Dyke, Go,* of starring opposite this butch, becoming the Fred Astaire and Ginger Rogers of the L.A. lezzie porn set.

And now, eight years later, here he was, chatting me up and asking if I had a hot date for Valentine's Day. "Well," I thought, "I do now." His porn career largely behind him, he told me he'd moved on to work as a male model in magazine fashion shoots. Documentary films chronicled his patient, thoughtful, continuing transition from lesbian to boy and from female toward male. I've always been drawn to masculine women and feminine men. When you have to ask, "Is that a boy or a girl?" is about when I get interested. The answer is less important than the question. So what could be hotter than having my genderfuck porn star fantasy come to New York on Valentine's Day to fuck me with his cock as hard as Cupid's arrow—the strap-on kind and the one he was growing himself.

He sent another enticing photo of himself modeling the detachable version—a primed, jutting, huge dick complete with balls in a smooth, inky, rich jet black that matched his harness. My own dyke Daddy Dirk Diggler. He called it the Big Black Nemesis. Simultaneously thrilled and terrified, I immediately did a Google search on the Internet for "big black nemesis," hoping to learn its exact dimensions to see what I was getting myself into. I'd been out twelve years, and knew my way around a dildo, even had the courage and audacity in moments to refer to myself as a size queen, but this was quite frankly the largest dick I'd ever seen, and it was more than a little daunting. It seemed enormous even against his six-foot frame. Here was my dream date offering himself to me, and I was scared I couldn't handle it. What if he was too big? What if I blew it?

Despite searching all the sex toy stores and bravely asking for it by name, I was unsuccessful in locating the exact measurements of the Big Black Nemesis, so I started training with my girly gold glitter dick, hoping I could work up to the Nemesis before its arrival. I popped in the video. That's the cool thing about dating a porn star—how many girls get to preview their lover before they actually meet? I'd never met him, yet I already knew his voice, the sharp sure thrusts of his hips, the sound of the smack of his hand on bare ass, how he looked fucking a girl, how he'd look fucking me. What I couldn't imagine was how it would feel. I hoped that in real life he'd growl, "Yeah, that's a good girl" if I sucked his dick just right like in the movie. I hoped he'd really pull his wifebeater up and back around his neck when he got all sweaty and started getting close, just like I'd watched him do countless times in series 4. I hoped he'd let me fuck him back, like he never allowed any of the girls in the videos to do.

In the days preceding his arrival, I came hard for him every night, bucking furiously against my own hand, his name rolling on my tongue. My fantasy went like this: I'm waiting for him at the airport gate. I'm wearing my slutty black minidress, low cut, push-up bra edging my breasts out of the top. Short skirt. I want him to see my legs immediately. I want him to know how they'll be wrapped around his waist soon. Very soon. Not soon enough. I stand by the gate, nervous and excited, tucking my hair behind my ears. In a blast, with no warning, the doors open and he's the first out—the doors seem to echo behind him and I hear my own breath in my ears. I'm wet for him already. His strides are long as he walks right toward me without looking around. Those eyes bore into me, so intense, that same stern, still blue from the picture.

He walks right up to me, his hands landing on my ass, and lifts me up to him. Before we say hello, before I hear his voice, before I can ask how the flight was or even confirm that it's me, his mouth is on me, devouring my tongue, probing my lips. He places me down gently and takes my hand without a word, leading me through twists, turns, and corners, like this airport is his home. He guides me to a dimly lit blue passageway and before we turn right, he leans down—he's so tall, I feel miniature beside him—and whispers his first words in my ear: "I can't wait." My ear is damp from the heat of his breath.

All at once, my back is against a brick wall and his hand is under my skirt. It's so fast, but I don't say no. I want it, too. He's horny, like a boy, biting my neck, pushing his tongue in and out between my lips, fucking my mouth and pinning me to the wall with an unmistakable hardness I know he chose for me. He grinds into me, chafing my thighs with his jeans. I wrap my legs around his waist. He pulls me up, positioning me over his cock, which has already found its way out of his briefs.

His hand is quick—the condom glides on and he nudges against me, butting up against my clit, which pulses dramatically. He kisses me gently, with tenderness, before biting my lip, not too hard, just enough to keep me on my toes. His fingers graze my lips. I catch his thumb and lick it slowly, sucking it into my mouth, pushing my pelvis against him and willing his cock to slip inside me on its own. His hand caresses my face, my chin, my neck, my hair so gently—then he slaps me. I lose my breath, then find it, and then his hand is between my legs, stroking me gently, then pushing in hard. He rips the fishnets I bought for this occasion, right up the crotch, just as I was hoping he might.

I turn myself over to his care, my breasts his to beat and bruise and bathe with his tongue, my velvety bare pussy his to invade, consume and display. He sears into me and my head, heart, cunt open to him, welcoming, buckling, giving way. His mouth clamps down on my neck as he moves inside me, the contrast of his impossibly soft skin enveloping solid muscle mirrored in his fucking: the hard, soft, rough, mean, gentle, sweet, vicious, tender, savage, voracious ravaging of my body just past breaking point.

His cock pushes sounds from deep in my throat. I grunt and wail—and he shuts me up, smothering my mouth with his. His broad hands hold me still as his narrow hips thrust over and over. He fucks me fast and hard and eager, like he's got to get off and I'm the only one that can do this for him. His cock claims its place inside me, burrowed deep, and I cry out, flooding us both with an orgasmic display that rivals the professionals. His name is spelled inside me in his cum, my sweat and tears. I did not know what need was. I have only wanted. As I come, I come to, in the safe, spent, warm release with this relative stranger who somehow already knows my body as well as I ever have.

He holds me to him for a moment, our sweaty skins melding, then, hands tangled in my hair, he is pushing me down where I belong, hovering over me. My mouth aches for him, needy, insistent, I suck at the empty air, searching with every breath for his cock. He tears off the harness and tosses it aside. I part him and discover the biggest boy-clit I've ever seen. I steady myself, holding onto his furry ass, and take his perfect mouthful of cock between my lips, sucking it against the roof of my mouth. He shudders and leans back against the wall, letting it support him while he pumps his little dick into my mouth. It lengthens and stiffens against the flat of my tongue. I circle the tip of his cockhead and it gives a little jump. He stops being gentle and slams against my face, furiously shoving as much of himself as he can into me. I twist and suck with a ferocious thirst to feed on him. I slowly pull off him, then my mouth finds him again, devouring, fiercely working his cocklet as the tension in his thighs builds and he clamps down, his legs squeezing the sides of my head. Only when he's done, only when he's heaved into me, leaning his full weight against me, does he finally relax, take my hand in his, still sticky with me, and we walk out, flushed and calm, impervious, untouchable.

I fucked myself to this scenario twenty-nine times in sixteen days, coaxing orgasm after salty orgasm from my sopping, aching cunt, and by the time he arrived, I was no longer scared of his Big Black Nemesis, I was hungry for it. I only hoped both would live up to my fantasy. When they arrived, I was waiting by the gate in my little black dress, having traipsed undeterred through six inches of snow in four-inch heels to greet him. I was rewarded at once. He was exactly as I imagined—a pulsing, vibrant version of the freeze-frame fantasy in my VCR. He leaned into me, the length of our bodies not yet touching, and his mouth melted my ear with his whispered first words: "I can't wait." My ear was damp from the heat of his breath.

The fantasy continued for four months without interruption. As he said, it's not about the destination. It's the trip. We didn't miss a stop on the subversive sexuality spectrum, stretching and expanding to fill the vast landscape of erotic possibility in the space between boy and girl, fantasy and reality. This lesbian porn star became my first boyfriend, and I found our inconsistency irresistible. I reveled in the dissonance, relished the in-between. Maybe that's what drew me to him. He was full of contradictions. He used the men's room with a driver's license that read "female" tucked in his pocket. He was a guy with ovaries. A dyke with a dick. The quintessential queer. The boi next door. The labels fell away as easily as our clothes, as gracefully as my fears. All that was left was throat-parching desire. Be my boyfriend, my girlfriend, my porn star, my lover, my fantasy, my special occasion, my every day, my habit, my ritual, my heat, my heart. Just be mine. And let me be yours. Your little angel baby girl, booty-call princess, girlfriend lover, slut whore bitch. For more than male or female, boy or girl, he was a Top. You can call him he or she, but I called him Daddy as I begged him to please, please, please fuck me, just like those girls in his movies. And he did.

My First Female-to-Male Transsexual Lover

Annie Sprinkle

This is an experience I had in 1989. I wrote this up as an article, and it was published in 1989 in Hustler *magazine, which I believe was the first F2M story in a men's magazine. That same year, I also produced a video reenactment of this story called* Linda/Les and Annie—the First Female to Male Transsexual Love Story, *which has become an F2M film classic.*

After twelve surgical operations, spending $50,000, weekly counseling sessions, lots of hormone shots, and a new wardrobe, a beautiful woman named Linda Helen Nichols became a handsome man named Les Nichols. Les's new surgically constructed penis was only two months old when we met, and he chose me to be the first to try it out. He would be my first female-to-male transsexual lover.

For Les and I it was love and lust at first sight. We caught each other's eyes at my friend Johnny A.'s F2M social. For the past year Johnny A. has been networking F2Ms through his newsletter, Rites of Passage. Occasionally he has a get-together exclusively for F2Ms and the women who love them. I had known Johnny when he was an F2M crossdresser.

The party was the best I'd been to in years. There were fourteen F2Ms and a dozen genetic women. Most all of the transsexuals looked totally like men—they take hormones that make them grow facial hair and give them very deep voices. We sat in a large circle, and people talked about their lives, their lovers, and their doctors. A few showed us their operations, and we ate pizza. The roomful of men with pussies gave this bisexual sex adventuress quite a thrill. Many of the "new men" were very attractive, and I flirted with several. Mostly I flirted with Les.

Les was kind of a cross between a biker and a circus performer. His background was French and Greek, which, according to him, makes him a Freek. Born thirty-five years ago, he is a triple Gemini, someone with many personalities. He has a fabulously sexy smile and the most beautiful, seductive, fun-loving eyes I think I've ever seen. Before long we were necking on the couch. His kisses were delicious, marsh-mallow soft, sensitive, and feminine. He possessed that incredible subtle power of seduction that women have plus an irresistible boyish charm. Before long he popped the question: Would I like to be the first woman to try out his brand-new penis? I considered it for about a tenth of a second. How could I possibly resist? Unfortunately, the penis still needed a bit more healing around the head: so we made our date for two weeks later.

At present it is possible for doctors to make a penis. The operation, called phalloplasty, is still in the experimental stages; it's painful, there are often complications, and it is very expensive. Most F2Ms don't get the phalloplasty. Only a few are done each year.

There are three types of phalloplasty. One is genitoplasty, in which doctors change the vagina, freeing the clitoris so it protrudes as a very tiny penis that can be urinated through. The genitoplasty clitoris/penis is very sensitive. Then there is microsurgery, which is the most expensive. Skin, fat, veins, and nerves are taken from the forearm and are attached with microsurgery. The resultant cock is sensitive and natural looking.

Linda (Les) chose the abdominal tube method—a simple operation—for his phalloplasty. A piece of the abdomen is rolled into a hollow tube and covered with skin grafts from the buttocks; the base of the neopenis is then attached at the upper line of the pubic hair, and the tip is attached just below the navel, like a suitcase handle. A second operation, a "tube release," follows, after that procedure heals for eight weeks. The top of the "handle" is cut loose, and a penis head is fashioned from another graft.

With some of these operations, a transsexual risks losing the new penis as well as all sexual sensation. Linda always loved sex and valued her sensitivity highly. Les told the doctor that if she lost any sensitivity at all, she would kill him. The doctor heeded the warning and decided to leave Linda's vagina intact. (Most transsexuals opt to have their vaginas closed up to form a scrotum.) So now Linda is actually a surgically made hermaphrodite. She had already had her breasts removed, a hysterectomy, liposuction on her hips and buttocks to make her shape more manly, and had two round saline sack implants put into her mons to make testicles. Now, no one would ever know that Les wasn't born a man, unless he told them. If he didn't tell a girl there was a pussy under his balls, she wouldn't think to look.

During the two weeks that we impatiently waited for Les's penis to heal completely, we carried on our romance by phone and by mail. (Les lives in Boston, and I live in Manhattan.) I asked him a million questions about his life and his sex change. He sent me photos of Linda. She had been a very beautiful, sexy, "femmy" lesbian woman with long brown hair, a pretty face, a curvaceous body with large breasts, and she wore Frederick's of Hollywood-style clothes. She joined the army at twenty-nine and became butch, cut her hair to a crew cut, started wearing men's clothes, and acted more masculine. Eventually, Linda decided to start taking hormones and make the complete change. Why? Lots of reasons. Perhaps the seed was planted as a little girl when she found herself attracted to other little girls. She thought she would need to be a boy to love and marry a girl. She had been abused a lot and felt she might be safer if she were a guy. She saw men getting more respect than women. She wanted the male privilege. She was attracted to heterosexual women more than lesbians and felt that a penis could better satisfy her lovers. She was always highly sexual, looking for sex with lots of partners—a behavior more acceptable for men. Linda imagined that being a man would solve a lot of emotional problems and improve her life in general.

Our long-distance phone conversations were mostly about sex and what we were going to do with each other once we got together. I was very aroused by the thought of making love with Les/Linda and could barely wait.

He drove down from Boston and finally arrived at my door. We planned to spend three days and nights together. After just five minutes, we were kissing, hugging, humping, rubbing, and getting undressed. Why wait? I would have wanted to fuck Les even if he wasn't a great kisser—or even if I didn't like him that much—just for the novelty of it. To be attracted to him was a nice bonus. I couldn't decide if I was kissing a man or a woman or both at the same time, a new twist on the ménage à trois.

Les undressed me, complimenting me on my figure, my softness, my perfume, and my smooth, white skin. He sure knows what a girl likes to hear. After all, he had been one.

I took off his shirt. His arms and chest were covered with tattoos. He had large, succulent nipples, the kind made for feeding babies. Below the nipples were scars where his breasts had been removed. I took a nipple between my lips and nursed, which he liked very much. I pulled off his pants and thought about how much of his life he had worn silky, lacy panties: now he wore men's briefs, which I then took down. There it was, his brand-new cock, with a shiny, red bow tied around it, presented to me as a precious gift. I was delighted with the gift and with Les's creativity and playfulness.

It was a fat, fleshy penis, remarkably large, considering it was all patchwork. The head looked very realistic, except that there were long hairs growing out of the tip of it, which I found to be a total turn-on. The shaft was quite scarred: it bent to the left, was natural in color and shape and very . . . unique. Like a typical man he asked: "Is it big enough?" I assured him it was perfect in every way.

He was considering getting another operation to get bigger testicles, and he asked my opinion on the matter. His balls were tight looking, yet very realistic. I liked them just the way they were. When I ventured down, it was there under his balls that I discovered a lovely treasure—a succulent, large, red clitoris with a huge purple head and a very moist, pink pussy. When Les proudly displayed both sets of genitals, I went into ecstasy, amazed by my good fortune. What more could a bi-girl want? I scooped his penis into my mouth and gave it a passionate, wet, suck. Then I licked and kissed my way down to his pussy and sucked that clit like I'd never sucked a man's clit before . . . and indeed I hadn't. It was wild and strange, like I was in some sort of parallel reality or hallucinating.

I informed Les that I was having the last day of my period. He said, "Great," found my Tampax string and pulled. What man could be more understanding and unintimidated by a little blood than a man who used to menstruate? He slipped his index finger inside me and went right to my G-spot, fingering my pussy like only a lesbian could. Les had no doubt been to bed with many, many women before me. He obviously loved women and their bodies.

Because we were both anxious for the defloweration we kept fore-play to a bare minimum. I lit some candles and incense and ritualized the initiation with an invocation of the Goddess, a blessing of the new penis and of Les for being such a brave pioneer, and then I gave a brief moment of gratitude. Never before in history has humankind been able to change people's gender so completely. I felt honored to be one of the first women in the world to try a humanmade penis. I prayed that Les's first fuck be joyful and healing.

We prepared the penis for penetration. In order to make Les erect, he must slide a hard plastic rod into the center of his hollow penis. The rod slipped right in. It was an instant erection, and it felt freeing not to worry about having to get it up and keep it up. Even though I didn't have to worry about getting pregnant (Les doesn't have sperm), we decided to use condoms for safe sex and to prevent any infections in case Les wasn't totally healed.

We considered what the most appropriate first-time position should be and decided I would get on top. I squatted over him, gave him my best kiss ever, took a deep breath and lowered myself onto the new-born phallus. I felt it push up inside me. My throat opened, and I groaned with pleasure. It felt fantastic. It really worked! But after just a few strokes we had to stop. The plastic rod had pushed its way up and out the head of his cock and through the condom. We had to go into the kitchen and cut an inch off the rod. (Thank goodness I owned a sharp, small saw.) In spite of all the modern technology that went into making Les's dick, we still had to work out a few basics. We laughed about it, and luckily Les did not seem alarmed.

Back in bed we tried we tried a variety of positions. Some worked and some didn't. The cock would flail right or left, or it would go to a bad angle and slip out. This first time would require some patience and compassion. I wasn't used to these newfangled penises, and, after all, it was Les's first time.

Les seemed quite happy with his new sex toy. He told me that watching the pleasure on my face made the pain of all twelve surgeries worthwhile. The penis had "surface sensations." He could feel my pussy muscles squeezed tightly around it, but most of his sensitivity was still in his clitoris, and I made sure to stimulate it while his cock was inside me—something I'd never done before.

We tried to think up a better system than using the rod. Les got the bright idea to try using his thumb; so he squeezed it into the shaft. I couldn't contain my laughter when I saw his cock with his thumb inside it (or his thumb with a cock around it). He joked: "It looks like I'm back to lesbian sex again"—using his fingers for fucking.

When I managed to stop laughing, I got back on top and rode the prick/thumb like a champion. Les had more control over its direction, and it was thicker, harder, and longer. It felt divine; I was on the brink of orgasm when Les screamed out in pain. I panicked. My heart skipped a beat. I thought I'd ruined his new $50,000 cock. I dismounted, and he screamed in agony as he removed his thumb from his cock. "Shit, you almost broke my thumb!" When we saw that all was well, we laughed hysterically.

Suddenly I was overcome with emotion, and my laughter turned to crying. I was so touched by Les's optimism, good humor, and lack of expectations. I was touched by how wonderfully freaky he is and how he lives his dream. I cried thinking about how much physical and emotional pain he must have suffered to change his gender. I cried for all the people who don't love their bodies just the way they are, for all transsexuals who have suffered, the many who have resorted to suicide, and for all sexual persuasions who are made into outcasts by our society. I mourned Linda Nichols, whom I know I would have liked very much; but by then she was virtually dead and gone. Les told me not to cry. "Look at all the adventures I've had and the places I've been. It's been a wonderful adventure. After all, I might not have met you."

We made love all night, until 7:00 the next morning. After all, his cock could stay hard for many hours straight. He told me I was the best fuck he'd ever had. I knew it was true. I was the only fuck he'd ever had. I loved being with him, and I loved being with a hermaphrodite. I wondered if I would become addicted now and no longer be satisfied with regular men or women. Would there be more hermaphrodites entering the world? Would there be a new community emerging, one of men with cunts? Would they become a new political force—women taking over the world, but as men? Would men now be able to become pregnant? I imagined how Les would look nine months pregnant. Would we eventually develop a new awareness of "transgender," of looking beyond a person's gender to his or her spirit, wherein society would no longer try and mold us into being plain old heterosexuals?

Having sex with Les was a constant mind fuck. I could put my finger inside his pussy . . . his pussy? . . . and feel her balls. His skin was soft and smooth like a woman's; yet he had hair on his chest. His hands were small and delicate, with a woman's touch; yet he wore men's rings. His eyes and lips—so sensual—were framed by his stubby beard. Although he protested, I got him to put on a pair of my high heels. He was the first man I've met whose feet were my size and who could walk perfectly in four-inch stilettos. Sometimes he dropped little hints to let me know he was still a woman deep down. He said that when he goes out into the world "it's like being a spy."

Sometimes I became the more aggressive, dominant lover. I reached for my favorite dildo, a four-inch rock-hard, quartz-crystal cock, and I slipped it up inside his pussy. He was so wet and juicy. Apparently the hormone pills make his pussy extra wet and give it a strong, musky odor, which I really liked. Hormones also greatly increase the sex drive. Perhaps this is why F2Ms are often notorious womanizers. Unfortunately, the pills are dangerous and very hard on the liver. His vagina was tight. He has never had intercourse with a man, so technically he's still a virgin. I imagined a threesome with Les fucking me while he was getting fucked by a guy. Les went for an orgasm. (We wouldn't want him to get blue balls.) I fucked his pussy with the dildo and gave his dick a hand job while he vigorously frigged his clitoris. It was so far out to see a man frig his clit. When he came, it sounded like a woman's orgasm, but with a man's voice. He was, of course, capable of multiple orgasms.

We took little breaks for drinks of sparkling apple cider, for a luxurious bath together, to kiss grapes into each other's mouths, and for talking. He told me about his life as Linda, the lesbian separatist, when she hated men and avoided them at all costs. I found it a little hard to figure out why someone who hated men so much would want to become one. Les thought it made perfect sense—a classic case of the "oppressed becoming the oppressor, with forced integration as a radical therapy," he said.

Since becoming a man, he likes men a lot more and has even been noticing a slight sexual attraction. Perhaps one day this lesbian separatist will become a gay man. Now he feels he gets treated much better and is constantly aware of the male privilege. "After all, men run the world and have their faces on the coins."

What does his mother think about it all? It must be hard for a mother to take. "She can't quite understand it. 'You were such a beautiful girl. You could have had any man you wanted.'" But she is fairly supportive, and she still loves him.

Has it affected his career? He's never really had one. Up to this point, he's always been a student. He's studied art and graphic design, has a bachelor's and master's degree in psychology, and at present is a PhD candidate in human behavior. He's considering careers in either video production, psychology, or pastoral counseling. Even though he was at one time a good Catholic girl, I can't imagine him as a pastoral counselor. Where he gets his money, he prefers to keep a mystery.

I hadn't laughed, played, and fucked so hard in ages. Les announced that his cock felt a lot bigger now that he'd finally used it. I was pleased. We stood looking out my eleventh-floor apartment window into the sky and watched the sunrise with Les fucking me from behind. I had several waves of cosmic, full-bodied orgasms. Time stood still; I became one with Les, the sky, and with everything. All I could think of was how amazing life is. Eventually we drifted off to sleep wrapped around each another, satiated.

When we woke up in the afternoon, Les read the *Times* while I made breakfast. He did the dishes while I made some business calls. Then he blew my mind one more time when he came walking into my room naked with a bunch of carnations sprouting from his cock and said, "Look, Annie; I'm a Greek vase."

I have the greatest respect for Les. I see him as a unique avant-garde artist whose medium is his body, whose subject matter is sex, and whose message is—as it is tattooed across his chest—FREEDOM.

Dancing with Three

Susan St. Aubin

The first time I saw this person was at a women's party, a private party in a club to which I had been invited by the daughter of a good friend, a twenty-five-year-old woman who was finally graduating from college. Her mother was living in Boston, so I suppose I was there as her representative, or perhaps her opposite: I am an artist, a never-married, childless woman who has loved both men and women, and has done what she wanted with her life, making her dangerous enough to be admired by the young. At fifty, the oldest woman at this party, I stood in a corner of the large room sipping a glass of white wine while watching the supple dancing bodies remove their clothing piece by piece as the evening progressed.

My mother always told me life is about choices, but so many choices are made for you: male or female, black or white, talent or none, even rich or poor. I've always been drawn to the spaces between classes, races, and genders, to places where form takes its most interesting shape, which is why my eyes were drawn to this person who danced alone, and who chose to leave her shirt on, though open to reveal a full-length body leotard. She—or it could have been he—wore baggy white pants which hung down over narrow hips, revealing the shiny purple leotard that hugged her body, molding her small, firm breasts. Or his. I was confused, though she must be the right pronoun because this was a women's party. She flung her long dark hair, silky and shiny as the purple leotard, over her shoulders, away from her face, as her body bent and stretched to the music.

I asked the hostess, who was dancing topless herself, who this person was. Her large breasts seeming to float away from her as she shook her head.

"I'm not sure. I think she came with Lara, didn't she?"

Her partner shrugged. "Probably," she said. "Everyone interesting comes with Lara."

I moved around the edges of the dance floor to get a closer view of her face or his, lost in the rhythm of drums, a face without makeup, full lips curved in a smile and eyes framed by the longest, curliest natural eyelashes I'd ever seen, eyelashes that caught the gleam of the strobe lights. The neck was long and slender, with an Adam's apple perhaps a bit pronounced for a woman, though not for a thin woman. The body seemed to stretch forever, past a long waist, long legs, down to feet in black Chinese slippers that scuttled delicately along the dance floor. When I tried to catch her glance, she looked away from me. I moved closer, wishing for an introduction.

"Which one is Lara?" I asked, waving an arm at the dancers.

"I don't know," she said in a husky voice, not breaking her own rhythm. "I've never heard of her." She moved away from me, dancing onto the crowded floor, embracing first one woman, then another, as she went. She appeared to know everyone, or pretended to, and no one objected.

Several of the women knew who I was, and came up to me to say how much they like my sculptures of wood and wire, enigmatic human forms neither male nor female, my signature work. Some I did outside with found materials, leaving them by the sides of freeways where they had come to be recognized as mine and left alone until they sunk back into the earth; others were on exhibit at local galleries or preserved in museums. No one asked me to dance, though, so I was left to imagine what it would be like to dance with someone who could be either male or female, or some combination. It would, I decided, be like dancing with two people at once. Turning to face me, there were breasts, small but soft enough to sway to the music, but turn around, and there was that firm, tight male ass. I could build a statue to create a different kind of Janus who was two bodies in one.

I didn't think I'd see that solitary dancer again, but two weeks later, sitting alone in a my neighborhood coffee house, there she was. Her blue silk tank top was low cut, showing the straps and lacy top of her bra. The smooth skin of her arms glistened over firm muscles. She still wore those baggy, low-slung white pants, revealing the soft, bare skin of her midriff this time. The white running shoes on her long, narrow feet, must be size ten or eleven, I thought. Her sturdy ankles were wrapped around each other as she sat and read a book while drinking black coffee from a heavy glass mug. She didn't look up.

Sometimes in such situations I'll sit and stare at the top of someone's head, willing them to look at me. It usually takes five minutes for them to turn around, but not this one—twenty minutes and still no response. On my way out, I walked over to her table.

"What's that you're reading?" I asked.

She looked up then, somewhat peeved at being interrupted. "A book," she answered.

The raw silk of that Tallulah Bankhead voice caressed my ears, but since I don't like being brushed off, I continued walking toward the door. When I glanced back, her eyes were on her book again.

She must have lived in the neighborhood because I saw her often after that, on the other side of the street, or in line at the grocery store, or in the café. I trailed him, convinced, now, that this was a man in woman's clothing. Only a man would walk with enough confidence to look straight ahead instead of continually scanning around, as women so often do. Only a man would have said, "A book," when I was trying to flirt with him.

I realized I was a victim of my own prejudices. Why shouldn't a woman walk with long, confident strides while staring ahead? Why shouldn't she brush off unwanted advances? Many times I tried to catch her eye, but, like a woman, she always glanced away, modestly never looking directly at me. Head up, eyes forward, she proceeded like a model on a runway, doing her job. The job, for him, was being a woman. But then, isn't that every woman's job?

I wanted to take this person home like a present to unwrap, not knowing what I'd get only adding to the excitement. I felt my desire shift from curiosity to need: I needed to run my hands over that smooth, possibly shaved, skin, feeling the firm muscles beneath. I wanted her throaty voice murmuring in my ears as I caressed her breasts, her firm ass, and the slick hair of her pubic bush, hiding perhaps a cock, or a cunt, or both. This was someone I had to know, someone I had to mold my hands around like one of my sculptures, feeling every possible protuberance and crevice.

In our neighborhood café, I stood behind her in line at the counter, measuring myself against her tallness, barely able to see over her shoulder. I brushed her arm as I reached for milk for my espresso and felt my skin tingle. I could see the pulse in her throat, could almost feel her life. Then she looked down at me, directly into my eyes this time, and smiled, causing my heart to contract and my face to flush with extra blood.

"Excuse me," she whispered.

I noticed she was with another woman, and watched as they took their mugs to a table with just two chairs. Yet our flirtation continued, for I never took my eyes off her even when she glanced at my body and lowered her lush lashes. It couldn't be him—the face, though not made up, was pink and smooth, and those lips, a natural rose. I left, certain that we'd meet again, which we did, at a party a month later.

It was the day after an election in which all my candidates, of course, had lost. This time we greeted each other.

"Hello!" she called as I passed. "My guys never win."

We laughed. She was wearing a tight blue sweater on this cool November evening, an angora sweater I could almost feel on the palms of my hands, though I didn't touch her. I took quick looks at her crotch, but her pants were too loose to reveal anything. They fit better when seen from behind, showing a distinctly firm ass that could belong to a man, or to a woman dancer.

There was food, there was music. "Dance?" I asked, and she took my hand, but when we reached the dance floor, she danced by herself, always just out of my reach. Even though I tried to keep up, she was still a dancer alone, just as I'd seen her the first time. Or maybe not so alone if she was a blend of two in one. Yes, she was all my opposing desires in one package: masculine, feminine, strength, beauty, dominance, submission. I could change myself to meet whatever she presented. I wouldn't have to choose because she could be my man and my woman, as well as anything in between. The permutations were fascinating.

When my eyes sought hers, she didn't look away. Her head turned toward me as I danced around her, trying to form a couple, or a triad, or more out of all that we were. The tall, lean body bent to me. In this dance I didn't know what I was: a woman to his man? Man to his girl? Girl to girl? Boy to boy? This was a dance of life that wouldn't end with the pulsing music. I could feel my heart beat like an echo of his. Hers. Those were the only words available to me—his or hers. Neither fit.

"Your name?" I screeched above the music.

"I'll give you my number: five-six-seven-seven-two-nine-eight," she said, dipping her head to my ear.

"Name!" I beseeched.

"Rain!" and then she danced away.

Rain? *She must have been born on some hippie commune,* I thought. *Born to a woman who must be my age now.*

When the music ended she came back with a card for me, printed with two lines:

REIGN

567-7298

What kind of name was that? A made up name, neither male nor female, but perfect for this person who danced away from me, tossing her hair over one shoulder. Her reign over me was all I desired. Or his reign. *Administer your tongue to my breast,* I thought. *Govern my cunt with your scepter.* But for now, there was only the throb of my heart, and the answering throb of my clit, the echo of my heart. I was ready for any gender organ she had, but she was leaving, a bright shawl around her shoulders, and a glance back. For me? I smiled while she tilted her head toward the door, and when she gave me a sideways nod, I followed.

Outside the stars and a sliver of moon showed brightly, with the faded outline of the full moon still visible—the new moon in the arms of the old. She walked quickly, without looking back to see if I'd followed, her high-heeled sandals clicking on the empty pavement. We passed my car, turned another corner, crossed another street as my heart kept pace with her footsteps, my feet with hers. Or his, I reminded myself as my heart raced past me, past her, into the dark, starry night even as my steps slowed, letting her get farther ahead. My house wasn't far from here, but when I was alone I felt safer driving, even for short distances. I was beginning to feel a bit nervous now, and quickened my pace to keep up.

When she turned into an alley, I followed, but she was gone. Had I looked away for a minute and missed her? There were back doors to flats and apartments, but none of them were open, none of them beckoned, none of them were hers. His. I began to feel confused—was this a mirage? Was I so thirsty for a person like this that I imagined him, like one of my statues come to life? Then at the end of the alley I saw a figure in a long, dark cloak and ran toward it, but it was only an old man, who quickly hurried away when I saw him. Whoever he was waiting for, it wasn't me. I looked behind, but there was only that moon, the outline so bright now it almost looked like it actually was full.

There was nothing to do but go home to sleep and dream of her, or, as it happened, of him. In my dream I'm on a bus crowded with commuters, men and women, all in suits. The women, of course, wear skirts and running shoes instead of their high heels, which they carry in their bags. I look closely at the man standing next to me, his briefcase on the floor between his legs, and see that it's Reign, but with short hair, wearing a man's suit and tie, reading the newspaper with his eyebrows drawn together in a frown. Then we're on the beach, the two of us alone, and he's something I'm creating, a life-sized statue I'm carving out of a rock—I work on his head first, then his shoulders and torso. He's nude, and as I work my way down he seems to emerge out of the rock. I think about how I'll carve his cock: how long, how the balls will hang, how much hair. Like God, I make these decisions. My hands feel the cool, gray stone and mold the curves of his ass. Suddenly the rock becomes a soft clay that obeys my fingers instantly, with no chisel or knife to get in the way. The figure seems real enough to be able to climb out of the lump of clay by itself, quite different from my usual abstractions.

I work my hands further down, but somehow I can't reach the genitals. The slick, wet clay turns dry on my hands and flakes off like dust. I dig and dig, but can't get to the figure beneath. My vision becomes blurred so that the beach and my statue both seem hidden in a fog so wet it wakes me up to a foggy dawn as gray as the clay my dream hands kept trying to mold. My fingers move across my pillow, which stubbornly remains a pillow.

When I called the number on Reign's card, an answering machine came on with no message: just a click, a silence, then a tone. *You know what to do,* that message said, without saying anything. I knew what to do: I always hang up. My message, too, was silence.

I know dreams can't predict the future, and yet, the next afternoon walking out of my dentist's office on a downtown street, I saw Reign in the guise of a young man on his way back to the office after lunch: short hair, and the light brown tweed suit of my dream, with breasts hidden beneath his jacket. Or breasts simply not there. This could be a brother or a cousin, with the same long legs, the same chin and eyes. I followed him around the corner into the marbled lobby of an old office building, but then lost him in a crowd of people entering a bank of elevators.

Of course, if Reign was a man, it made sense to work as a man. Even if he wasn't a man, it made sense because he'd certainly get more respect and more money as a man. When I needed cash, I used to work as a file clerk or as a typist, but if I had a choice, if I could play male as well as Reign seemed able to do, I'd prefer to be an administrator or a junior executive without having to claw my way into the job as women do. But lately I've been successful enough with my sculpture to be able to stay away from downtown, except for trips to the bank or the dentist. But now, in search of Reign, I took the streetcar downtown every day and when I finally saw him again, I smiled and said "Hello," wondering what his baffled look meant. Did he know me? Or was he just pretending not to recognize me as he walked past with a nod that didn't quite acknowledge any relationship?

Since I was always going downtown anyway in search of this male incarnation of Reign, I decided I might as well sign up with a temporary agency and earn some money. I went into one that was on the ground floor of the office building where I'd seen him get into the elevator. It turned out I'd used this agency years before, in a different location, so they didn't even test me, for which I was thankful because, although I'm a fast typist, my computer skills aren't so great.

"Any jobs in this building?" I asked.

"Hmmmm . . ." the woman clicked through several computer screens, looking at their listings. I could almost hear her think that maybe she should test me since it had been so long, to see if my skills were up-to-date, but then she shrugged and said, "How about receptionist? Lots of companies in this building need receptionists."

Fine. I could do that. She gave me the name of a lawyer on the eighteenth floor.

It took a week, but finally I saw him—her—in a crowded elevator, looking at me as we ascended one morning. He quickly looked away when I noticed him, so I knew it must be her. The man next to him said, "So, Richard, what did you think of that meeting yesterday?"

His answer came in a voice so low I couldn't understand what he said. When the elevator stopped at the twelfth floor, he and the man got off together. Before the doors closed I watched him walk down the hall, a masculine walk, two men pounding their feet on the tile, facing each other to talk, not looking where they were going, trusting, like men do, that the group of women coming toward them would part to let them pass.

Every time I saw him I stared at his chest, just as I'd once stared at her crotch, to see if there was something there, something to definitely identify the gender, but any breasts were bound out of sight and his pants were as baggy as Reign's had been. There were no clues on him.

One day I overhead Richard name the company he worked for, so when my job ended, I went back to the agency and asked for a job there. They had several simple filing and receptionist jobs, but since none of them involved anyone named Richard, I picked one at random and signed on. It was in the file room, where people came and went all day in search of files, so it was a good choice: Soon he came down to request a file.

I smiled and said, "Hello," and though he pretended not to respond, I could tell he remembered me because his eyes seemed to deepen and darken as he smiled back, without looking away. When I brought him his file I let my fingers brush the smooth skin of his hand, so much smoother than a man's would be though the hand was certainly as large as a man's. There seemed in that instant to be a vibration between us, but he was suddenly gone before either of us could say anything.

At night I dreamed of that skin, running my palms over the smoothness of his arms, gently molding the flesh beneath to feel the muscles, which were Reign's. Flirting with a man, even a man who might possibly be a woman you've flirted with before, is a game all its own. I kept calling Reign's number, but never got a live person of either gender. Every morning I hung out by the elevators until Richard arrived, then followed him in. The company took up three floors of the building, so I got off first. I found out by consulting the company directory that he worked two floors above me in the executive offices. Most of the men worked up there, and the women—receptionists and file clerks—worked on my floor. Richard Coso, the only Richard in the company. I wondered if Reign used that name, but there were no Cosos in the phone book.

I smiled a lot, as women do, especially women dealing with a man twenty years younger. As a woman, Reign's youth didn't seem so extreme, but with Richard I was truly ashamed of my fading hair, and the lines that stayed around my mouth when I didn't smile. It felt like three of us were in this dance, me, Reign, Richard, all of us toying with each other. But Reign was hidden. She must have moved out of my neighborhood because I never saw her in the streets around my house, and I only saw Richard downtown.

Then I saw him one Sunday morning in the café where I used to see Reign, wearing Reign's baggy white pants with a tank top so loose I couldn't see any breasts. He—or she—sat alone at a table with one extra chair pulled invitingly out, an opening Reign would never have left. Humble and smiling, I asked if I might join him, and he said, "Well, hi there, sure." Definitely a man, competent, unafraid, with a deep voice that pretended nothing. As we chatted, I watched his throat, which gave me little information: The Adam's apple was there, but not too large for a thin woman or a small man. He asked me about my art, leaving me to wonder how he knew I was a sculptor as well as a file clerk. Reign would know.

"I have this friend, Reign, who looks just like you," I finally blurted.

He raised one eyebrow over his coffee cup.

"You could be brother and sister," I went on.

"I'm an only child," he said in a voice that seemed, suddenly, higher.

We both laughed, a quick, choked, uneasy laugh.

"They say everyone has a twin." He stared into my eyes the way Reign never did, and yet I felt these were her eyes. "Two halves of a soul yearning to be joined, male and female, brother and sister. It's up to each of us to find our other half."

"I don't think I have another half," I said with a light smile. "This is it, right here." I stretched my arms out wide. I knew there was truth in what he said, and I knew he was one of the rare people who can be both halves, but all at once I was reluctant, almost frightened, of Reign/Richard, and the way she kept staring at me.

"But I see you looking. Searching. Following me, following something in me that would complete you."

The words hypnotized me as the tender black eyes with their long lashes caressed me, levitating the fine hair on my arms. I almost dropped my coffee cup.

"No harm in that," he went on.

You're two, I thought but couldn't say. *Together we'd be three.* This was more than complete—The mathematics of the situation was getting silly.

I couldn't decide if he was or was not Reign. "I paint," he said. (Did Reign paint?) "So I know that all art is a search."

I flexed my hands, feeling his flesh there, like raw clay. Her flesh. Would he admit to being Reign? Did it matter?

"On the weekends I can be anything I want. I'm the artist of my life, my own man."

Or woman, I thought. *And how did you manage your long hair at work before you cut it? Pin it up under a wig?*

"I had a year's leave," he went on, as though he had heard my thoughts. "I lived as I wanted. And then, a month ago, it was back to work. There's something I want to show you. My place isn't far from here."

"Your paintings, right?" I said so we both could laugh at our situation, so absurd and yet so typical.

"I wasn't thinking of my paintings, but yes, of course."

He stood, taking my hand in his, a gesture that asked me to go all the way in this dance. The light silky tank top clung to one of her small breasts as he moved, as Reign tossed her bangs out of her eyes and headed for the door, my hand in hers.

"Don't get lost this time," she warned in her Tallulah Bankhead growl. "Keep your eyes wide open and come all the way with me."

My fingers were wrapped in her soft moist skin. This time neither of us would let go.

Finding America

Jean Roberta

So many writers had lusted after her, from John Donne in the 1600s to Whitman and Thoreau in the 1800s, that I should have known I would meet her some time, somewhere. I just never guessed that she would appear to me in the dark.

While a summer storm rattled the windows of the queer bar, I told my friends about the return of my old nationality, the one I had left behind in the 1960s when I was a teenager. Years after moving north with my family to save my brother from being drafted into an ugly war, I had become a Canadian citizen so I could vote and apply for government jobs. When I swore the oath of loyalty to the queen, I believed that my American self died, the last citizen in a 200-year-old family tree. I had been warned that I couldn't belong to two countries at once, and I had made a rational, adult choice. I prided myself on being immune to girlish sentimentality and to good-son patriotism of all flavors.

"Have a drink, Carrie," offered my friend Greg at this point in my story. A gin and tonic appeared in front of me, glowing eerily in the dim light of the bar. "Who'd want to be a Yankee anyway?"

"Yeah," muttered a chorus of the politically conscious. I recognized a dyke in the group who had been turned back at the border on her way to the Michigan Women's Music Festival.

"Who wouldn't, man?" demanded a drag queen who longed to be a star in New York and a star in L.A. My listeners seemed restless, as though they were about to separate into hostile teams.

I took a swig, and felt the gin burn pleasantly down my throat. "I got it back," I bragged. "The law changed. I'm not sure if it was ours or theirs, but all of us who came up in the sixties were allowed to reclaim our old citizenship. My brother found out we could be dual. It's like another amnesty. I have two passports now."

I wondered if I was imagining the unusual bitterness in my drink, or if I was just tasting the contrast between tonic water and the fruity lozenge I had been sucking earlier. Or tasting the atmosphere.

Everyone seemed to be looking at me as though a design of stars and stripes had appeared on my forehead like the mark of Cain. Most of the bar veterans had known me for twenty years, but few had known or remembered where I had spent my childhood. I wondered whether I looked tougher or more glamorous as an American dyke than I had before. I wondered whether I was now under suspicion as a CIA plant.

The crack of thunder interrupted the velvety recorded voice of a dyke singer-songwriter from an industrial city in the United States. The lights flickered and went out, leaving us all in a lush dark silence.

My head spun wildly, and I struggled to stay upright. I walked shakily forward, touching the wall.

Relief flooded through me when I touched solid wood and saw the glint of the sign with the women's symbol on it. I pushed the door and found myself in a cave lit by candlelight. The impersonal room full of metal and mirrors now looked seductively mysterious, as though the ambience of many furtive gropings had become visible.

The person who came toward me looked vaguely familiar, and a name like "Andrea" flashed into my mind. Or "Androgyne," but I doubted if that could really be anyone's name.

"Carolina," she welcomed me with the name I had chosen in eighth-grade Spanish class. "You've come back." I wobbled, so she held me close with a pair of steely arms.

She must have been at least six-feet tall, with golden-brown skin and shiny black hair that hung down her back. Her almond-shaped eyes suggested Asian or Native or Latino roots, possibly all three. I wasn't good at figuring out such things. Then a chill shot down my spine like lightning. She looked approximately 12 percent African. The other ingredients all seemed to be in the right proportion. She was the one I had dreamed about.

She was pushing me against the wall, and her full breasts were mashed against my smaller ones. Hers felt like human flesh. Had I really seen her in the bar before, and was she really a woman? Her lips were hot on mine, and her face felt as smooth as a girl's.

"Uh," I gasped, vaguely trying to push her away. Whatever she was, she was taking too much for granted.

"Twice as good, honey," she chuckled in my ear. "Twice as strong too." I could feel the hardness of her thighs through her simple black knit dress. How could those legs not belong to a man? My suspicion seemed confirmed when I felt another hard thing pressing against my stomach.

At five feet four inches and 130 pounds, I had always felt small compared to most of the other bar dykes, but the pressure of my new companion's body made me feel tiny. I was wearing three items of clothing which felt like no protection at all.

I panicked. "I don't even know you!" I yelled into her face. Her grip loosened just enough that I could tear myself away, rush into a stall and slide the bolt home.

The washroom seemed to be filled with pregnant silence, a suspenseful absence of sound. Sitting on the toilet, I was surprised to realize that nothing needed to come out of me. Or I was really scared shitless.

I could hear my own breathing as I waited for her to leave or for the lights to come back on.

Was she gone? No. I could feel her presence, patiently waiting. "Carolina," she crooned. "Why do you want to stay in there when I'm out here? You know me, babe. You don't have to be afraid of me. We could talk for a while, if that's what you want to do. Anything you want, honey."

I cautiously opened the door of my stall. The candles were still burning, and their flames were reflected in all the smooth, hard surfaces. "You sure?" I asked.

She showed me her teeth in a feral smile. "No lights, no music," she clucked. "We just have to entertain ourselves for the duration. Let's go upstairs where it's more comfortable." She picked up a brass candleholder that held a tall white candle and opened the washroom door. She looked at me. As she expected, I walked through first. I thought vaguely that I would be safer in a larger space.

Outside the washroom, the bar was eerily quiet. I could hear a few echoing voices in the space closest to the window, where a little moon-light seeped in like water. Most of the regulars seemed to have gone home.

My companion led me up the creaky wooden steps to the second floor, knowing that I would follow her light. She walked into the dressing room of the drag performers, queens and kings. Her candle cast a glow on scattered wigs, gowns, suit jackets, and winking glass jewels, giving everything an aura that it never had by electric light. She set her candle on the dressing table and walked to the old chintz sofa that the manager had donated. She stretched herself out on it, making sure that I noticed her long, smooth legs. She kicked off her sandals so I could see that her bare legs ended in two sets of gleaming red toenails.

I sat gingerly in the space she had left me. Looking into her dark eyes, I was startled to see whirling golden pinwheels in them until I blinked them away. She picked up my nearest hand and pressed it between both of hers. "I'm not a freak, girlfriend," she assured me. "No more than you." The warm weight of her voice was exactly like that of the dyke diva whose songs were played by the bar DJ night after night. A flowery smell of roses and gardenias wafted from the person beside me, seeming to come from her mouth.

She was like several people I had loved and lost, and several more I never expected to meet. Yet she wasn't exactly like anyone in particular.

"I'm not pure," she explained, as though answering my thought. "A little of everything." She touched my face, and this time I didn't pull away. "So white," she mocked. "But not really. Not unless you're straight from Europe. And you're not straight in any way. All your ancestors wanted what they didn't have," she taunted. "And you're the same. Like them, like me."

She stretched a long arm in my direction and tugged my T-shirt out of my shorts. "Show me," she ordered, and I pulled the shirt over my head. My nipples immediately hardened under her gaze. I forced myself to look back at her.

In a few quick movements, she pulled off her dress, showing me a pair of breasts like basketballs. She pinched her own nipples, and I thought I saw them squirm like live animals. On a reckless impulse, I leaned toward them, and she covered them in a sarcastic imitation of Venus rising from the waves.

She stood up and slowly pulled down her tight panties. As the hard fabric released her flesh, I saw the head of something that looked too small to go with the rest of her, but it was definitely male. "I'm dual," she informed me. "They changed the laws. Do you like it?"

I focused on breathing evenly. "Yes," I sighed, surprising myself. "You look—complete." I was aware of my still-covered hips and butt, which were a size larger than my top half. I remembered the delight and held-in disappointment of various ex-lovers when they saw me naked for the first time. The hair on my head was an artificial shade of oak-blonde. "Normal," I realized, is a relative term.

"Take off your shorts," she told me as though prompting a lazy child. I took my panties down with them, and showed her my humble bush. By daylight, it was greyish-brown, my natural hair color. I couldn't read her expression.

"Come here," she cooed. She was rolling the tip of a condom over her womanly cock, or her outsized clit. My curiosity outweighed my fear.

I kneeled in front of her and pulled her flesh root carefully into my mouth. As I licked its roundness and tasted latex, it responded as well as I had hoped. She pushed with her hips, and I was grateful that her cock couldn't reach the back of my throat. I sucked, and she moaned in response.

I wondered whether she regarded me as a natural resource for the taking, or a local labor force that existed to please her. "That's it, baby, keep going," she encouraged me. At least she was pleased. I steadied her short shaft and balls with both hands, and was surprised to feel a furrow behind them. It didn't seem as deep as mine, but I was afraid to find out. I had no idea what it could do.

I willed pleasure into her cock, as I thought of it, and soon she was clutching my head as she thrust and groaned. When I finally pulled away, my face felt as wet as though I had actually been tasting a woman.

She pulled me upright, and that's when I wondered whether she preferred to come standing up and whether she needed more attention. Nothing seemed likely to surprise me at that point.

"Up here," she directed me, gesturing at the sofa. I tried to sit, and this annoyed her. She grabbed me by the waist and positioned me, like a doll, on all fours on the cushioned seat. She pushed my head down on my arms so that my butt and my wet bush were on display. I suspected that even my inner lips were visible to her by candlelight. She seemed to have sharp eyes.

"Mmm," she commented. As I shifted my weight to make myself comfortable, my ass must have wiggled in her face. I heard a throaty laugh just before two long fingers pushed smoothly into me as far as they could go, and stopped moving. More fingers stroked my clit as lightly as the wings of a passing moth. I knew I was growing wetter, and I moved my hips with increasing urgency while she snickered.

"What do you want, girlfriend?" she teased me.

"Fuck me," I muttered. My face felt hot, not only from the position I was in. "Please," I added. She granted my request, plunging in and out of me with long, dramatic strokes. When she pinched my clit between two fingers, I erupted like a volcano.

Afterward, we sat together as she held me close. "Miss me?" she asked sentimentally, rubbing one of my nipples as though it could give her an answer.

"Mhm," I answered, not knowing if her question referred to the past or the future.

"I can't stay," she sighed. "I have too many places to go, people to meet." She made "meet" sound sexy and uncouth. "I have a brother, though," she added. "He can keep you company sometimes when you're both in the same place."

The lights went on, and I felt suddenly blinded. The phrase "a blaze of glory" flashed into my mind as my eyes struggled to adjust. Once I could see again, a slim blond young man in a tight white shirt and pants stood in front of me like a commercial for bleach or some antibacterial household cleanser. I felt as funky as a cockroach, but his expression was friendly. He handed my clothes to me, and I noticed that they were limp and pungent with sweat. He watched with open interest while I awkwardly pulled them on.

"My brother, the star," announced the person I thought of as "America." I remembered that in the realm of mythology, actual stars could become human and vice versa.

"How do you do, Carrie? I'm the spokesman for the family," he grinned as though for a TV camera. "You can call me Adam. They say I'm the spittin' image of God." He had the pleasantly husky voice of a teenage boy or a dyke with a cold, and his tone seemed to remove the arrogance from his statement. He seemed well aware of the irony of being judged by one's appearance. "Do you need a ride home?" he asked. Apparently he was a gentleman.

I didn't know whether Greg or anyone else was still around, and I knew I couldn't get home safely on my own. "If none of my friends are here," I answered.

The three of us went downstairs together, the sister and brother each holding one of my arms. I was still too dizzy to walk a straight line, and it must have been obvious.

On the main floor, I discovered that the bar was empty and locked, although no one had thought of turning the lights off. I turned off the ones we didn't need to see our way out. I knew that the back door could be unlocked from the inside. We filed out that way, leaving the queer bar open for any lost souls who might need its shelter. This seemed dangerous and appropriate to me, even though I didn't have a choice because I had no key.

In the parking lot, I was ushered into the back seat of a car I had never seen before. I gave directions to Adam, who drove accordingly. His sister kept up a stream of talk that sounded irrational but strangely comforting. I welcomed the distraction. I put off wondering who these people really were, and decided to reconsider the mystery in the sober light of day.

The motion of the ride aggravated the motion in my head as the lights of downtown slid sickeningly past, and gave way to the soothing dark shapes of the trees in my neighborhood. When Adam pulled up at the curb, I wondered how I could walk up two flights of stairs to my apartment. Without an invitation, my new companions handled the situation by holding one of my elbows apiece and moving me forward.

I hadn't expected company, and the mess in my apartment embarrassed me, but I was in no condition to do anything about it. My guests didn't seem to mind. The woman moved about my kitchen making coffee, looking especially tall in my compact living space. She made herself at home by turning on the radio and dancing to some earthy number by a female rapper.

I became aware that I was sitting beside Adam, who was holding my hand like a high school date. "We know you're a decorator at heart, sweetie," he was saying. "It's an artful arrangement. If you show me the bedroom, I'll show you something interesting."

"Something to perk you up," offered the woman, handing me a cup of coffee. "We can't have you falling asleep yet." The caffeine disturbed my stomach, but its rush gave me more energy and helped to clear my head; the tradeoff seemed worthwhile. Adam gleamed beside me, looking almost transparent, but I could see a fine golden fuzz on his cheeks.

He rose to his feet, apparently without effort, reached for my hands, and pulled me up. We seemed to float into my bedroom, where an anthology of lesbian sex stories still lay on my night table, and my favorite dildo lay half hidden in the unmade bed. I told myself that I was beyond embarrassment.

Adam was only a few inches taller than I, so when he wrapped his arms around me and kissed me, our bodies fit together comfortably. He exuded heat and the breezy smell of men's cologne. "Are you curious, babe?" he asked me, unzipping my shorts. "I've seen you, but you haven't seen me." He helped me to pull off my clothes, then he pinched each of my nipples as though responding to their assertiveness. The tingle rushed to my pussy.

The young man took a step back and wrestled his own shirt over his head as though fighting off an attacker. He threw the shirt onto my bed while shaking his charmingly tousled hair. Smirking at me, he slowly unzipped his spotless pants and shimmied as he pushed them, inch by inch, down his legs. He kicked the pants aside as though he would never need them again.

I seemed to be looking at a eunuch. The lines of his body were clean and almost straight. His chest was lightly tanned and lightly muscled, but almost hairless. His lean stomach led to a crotch that looked as smooth as glass until I stared shamelessly and saw the unmistakably female slit. He grinned at my stunned expression.

"So who's a real man, Carrie?" he asked softly, holding my chin so he could look into my eyes. "Do you want one"—he gestured at my bed, letting me know what he had seen—"that's permanently attached to some guy who lets it do all his thinking? Don't you call yourself a lesbian?"

I hadn't called myself anything since the lights had gone out, so I thought his question was unfair. Still, it deserved some thought. If I hadn't lost my identity by gaining carnal knowledge of a woman with unusual plumbing, what did I have to lose now? I realized that trying to determine sexual taste for a lifetime was like trying to determine how many angels could dance on the head of a pin.

"Angels," I said to him. "They're supposed to look more like you than anyone else."

He easily pushed me onto the bed. "Then aren't you lucky?" he laughed. He lay on me full-length, and he felt heavier than he looked. "Not everyone gets a visit from an angel."

I knew then that I had read too much nineteenth-century American literature. "Ah," I sighed, trying to sound more savvy than I felt. "This is a kind of allegorical vision, isn't it? I bet you're here to tell me that we're all queer and we're all doomed. That even if we escape from one war, we get hauled into another one. But if we all join hands, we can rediscover the promised land, right?"

"Prob'ly," he responded agreeably. "Spread your legs, girlfriend."

He had picked up my dildo, still smelling faintly of my own lust, and guided it into me. I couldn't believe how different it felt when someone else was wielding it. I soon became so wet that I knew I would leave a puddle on the bedspread. "You want it harder, don't you?" he asked gently.

"Yes!" I gasped. There was something strangely angelic in the way he responded to my movements and my need for friction in particular places. His rhythm perfectly matched my own until I was about to explode, and then he gracefully set things off by rubbing my swollen clit.

He kissed me and stroked my hair in the aftermath. His smooth, damp chest slipped against my breasts like a silk teddy. "Don't you want anything?" I asked shyly. I had never met anyone who seemed so unselfish, or so stony. In response, he reached an arm over the side of the bed to pull something out of a pants pocket. With elaborate care, he stroked himself between the legs.

"Kiss it, babe," he suggested. He moved so that he could lie on his back as I bent over him.

Burying my nose in the innocent-looking slit, I was surprised by the ocean-fresh smell and by the size of his clit, which must have been several inches long. It was covered by a gossamer substance that probably wouldn't have been visible if it hadn't sparkled like glitter. As I pulled it into my mouth, he seemed to hum all over. I tried to slide one finger into him to heighten the effect.

"Uh," he warned me. "That's off-limits, babe. Too sensitive." I had always wondered how too much sensitivity could be more of a problem in bed than a thick skin or a tendency to lose concentration, but then I realized that these opposites might be two sides of the same coin. In a burst of tenderness, I decided not to trespass on private property.

As I tried out various tongue movements on the worthy organ, he reacted with shivers of pleasure. I soon discovered that he was sensitive all over, and liked being gently scratched over his ribcage and narrow hips.

I wondered if light grazing with my teeth would affect his love-stalk the same way. I inhaled deeply through my nose, and tried it. I was rewarded by vibrations on my tongue as grunts and moans tickled my ears.

I fit my head into the curve of his shoulder and snuggled against him as though I were resting on a cloud. He let his arm slide around me until his hand rested warmly on one of my lower cheeks. As I began drifting off to sleep, the occasional squeeze woke me up and reminded me that I was not alone.

When another body climbed into my bed, I recognized the woman by her smell. She pressed against me, making me the filling in the sandwich. "How you doin', baby?" she crooned in my ear.

In the morning, I was alone. My head hurt, but the fog seemed to have lifted. In my mouth was not the sour taste of a hangover but the rich, salty taste of a cunt that made me smile as I swam out of sleep. An earthy smell clung to a white candle that lay on my bedspread.

My phone was ringing. "Carrie, you're there!" gushed Greg, as though he had reason to believe I had been abducted by aliens. He was wallowing in guilt because he had left the bar without me on the assumption that I had already sneaked out alone, an act that he thought was characteristic of me. He claimed to have worried all night while phoning me in vain. He wanted me to join him for brunch, supposedly so he could see for himself that I was alive and unharmed. He could never resist the promise of a good story.

The complete truth, some say, is beyond the limits of the human mind. I knew that my memories of the night the lights went out would change and shift over time, like the colors of a gemstone under different kinds of light. One thing I learned for sure, however, is that duality is more widespread than I ever knew.

Dee and the Fire on a Train

Ralph Greco Jr.

I put on the wig and Dee looked back.

"Perfect," she puckered.

Soft pink lipstick even on thick lips. Brown liner easy on the bottom with a deeper line on top; green eyes radiant to an impossible jade luster. Skirt falling to just the top of her knee; silky blouse billowing over a thin, quiet frame. Heels barely two inches, enough for her five-foot-nine-inch height. Stocking seam straight up taut lines of recently waxed legs.

Ready, Dee flicked off her apartment light, shut her door.

Late Saturday night was the best time for the boys. Sunday allowed for so much abandon and unlimited drinking; everybody was loose.

There were the cocky, flannel-shirted, low-waisted "hip-hop" crowd, all sinewy muscles and impudent frosty stares. Dee had occasion to rub against one or two of these macho, trying-to-be-anything-other-then-white-middle-class kids, the little proud darlings sniffing at her like a cat when she walked by. They were great for a diversion, a quick pump to the ego. Hot live skin whispering with sweat from the oddly native "dance" these boys assumed they could perform until 3 a.m. It was many a night Dee slunk home with the taste of one of them on her lips, lay down on her muted pink bedspread, and pulled her skirt up to her waist.

Then there were the gym geeks, poured into suits and T-shirts, and any other tight-fitting garment they could find still in fashion; hair as sharp as their tongues; reason bulging south with their biceps. Yes, a big bicep was great, a rock-hard ass a pleasure, but Dee could never really stomach these body-without-mind men.

No, this night Dee's prey was the biggest, most elusive game of them all: the kings of this three o'clock train; the arrow-straight college boys, yuppie wannabes, the college crowd, blue bloods. The young men who traveled at least five to a pack, smoked with an almost feminine twist of hand, and spoke of law offices, stock reports, and master's degrees. The clean-shaven lads, so much more interesting than their older counterparts, the true young businessmen. These younger boys, fresh out of college (or some still in), living with Mom and Dad still, bright eyed and just a little fearful of this train ride from New York City.

Dee wanted—no, *needed*—to capture the youth of one of these straight-backed young men. She needed a quick stare, a coy play-it-cool smile, a turned, slightly stubbled cheek; the conspiratorial roll of muted urgings as "they" looked at her. She needed to prove to a boy that he had made a perfect score on his ride back to his quiet neighborhood.

On and off, a jumble of the club crowd. In her twenties, Dee had tried all those clubs: gay men's bars, too heavy on leather, too loose on talk; straight dance clubs, too many frosted-haired bimbos and their posing boyfriends; neo-post, cum-disco raves, more heroin pass out than fun. All of it had bored her so quickly. All of it so intrusive on Dee's delicate balance of desire, walk, and test. The lights, smoke, and assault of those cavernous clubs were too much for her in too close a space. In the city, or in her own neighborhood, a club was a club was a club. Dee would rather the consistent, quiet rumble of the train she now waited for, pulling from one stop and taking to the next; a fleeting connection of flight and speed. For Dee needed movement above all else, as much away *from* as going *to*. She needed the physical limitations of strutting on the shimmying metal floor, occasionally losing balance and catching an eye, or better yet, a hand to help her.

"I've always depended on the kindness of strangers," she always wanted to say.

If only one of those boys would reach to her. If only she was crazy enough to let her feet dangle for the briefest of moments. If only she could allow herself to yield to the expected stereotype of a woman walking late at night, alone on a busy train.

Of course Dee was no stereotype, or maybe, very strangely, she was. How many men wore a different face, a different garment, a different attitude at night than they did during the day? Away from the grind of the lunch crowd at Angelino's, Dee was a quiet butterfly, perfumed and primped. Far away from the stoic, curly-hared waiter who spoke low and performed tai chi on the back deck of his upstairs studio apartment on Sunday afternoons; Dee was no "David," she was sure of that, but she was not so unlike everyone else who shed their daily wrappings to find true heart in the velvet confines of their night. The silk G-string, the black garter, the push-up bra, high heels, lipstick, and rouge were clothes that covered, concealed, and reformed to reveal Dee.

She sauntered (never her very best thing); Dee felt best when not in motion. The train could move, the car could glide, the roller coaster could climb as she placed a hand on Earl Anderson's half-thick member in tenth grade, but Dee wanted to stay seated or steady standing. "Let the machine do the work" was her motto at work with the grinding pasta maker and her little home laptop. Dee wanted to preen. Dee would dance in place, set herself a spot and command from there.

Luckily, there was a plastic form (on these trains the seats were more like "plastic people rest forms" than actual seats) open only two steps down from the sighing open door and Dee took it. And luckily, five boys sitting around her (one on her immediate right, one a few seats down, and the last three across and down the train side) noticed her passing. They were together a draped group, but solid, a mass, linked by cologne and kinetic desire. If Dee was lucky, if she played this right, this tight little group of yuppie seedlings would be coalescing for her attention before the next stop.

The car was not as full as Dee had seen it most Saturday nights at this time. Summer was on its way and suburbanites used their weekends for further trips then a twenty-minute ride into the steaming city. Other than the group of chinos, loafers, and pastel shirts, there was only a young couple, a myriad of piercings between them, seemingly locked in an embrace at the far end of the train.

Dee knew that if somebody could ever tell (and the odds were low indeed) it would be a couple like that one. People who lived their entire adult existence dodging stares (piercings that numerous were impossible to ignore) would be perceptive enough to see under things others couldn't. Maybe God allowed them a special X-ray vision, a seventh-sense compensation for being born into a world where their deepest need surpassed the majority's "judgment."

Metal doesn't travel well on a dead-end street.

The true freaks of this world, inside or out, battling it or living it, needed as much as they could get in the way of defenses. Most people rationalized that that much hardware in a person's face *was* a defense, a raised-middle-finger cry of freedom. But what all the true freaks of the world were really doing was living the only way they knew how . . . by their hearts. They had no where to go, no place to be, couldn't escape the fire that licked at their tails because that fire was them, burning away all semblance of time and place and honor, glory and property. The fire moved as they moved, from libraries to school gym locker rooms to Friday night movies. The fire burned so bright, so white hot that the only salve a true freak had was his or her kindling spirit.

All that could be done was to look into the snapping flame and welcome it as Dee had welcomed leaving home at seventeen, ignoring the whispers of Ohio and Earl's confused yelling and coming here . . . close enough to New York, but far enough away. So, would that couple care to tell even if they could? Dee paid them no more than a passing glance and a tight smile as she suddenly felt the boy next to her flick his finger down her skirt!

He wanted to play; had his friends noticed his advance? Dee couldn't be sure, but she sure wasn't going to look at the curly-haired boy. He didn't need to be recognized just yet. He was brazen enough to touch a strange girl on a train; he had been cocky enough to imagine Dee would enjoy the touch. This was a treat indeed. Usually these kids were only forward with their mouths, spewing frat jokes or esoteric humor they thought only they understood.

Let him play, Dee thought. *I'll show him what a real woman is like. Take him out to the wire.*

Dee moved a whisper of a fraction on the train's next lurch; her taut upper thigh rubbing against the boy's soft hand. The kid hadn't moved, probably hoping at another pass, another slight touch. Dee looked down ever so demurely and traced the boy's pressed tan slacks to his tucked-in blue cotton shirt and then to the half-smiling face looking at her in shock.

"Sorry," Dee sighed. "Didn't mean to . . ."

"No, no," the boy protested, his slightly angular brown eyes staring down Dee's tight frame and then back up again. "The train just lurched and I . . ."

"I didn't say I minded," Dee cooed and smiled what she knew to be the second best of the three versions in her arsenal; mustn't blow him out of his socks right away. The object was to get his tongue in her mouth after all; that third smile would have been too intense right then. The kid needed as much confidence as he could muster.

Have to keep him interested and then pull him in, Dee mused to herself. *Hook, line and sinker* in, *and* out.

"I don't mind either," the kid responded with a wide smile of his own.

He had a deep dimple in his strong, slightly square chin, and chubby cheeks. From what Dee could spy of his body the boy was just on the other side of husky, maybe even a little chunky, but he was darling and . . . daring.

"Mind this?" Dee asked, placing her soft hand between the outside of her leg and the boy's. Fingers touched, palms arched and soon the two were holding hands.

"Wha . . . what's your name?" the boy asked.

His four friends moved like mercury; undulant and staring.

"Dee," she said, smiling still. "And yours?"

"Chris," the boy confessed, aware of his friends but keeping his eyes on the tall girl before him.

"Where'd you boys go tonight?" Dee asked loudly enough for the group to hear.

"No place, just a few bars," Chris admitted softly, hoping to engage Dee back into their private confidence.

Yes, Dee reminded herself, nearly forgetting because of Chris's brazenness. *Boys like this don't need an audience, even if it is their friends.*

"Why don't we sit by ourselves?" Dee whispered in Chris's ear. The couple stood, slightly touching hands as they walked to the far corner of the train; now there was a "pierced couple" in each end of the car!

Of course Chris's friends watched them, but Dee made sure to sit with her face to them; she'd stare them down if she had to. Two minutes from their destination—she had to work fast. She couldn't get off the train with Chris (if indeed the next stop was his) and she didn't know how long she could keep his attention. A boy this age, although ruled by the tightness in his pants, could very easily get overconfident or silly with the approach of the station that signified home or even a respite. No, Dee had to act now.

"I don't really go in for picking up men on trains," she began her speech. "But I just had to walk over and sit next to you."

"Thanks," Chris responded, looking down quickly then back up again.

"Do you mind if I ask you for a kiss?" Dee asked.

No place on God's green earth, from the wide acres of his family's south Ohio community, to the high crazy streets of San Francisco, to crowded Roman streets, had Dee ever known a straight man to refuse this simple request from a lady.

"Uh . . . yeah. I mean . . ." Chris started and in full view of the New York/New Jersey transportation posters and Chris's horny friends Dee liplocked the boy and found his tentative tongue just as the train pulled into the station.

"I, I . . ." Chris tried as his friends sprinted off the train giggling. "Give me your number. I'll . . ."

"Doors are gonna close, honey," Dee said and like a buffalo the boy followed his friends and jumped off the train onto the platform.

Dee smiled as Chris's friends literally grabbed their chubby companion and encircled him with wild stares and high fives. The buzzer sounded, the doors closed, and Dee smiled at the crisp college boy who stood licking his lips quietly for one last taste of the incredible woman he had just met.

The pierced couple hadn't looked up once. Going to the last stop, no doubt, where Dee would walk across the platform to catch a quiet train going the other way. Two stops and back home, savoring Chris's high sweet smell, his quivering lips, and the knowledge that a fire was burning and Dee had once again fed it her own brand of kindling.

Holes

Patrick Califia

It was a rare Saturday night when I had been able to hold depression at bay, as well as a clingy neurotic girlfriend who hated it when I went out alone, and put together the right combination of sexual need, adrenaline, and a little stash of MDA to go to the Saturday night party at the Catacombs. It was only three doors down the street from my house, but the prospect of having to take all of my clothes off in front of 100 or so sweaty, naked men (even if most of them were too lost in their own white-hot couplings to be aware of anyone but their mate in rut) was a challenge I often could not meet.

Catacombs parties happened every Saturday night, so it was easy to persuade myself that next week would be a better time to go. I was young, and had lost only one friend to suicide, a bitter woman I never expected to live out the full course of her years. To me, this was the apex of tragedy. I had not yet been slapped around enough by death to know that there is no such thing as a friend you can count on seeing again, and I had not lived through enough election-year crackdowns to know that a space for perverts will not necessarily be open next time you need to strut your wicked stuff.

The door to the insular world that called to me with a (butch) siren's voice was below street level. I carefully picked my nearsighted way down a few concrete stairs in the dark, barely touching the wrought iron handrail. The building was a unique dark blue-green, one of the less tarty painted ladies that marked San Francisco as a queer town. A brusque brass plaque on it read, "If you have not called, do not knock or ring now." (These parties were by appointment only.) Since I had duly made my reservation, I rang the bell, and was greeted by Steve McEachern, a tall and handsome man in his early thirties. I followed him into a tiny entry room that protected the rest of the space from view if you were standing in the doorway. In three steps I left the chill of autumn behind and entered a super-heated and humid world where everything smelled of testosterone, leather, amyl, and Crisco.

Steve had the biggest rings in his nipples that I'd ever seen, solid gold, and an even bigger one ran through the head of his shapely average-sized dick. His chest was nicely muscled, without being gym-shaped, built up, I suspected, solely with marathon sessions of whipping and fucking. He had a jaunty, short- but-unruly beard, and the devil's own twinkle in his eyes. I signed in, handed over my money, bought a new bottle of poppers, and greeted a few regulars whose names I knew. The door was going to be open for another hour, so everyone was pretty much still clustered in the front room, which had a long bar along one wall, and benches along the other walls. There were long sheets of facing mirrors which made the room seem much bigger than it really was, and gave you no escape from yourself. The sound system behind the bar was pumping out one of Steve's excellent party tapes, driving dirty disco music that made me want to get stoned and fuck somebody's lights out. I hoped this was not one of the awful nights when I would stand apart from the feast, unable to connect and embarrassed by my own thwarted longing.

Steve's ex-lover George, a drunken thug with a handlebar mustache and what we then referred to as "the dick of death," was holding down the far end of the bar, and made some obnoxious slurred comment to me that I ignored. Clustered near Steve and his clipboard were his current boy toy and Cynthia Slater, who had introduced said trickette to the Catacombs. This had happened more than once. She knew exactly what kind of men Steve would fall for. Right now she was in a good mood because they were a threesome; her swain had not yet left her and moved in with the twisted, high-octane fag whose gifted hands were her obsession. (And mine, though I was too cool to drool over him in public.) She had become a fixture at the Catacombs in part because she was as sexually outrageous as any guy in the place. Steve was genuinely fond of her and enjoyed playing with her from time to time. He had pierced her nipples because he knew it was something she really wanted, and nobody else would. But he was not the ardent, bisexual lover that she later described as her ideal master, when he was not around to contradict her.

Having revolted the Castro clones by being a fist fucker, and then having outraged the fist fuckers in a previous club by also being into S/M, Steve enjoyed asserting his independence by pissing everybody off again when he included her on the guest list. The gay men who came to these weekly events were amused or impressed by her epic sexual performances and intake of mind-altering substances, and sometimes surprised to find themselves attracted to her. A lot of them also just resented and ignored her. They wanted the Catacombs and the rest of their gay world to be a refuge where they would be protected from women and the fucked-up expectations of heterosexuality. Cynthia had first brought me here as her lover, and that had taken some of the tension out of the atmosphere by visibly making her as queer as the guys we jogged elbows with.

I turned my back to the bar to undress and stow the regulation boots, jeans, T-shirt, and flannel shirt that I had thrown on before my stressful five-minute trip down the hill. The men who came to these parties wouldn't be caught dead out of full leather if you saw them in the Brig or the Ambush, but they rarely bothered to wear more than a leather vest or a jockstrap to the Catacombs, because it was a rule that everything got removed within thirty seconds of signing in. "Prissy queens" who tried to keep their clothes on were often relieved of their finery against their will. You might have thought that Cynthia's presence up front, with her gorgeous full bosom and cute little ass and long black hair, would have made it easier for me to be naked there, but we did not feel the same way about our bodies. She had a sexual style that was stereotypically masculine, but she occupied her feminine body completely and boldly. She was there as a woman, and I was there as someone who wished I was not.

Covered up, it was so much easier for me to maintain an illusion of masculinity. I was the only dyke I knew who strapped on a dick to fuck or made my bottoms call me Sir. As much as I enjoyed seducing butch female bottoms, I wanted to be here, with leathermen who locked other men in cages, flogged and insulted, and came inside their chosen prey. Too often, I felt more like one of them than I did like a lesbian. I was soothed by the ease with which they slid past one another, somehow being able to read whether a hand on the butt or a tweak to a tit would be welcome. I could not imagine this sensual treatment of strangers being allowed among a group of women. I loved the leathermen's utterly masculine bearing (often interspersed a few seconds of camping it up that only underscored their maleness) and unabashed homosexuality. Nowhere else but in San Francisco had I seen this unselfconscious and frank desire which was not only gay but deeply perverse.

At leather bars, and at more select gatherings like this one, I was a curiosity. There were men who resented my presence and tried to exclude me, men who felt I belonged there because I was also an enthusiastic practitioner of restraint and torture, and only a handful who were able to articulate some confusion about my gender. It's amazing, actually, that any of them mentioned this to me, because I could hardly bring it to the front of my own consciousness.

Naked and therefore doomed to endure whatever was about to happen next, I oddly felt better. I was only one naked person among many, and far from the only imperfect body. The Catacombs was not a place where you had to be thin, white, well-built, or young to get cruised. Sexual skill was valued as much as a handsome face. My party attitude switched on, a shift in values that made bare skin seem like a bold statement, an act of bravery that proved I belonged. I went back to the bar and deliberately slid between George and the person next to him to get a Styrofoam cup of coffee. He was smoking a cigarette and made as if to grab my tits. I fended off his touch, which wasn't very difficult because he just wanted to provoke me, not grope me. George got what he wanted by being such a crappy and belligerent top that eventually somebody who didn't have anything better to do would throw him on his back and fuck him. "Is that a donkey dick," I asked, wrinkling my nose, "or are you just a jackass?" A few men nearby laughed loudly, so George stood up and jiggled his big, floppy meat at them. Like he ever used it for anything other than a handle.

Bob was also at the bar. We were always glad to see each other. He was a slight, middle-aged guy with a bald patch in the middle of his head. Bob was thought to be a little peculiar because he attended the Metropolitan Community Church on a regular basis. But he was always quick with a bawdy jibe, so his Christianity didn't seem to be holding him back much. He was the first balding man I ever had a crush on. It was, after all, something that only happened to men, so it was virile and sexy. He didn't try to hide it, he just kept his hair short and didn't trip about it. I always enjoyed looking at his scrumptious ass, but the magical spark never flew between us, for some reason. I don't know that I ever even saw him play.

Everybody there was already high, and I wanted to catch up. I stirred a drizzle of white powder into the sweet, milky coffee and drank it quickly. While George bobbed and weaved over his stein of beer, I stood beside him, unable to get the size of his cock out of my mind and equally unable to imagine ever touching him. My skin, flesh, bones, and spirit vibrated with tension and ambivalence about his ruined alcoholic craggy face as the MDA took effect. I had brought an empty glass spice bottle with me, and poured just enough poppers into the bottom of it to be absorbed by the cotton ball inside. I had been taught not to leave any surplus liquid to slosh around. It might burn someone who was too high to keep track of the contents of the bottle while they brought it to their mouth and nose.

Just as the music was melding nicely with my heartbeat, and the edges of my vision were beginning to acquire a heavenly glimmer, I saw him. And he saw me. Jim, the deaf body builder. He had just finished a quick sign-language conversation with his small, dark-haired lover, who gave him a peck on the cheek and disappeared into one of the back rooms with a prospective bottom. I had seen Jim at parties before and felt a little self-conscious about his disability, but always gave him a smile. He was gorgeous to look at, thick chested, heavy strong legs, arms that could crack an ox in half, and yet he carried himself with a cheerful and even humble openness. There was no shred of snotty attitude about him. As he grinned and swam toward me with the slow grace of a muscle queen, I knew that we were going to play. The eye contact which usually sufficed for Catacombs regulars to make their dates had, for once, worked the way it was supposed to work for me.

I don't know how he did this, but even though Jim towered over me and probably outweighed me by at least 200 pounds, this sweet monster with his shaved head managed to convey a submissive attitude. As he came toward me, he flexed his arms, just a little. It wasn't a studied pose, just an anxious reflex, perhaps reminding himself why he might be an acceptable offering. He made a guttural, indecipherable sound that I think was involuntary. It reminded me of the cry of a magpie whose tongue had been cut out. I wondered what it was like to be born without hearing, to never know that sensation. It didn't seem sad to me as much as it seemed an attractive challenge, a difference that I was determined to bridge.

I reached for his face, and he put his arms on either side of the bar, creating a little cave where I could focus on and touch him. I could not see around him, and enjoyed being ensconced safely behind the bulk of his well-disciplined meat. We kissed each other for a long time, long enough I think that he was surprised. His lips were as muscular as the rest of him, but his tongue was small and shy. When I stopped kissing him, it was only to put my mouth on his neck and shoulder, to lick the bitter-flavored sweat from his sandpapery skin and bite into his muscles. One of the things I loved about fisting was the way that it resembled and yet differed from sadomasochistic role-playing. As an S/M top, I was expected to be distant and formal, but fisting tops got extra points for being hands-on, sensually giving, and physically involved. I once heard Steve, our sensei in depravity, say, "Why the hell would I fuck somebody I don't want to kiss?"

The attention in the room had shifted subtly in our direction. Any hot scene in the Catacombs drew voyeurs like a sprinkle of fish food on the top of an aquarium. The assembled body of experienced fisters had eyes in the back of their collective heads for other people's pleasure. Perhaps because we were all so loaded, it seemed as if we could experience a portion of one another's bliss. Watching somebody else get expertly plowed was a fine form of foreplay, a rare bit of pornographic eye candy that could never be replayed. This shot of peer attention gave me a burst of confidence and energy. Eighty-five hungry assholes can't be wrong. Getting my hand into Jim was going to be a very good time indeed.

Many pairs and threesomes had already left the front room ahead of us. There were two more rooms (not counting the tiny bathroom, where I often perched on the sink to pee, to the consternation of whoever was douching out in the shower). The very back room contained "sling alley," a half-dozen leather butt baskets and stirrups hung facing each other on heavy chain, with studded leather holders for cans of Crisco swinging conveniently at the side of each station. I could already tell from the volume of oinking and the resounding chains that all the available slots in this room were taken. There was also a bondage cross there, built out of heavy eight-by-eight timbers, but that was not where my scene with Jim was headed.

The middle room had several platforms around the walls, each containing a thin plastic-covered mattress. A wide waterbed hogged center stage, and a gurney hung from springs and chains at right angles. I saw a vacant platform to the left and just inside the doorway, and steered us toward it. Jim was alongside me, making faces of sweet anguish as I toyed roughly with his pecs. We were so in synch with each other that I didn't seem to push him onto the bed; it was as if I had lifted him and placed him there, like a perfect slice of pie on a little white saucer. I had already grabbed a pile of towels, from exactly where I did not remember. We settled into the missionary position of handballing—he was on his back in front of me, I was sitting with my legs under his thighs, tucking a towel underneath his massive ass. He had shaved all over before coming to the party, but his skin was still slightly abrasive. To my ripped hands, his skin felt both downy soft and yet had a texture that was elusively pleasing to explore. Jim relaxed completely and let me touch him everywhere. He gave me a lazy, trusting smile, in no hurry for me to shake hands with his joy spot.

When people think of getting to know somebody, the image they have is of talking to that person. But there are other ways to acquire knowledge about another person and make yourself known to them. As I took my time to single out and massage each one of Jim's muscles, from the top of his head down to the soles of his feet, his body was reassured and befriended, the same way that a cat comes to accept the comfort of a knowledgeable stranger's lap and fingertips. I was so lost in sampling every inch of him that some of our voyeurs moved on to more ebullient scenes. But men with a similar style of play were taking places near us, creating an invisible temple of silent seduction. With our hands and heaving hips, we were weaving pleasure that filled the air, and each sensation that brought someone joy got the rest of us higher.

A sexual touch can say, *I want you,* but it can also say, *I care for you,* and in the long moments that I was enclosed by this man's scent and the visual delight of his body, I was not in love with him, but I was loving him. It was something that we didn't have to say out loud, he knew it by the look on my face and the quality of my caress. He put his hands on either side of his cock, showing me how fat it was, and made one of his incoherent cawing sounds. The tendons of his neck popped out with the tension of arousal. I am not ashamed to say that from time to time the edges of my eyes stung from unshed tears. I was amazed, yet again, by the power and generosity of an unabashed bottom. I've never understood how someone can do that, simply let go and invite me into their psyche and their orifices. And as much as I want to glory in that gift, I never feel quite worthy of it. But with Jim I was not intimidated. He was letting me know again and again that I was doing everything perfectly, that he wanted exactly what I had for him.

The smooth surface of the freshly opened can of Crisco was cool and creamy, with a comical little peak, the tip of which curled over and nearly touched itself again. The pointed fingers of my left hand dipped into and destroyed that snow-white, virgin plane. The fistful of grease I took away with me left a hole behind, a pit with a rippled edge that was almost as big as Jim's asshole was going to stretch to receive me. I rubbed the Crisco onto his chest, down the six-pack of his abdomen, and smacked on his pectoral muscles a little, making the skin red. He groaned and nodded, and lifted his legs. Because he could not say "please" out loud, his entire body was shouting that wish.

Time slowed as I ran my slippery fingers down to his navel, and around his cock. I would have been happy to jack him off or blow him, but Catacombs sexuality was not dick centric. I rarely even saw a hard cock until after 4 a.m. I wondered if being able to get an erection was adequate compensation for coming down from whatever cocktail had been chosen for this evening's chemical backdrop.

When I closed my fist around Jim's full, heavy nutsack and squeezed, his face twisted with a little pain and a great deal of wonder. *So this is how much I can feel,* he seemed to be saying. *That, yes, and that, yes, more, yes, that.* Wanting to hear his guttural cry again, I dabbled at the outermost rim of his anus, tickling it, and the strange noise pealed out, a permission and a plea. My other hand wandered across his chest, keeping his nipples hard, while my index finger circled a half-inch inside him, the preliminary move to creating a slick funnel that would admit all of me. I wanted to punch into him, and containing these fierce impulses was like being perpetually teased and kept right on the edge of coming.

As we played, my hunky accomplice would sometimes hoist his own thighs aloft, to give me greater access, and sometimes allow them to rest upon my legs again, when his arms had tired or he was being sent into some other world as I entered the private world inside of him. I moved around too, sometimes sliding back so that my arm was parallel to his body, scooting to one side to obtain the proper angle, looking for a moment of relief from fatigue so I could keep my forearm moving. Everything that we did was reciprocal, like a dance. There was no force, just an invitation to press on, as he opened for me, trusting me with his pleasure and his life. And I could not get enough of him, I wanted him to fly and gasp and experience release after release, until he had enough. And by that I mean, really enough, not the polite excuse that a self-conscious bottom will make when he fears that the top is tired or losing interest, or is ashamed of needing too much. I thought that getting too much of Jim might almost be enough.

I loaded the palm of my right hand with grease and poised both of my hands side by side, trading off, going in and coming out, changing the direction and pressure so that I did not make him sore. Each time he made way, I rewarded him by advancing a bit more. I felt as if I were being drawn into a labyrinth that was flushed dark pink with blood and lined with a material smoother than satin or glass. My hands were only halfway into him when I began to feel the pulse of his heart, resonating even here, governing the rhythm of our coming together. I do not think I could have dawdled any longer without losing the momentum of growing arousal, but still, when his sphincter swallowed me, it was too soon, too much—for me, not for him. I gasped out loud, and almost fell on top of him.

I've heard fisting described with horror (or with faux scientific objectivity as "brachiopractic eroticism"). I am at a loss to understand this ignorance and repugnance. We are afraid of holes and their dark secrets, which they might someday tell—contrary holes, holes that will not open when we want them to, demanding holes that cannot be satisfied, dirty holes that no one is supposed to look at or lick or touch (yet still receive adulation). It occurred to me, however, that sometimes holes are filled with light. Sometimes the things they have to tell us are wonderful. The empty place within Jim was akin to a forest grove or a cathedral. We need such quiet places in order to hear the voices of the forces that made us.

For a man to allow himself to be penetrated is for some people the equivalent of the sky falling. It is a disaster; nothing could be more unnatural or threatening to the social order. The world does not want the spiritual child that is born from the trusting and magical bowel of a man who is not afraid to be a hole, and a very large hole at that. But I wanted that birth, I was Jim's impregnator and midwife. As Donna Summer wailed like a deranged witchy nymphomaniac, we jousted and joked with one another, each small movement of mine inside of him triggering a wealth of thrills. I tapped my forearm, hard, and his abs vibrated. I kept at it, knowing I would have bruises the next day halfway up to my elbow. Jim put his hands behind his head, holding it up with bulging forearms so that he could see what was in him, and urged me on in his own untranslatable language.

His mad, rolling eyes and excited calls made me hard and wet. It was as if my arm was a cock that was long and rigid enough to make him levitate. The need to cum built in the pit of my own stomach, and he saw me delay my climax again and again so that I could stay with him and go a little higher toward heaven. I would see a flash of gratitude on his face, then disbelief as we continued, gently but relentlessly, finding new nooks and crannies, new degrees of being utterly stuffed, fucked, had, fondled internally, and loved senseless.

His cock had slowly continued to get thicker and thicker, but not longer, and I had glanced occasionally at this partial hard-on, wondering at his ability to manage such a thing when all of his nerve endings were otherwise occupied. He was covered with a visible gel of sweat and Crisco, and the stench of poppers was making me dizzy. He groaned again, a series of bass notes forced from the pit of his gut, and began to piss. I found his prostate and pressed on it, moved back and forth across it, making sure this expulsion of water felt like the weirdest and most intense orgasm on earth. The hot fluid was almost clear, and didn't smell like urine. It was distilled from his body in a mysterious way that bypassed all the usual processes that make cum or piss. I leaned forward, grinning ear to ear, and he shared it with me, so that we were both laughing and tripping in the hot fountain my hand had milked out of him.

Three times we built up to a point where his body was driven to release some balmy, liquid evidence of his extremity. Each time, I let my posture and facial expression indicate that I wanted to share this communion with him. Jim could not tell me how he felt, so he shared his piss with me, a sweet-smelling gift, playing it across my chest while I shivered and laughed and admired his feckless bulk, joined to me like a Siamese twin. These outbursts came at shorter and shorter intervals, and I began to think that we might eventually have to separate. The texture inside of him had changed just a little, but even such a small effect made me nervous. The fragility of the lining of his channel was something I never forgot. And his color had changed too; he had acquired a pale tone that made me think he needed a rest.

Then there was a break in the music, and every bit of action in the club hung fire. The gut-wrenching bellows of "Yeah, you fucker, yeah" and "You can take it, take it all" stopped. We had been caught in the music, everyone unaware that they were moving in time with it, and it had created both a feeling of unity and pockets of privacy in our butt-pumping frenzy. After a long silence of five seconds, we heard three sharp slaps, then the extra-loud sound of a baby crying. When the music resumed, it was as if the power had come back on.

"Yeah, you fucker. Fuck you!" Creak, creak. "Take it all!" Enough of us started laughing to break the dramatic tension that had kept Jim and I hard at work. He put both of his hands up and touched my face, squeezing it to say thank you, and made a regretful gesture indicating that I had to begin my departure.

Considering how much I love getting inside of someone, I am usually in no hurry to leave that warm and responsive shelter. Even if it would have been safe to quickly slip my hand out of him, I would not have been so rude. I stopped thrusting or turning my hand from side to side or slowly opening it a bit and closing it again. His guts stopped contracting around me, and his heartbeat slowed. As the tunnel ahead of me slowly collapsed, I withdrew, only turning my hand when I had to negotiate a tiny glitch in the passage. There was a final outcry from him as his rectum shrank and shat me out, but there was no disappointment in it, only victory. His asshole looked like a crimson rose in full bloom.

I laid down on top of him and we kissed again, relishing each other's naughtiness and stamina. I told him again and again how hot, handsome, and fun he was, but all of these words sounded trivial. He had taken me along, allowed me to vicariously experience his bliss, and granted my every wish for a man whose need matched my own. That was the hole that I had needed to fill. For a long time after that fuck, I knew that I mattered in the world. I knew I had something good about me, that there was a reason for me to exist, my counterpart was real and not some insane figment of my damaged sexual fantasies.

We staggered out to the front room to get something to drink and receive quiet congratulations from friends who had enjoyed watching us enjoy one another. I perched on one of the padded benches, which had become so slippery from contact with a series of well-greased buttocks that even a brand new towel was no guarantee that I wouldn't shoot off my seat like a burlesque banana fired from the cannon of its skin. I had forgotten, while I fisted my bodybuilder bottom god, that there were breasts swinging against my arms and getting in my way, forgotten my cunt, forgotten that I was not a man he would want the way gay men yearn for one another. I knew what my cock looked like, but if I reached down for it, it would never be there.

I don't remember the rest of the party. I only remember what happened afterward, when I had to leave that camaraderie behind and go home. My lover had waited up for me and was impatient to hear the juicy details. She was titillated, but jealous. "You let some man piss on you?" she jeered.

I was abruptly plunged into a worldview where the things that I had just done were noxious rather than blessed. Walking home, I felt like a flawless topman who had triumphed over the tight-assed forces of evil. She didn't want me thinking I was a faggot, even if she called herself a daddy's boy in bed. She had to force me to see that Jim and I were on different sides of the gender divide. He was supposed to be the enemy, someone I held at bay lest he gain some toxic advantage over me. The flat chest that I had unconsciously assumed in my imagination as I walked home, and the weight of my cock and balls in the left side of the crotch of my jeans, were not spoken of, but violently exorcised just the same. I made some kind of sarcastic retort, but shame stuck to me and burned, like napalm. It is too easy to take judgments to heart when the people who issue them also say they love us.

Approximately twenty years later, I place a lot less stock in "love" like that. I am no longer willing to be in a relationship where I do all the things that men are supposed to do while I pretend to be something else. I won't take any shit for being a cocksucker and a man who desires other men. My beard is on the outside of my face now. People have accused me of cutting off my tits, but they don't understand that the surgery, for me, was about what I gained, not what I lost. The flat chest that I wanted is mine now, I don't have to imagine it, I can touch my pecs whenever I want and when I embrace someone, I can relax into full-body contact without wincing away. My cock is still hiding, but hey, I could always win the lottery. In the meantime, I have the pleasure of men who want to be fucked the way that I can fuck them to prove that my dick is real enough. If fist-fuckers who wear their red hankies on the right can be big fierce queer studs, I can try to be as proud of my holes as they are of theirs.

The next time I went to the Catacombs and Jim was there, he smiled at me and came over for a hug. I was happy to see him and embraced him in return, but my girlfriend had come with me, and so I deflected his unspoken invitation. The next time we met, I was available, but he was not. We never played again. We both thought, no doubt, that we had lots of time to revisit that mattress, or perhaps even grab the waterbed.

He is gone now. He died, I think, in the first wave of men who died, of a disease that had no name. Steve had a heart attack and was spared the ordeal of witnessing that epidemic. Cynthia died many years later, because she was just enough of a faggot to share a virus with the men who never really accepted her. The Catacombs has been closed for decades. And I find that it is pretty difficult for me to go looking for another grinning, good-natured sex pig to wear for a bracelet. Would it be the same without the drugs? Could I work my whole hand in and out of a shivering, gulping sphincter without being cut in half by grief? I feel like a dog who has lost his master, who mourns without understanding. But I also continue to remember, and be grateful. Within me, still, Jim's shameless virtuoso one-person gang bang is an eternal miracle, a seed of joy potent enough to turn the whole world into a bacchanalian garden. Do you have a furrow worthy of that seed? And if you accept it, where will you sow it in your turn?

Getting Real

Chris Jones

I sometimes wonder if I would be a gender queer if I weren't Hite Masturbation Type III. Maybe if I was, say, Type I where you're touching your clit all the time, I would have been more sexually aware of myself as a woman. But in classic Type III style I always find myself face down on the bed, ass in the air, and something clutched in my hand (usually a bunched-up blanket) that makes me feel so good.

It probably wouldn't have mattered though. I was a boy in my fantasies before I knew about penises or that the things I was imagining had anything to do with sex. When I learned about penises and erections at age ten, I incorporated them into my fantasy life. My poor, fantasy boy self was always getting himself into situations where his pants got pulled down and his erection was exposed and touched. Or worse, he was forced to touch it himself. What an embarrassment.

About the time I started getting interested in boys, so did my fantasy self. Then I found out about homosexuality, and things got very scary for a while. I'm not really sure what I fantasized about in my late teens, but I remember that I made up a whole list of things I wouldn't let my fantasy self think about, including other guys' erections.

By my early twenties some of my gay male friends were starting to come out of the closet, and the fantasy of being one of them no longer seemed so bad. Also I had learned about fellatio. So now my internal young man not only got his penis touched, he also got to put it in the occasional mouth, when he wasn't down on his knees sucking someone else's cock while jerking off.

By my thirties the sexual revolution had gotten far enough along so that there were sex manuals for gay men as well as heterosexuals. By sneaking peeks at my friends' copies and finally working up enough courage to mail order one for myself, I finally got a pretty complete picture of all the things two (or more) men could do with each other, and I incorporated a lot of that into my fantasy life. But my favorite fantasy was still having my cock in my hand, making it come. And fantasy it stayed, since I couldn't find any way to actually do it.

As you can see by the progression of decades, I was not on the fast track to becoming a transsexual. At some point I stumbled on enough information about female-to-male surgery to be sure I wasn't going to get a real, functioning cock out of the deal. Besides there are things about being a woman, including having regular hormonal cycles, that I found (and still find) very appealing and didn't want to give up.

But it wasn't practical considerations that kept me from buying a dildo until I was in my forties, only lack of imagination. I thought they were some leftover anachronism from the era when vaginal orgasms were in fashion and women didn't know where their clits were. I couldn't imagine what any sane woman would do with one.

Until I saw Carol Queen's, that is. There she was on the screen, dildo strapped on, her cock up her boyfriend's ass, and coming against the base of the dildo! It was just like the bunched up covers—only better. Much better. I ordered one immediately.

That sounds nice on paper, but in reality it took a bit longer. There are lots of different kinds, in various price ranges. Since I wasn't entirely sure if this would work for me, I didn't want to spend a lot of money. I was able to find a realistic looking, inexpensive, rubber cock with a partial scrotum attached. For some reason, probably due to not actually seeing a naked man until I was twenty, I never incorporated balls into my fantasy self, so this was attractive not so much from the fantasy point of view as it was because it gave the dildo a larger base, giving me more surface area to work with.

There was also the problem of harnesses. The women in the video all had one, but the harnesses in the catalog were expensive, especially the hand-crafted leather ones. Fortunately a helpful book explained that if you're not going to fuck anybody and you just want to wear the dildo, you can stuff it in a pair of briefs and it will stay quite nicely.

I had a bad moment when the package arrived. The helpful book that had explained about the briefs also wasn't too keen on rubber dildos as opposed to the more expensive silicone ones. They described the rubber ones as giant novelty pencil erasers. And I had to admit when I opened the box that it definitely had the look and feel of an eraser. A very large eraser. I had a vision of using it for one if it didn't work out as a masturbation toy. I'd just start with the head and rub out my writing mistakes while wearing down the phallus . . . it was not an erotic picture.

To get past that I had to spend some time with the dildo. I stroked it, ran my finger over the piss hole and the smooth glans, found the vein running down the shaft, then made my way back up to the top. It didn't take long before I could start to think of it as a cock again. My cock.

Much as I wanted to check it out right away, I also wanted the first time to be special. I waited for an evening when I had the house to myself. I got out a flannel shirt, a pair of khakis, and a pair of my husband's briefs. Discarding my woman drag, I put on the shirt and then slipped on the briefs up to my knees. I was already hot, thinking about putting the dildo up against me. I picked it up and placed the base against my wet cunt. It was electric. But I wanted more than an orgasm. I wanted to be my aroused man self. I drew the briefs up and settled the dildo into place so that my hard-on created a bulge in front. Then I put on the pants.

My rampant cock was already making me ache, but I forced myself to walk around a bit, stroking it through my pants with loving fingers. I lit some candles, laid down my bi-gender talisman—a bear carved in tiger's eye with a tiny fault line running through it diagonally—and made sure the shades were down and the curtains closed. Then, I lay down on the bed and unzipped my pants, stoking my cock through the briefs. I pulled it out through the hole and spent a moment admiring my erection. I was hard, I wanted it bad, and I knew that this was going to work for me.

It took a little experimenting to get the stroking right. While real cocks like the most attention paid to the head, mine needed firm strokes up and down the whole length, especially firm when I got to the base. What seemed best was using my fingertips at the top, then tightening my hand and thrusting my cock up through my fist. I followed that with a gentle trip back to the head and repeated the process. About this time I realized the candles were throwing distinct shadows on the wall, and I knelt up on the bed and watched the shadow of my hand caressing my very own penis. It was more real than any fantasy I had ever had.

I wish I could say I came that way, but I really am a Type III and I need to be face down, pushing into something in order to come. So I bent over, put my ass in the air—the classic gay male bottom begging to be fucked—and thrust my cock down hard into my hand. Shortly after that I lost focus. It wasn't about my position or my hand or my cock anymore. Things were just really good. Then I came, the way I always come—with my clit.

It's not that the dildo failed to make my fantasy real. It was much realer than it had ever been. But any meaningful play is bound to call forth profound truths. I am a bi-gendered person. I need my cock, whether in my head or in my hand, to come, but I need my clit as well. Acknowledging that isn't a failure on my part to be the man I want to be. Instead, ignoring it, as I have done so often in the past, is a failure to be my true self, both man and woman. I'm very lucky that I didn't wait any longer to find that out.

Shoes

Shaun Levin

Imagine. Red leather shoes with shining gold threads hugging the tips, stretching along the sides to circle the slim high heels. Soft and smooth like the skin of an unwashed peach. The touch you can feel without touching. Imagine the leather pressing against your skin, cuddling your toes together, holding onto the sides of your feet. Imagine being lifted. Head high and towering above the rest. I'm here at the window, my nose against the cool glass, watching the shoes beckon me like an open palm, waiting for me to slide my feet in. One at a time. Slowly and lusciously like a knife into summer butter.

My hands are sweating against the glass, a circle of mist has formed around my nostrils, and my feet are so tired. Heavy like lead in these flat heels. The day began months ago, and I need to rest. How I long to walk into the shop and buy those shoes. For a split second I can picture myself. I see myself walking in, parting the glass like saloon doors. I'm here. Serve me. Now.

But I can't. Not anymore. People recognize me in this city.

The last time I bought shoes like this was back in high school, in the days when I could hide from the world behind family. I'd take the bus into Tel Aviv where the buildings and the streets and the hot smells were so beautiful and the people were all strangers to me. It was safe to do that then. I could tell the salesman that they were for my sister, please, or for my mother.

"Should I wrap them, then?" he'd say.

"Oh, yes, please," I'd say.

And I'd watch him cover the box with wrapping paper and ribbons. I'd watch him slide it into a sturdy shopping bag and I'd take it from him like a gift. On the bus home I'd sit with the box on my lap, rubbing against me to the gentle vibrations, my cock getting harder as it chiselled its way into me. A sixteen-year-old boy's anticipation of womanhood. These were my antidotes to fear and shame.

Before going inside I'd dump the bag, the box, and the wrapping paper; hide the shoes in my jacket, under my armpits, and go straight up to my room. Buy anything nice in Tel Aviv? my mother might call from the kitchen. Just walked around, I'd say, stuffing the shoes into the back of my cupboard, covering them with the spare mohair blanket I kept there. Each night I was surprised to find the treasure beneath the yellow and faded blanket. Each night I'd rediscover the shoes, safely stashed away like stolen goods. Each night was the same journey, each time a little closer. My first pair were. Imagine. Black platforms with golden stars set in thick Perspex heels. Always a man of extremes, my mother would say.

I'd sit at my desk, right leg over left, feeling the gentle weight of the shoe as I swayed my foot up and down. Up and down. Impatiently waiting. For something. To happen. I'd file my nails with the emery-boards I kept in my desk drawer, stroke my long straight hair with the ivory brush. Eyeing myself in the mirror, I'd run the tips of my fingers along my legs, down to the shoes, caressing the leather that pressed snugly against my toes. And hugged the sides of my feet. And I'd cup the heel in the palm of my hand. That cool transparent texture. Like glass. Like glass it was.

Then I'd walk slowly across the room, a white sheet draped over my body, keeping to the carpet, careful not to let the loud heels touch the floor. With heels like these you can't walk too slowly. And if you don't keep moving, you lose your balance. Stop pacing up and down, my father might shout from downstairs. I'm doing my homework, I'd say.

I only stop now at windows with shoes for men and for women. With my face gazing at the rough boots and indelicate Italian shoes, I let my eyes feast on the long shining black boots and the thin heels on the slim blue or white or orange shoes. Not shoes. There should be another name for them, something to distinguish them from all other footwear. They have these tiny silver studs. Imagine. They have gold-tipped points. I've got used to doing this. Facing one way, and looking the other. If the winds change I'll probably remain this way, squinting to the side, my face to the front, for the rest of my life. Never make faces, my mother would say. The clocks strike, the winds change. You never know.

I can't just walk into a store, buy the shoes, and take the nice and easy breezy route home. The route that's green and tree lined and no one sits on park benches and calls out to you. Hey! those beautiful high-school boys you want to look like, but cannot, will shout. They point and jeer. The sound of their beer bottles ringing as they bring them together, cheering: *Le'chaim, motek.* Sweetie pie. Throwing their heads back to laugh and gobble down warm beer. Hair shining in sunlight, and tight skin, unblemished, clinging to their bodies like lovers. Skin you cannot touch. You see nothing. You hold your hands tightly at your sides. Your insides tightly in your hands. The way Olga smuggles her drugs through customs. Just walk. Just keep walking.

It's a sunny day. Imagine. The sky is blue and the sidewalks are clean. I walk into the store and the salesman, nice jacket, open-necked shirt, light wool trousers and, ooh, bulge, approaches me, respectfully.

"Sir," he'd say. "May I help you?"

"Those there," I'd say. "The red ones in the window."

"They're you," he'd say, and smile. "Would you like to try them on?"

"Ooh, yes," I'd say. "Thank you."

That's how it would happen. Nice and easy. Just like I said. Sometimes it's not enough to do what you want in the safety of your home. You want to take it with you onto the street. Sometimes you become so afraid of an open door you stop the thoughts from venturing out. You chase away the voices begging to be let in. Sometimes I think pacing up and down in my green knee-high boots and threadbare denim shorts is not real if no one can see me. I can stroke myself in front of the mirror. I can knead my chest, push on the muscles, press against my nipples. I can pull my stomach in. I can hold my head back and feel my hair brushing against my spine. And it's just me looking at me.

I want those shoes. I want them like a man who wants a man cannot live without a deep voice so close he can breathe its soothing sound. I want them like a cynic longs for beauty and a joker longs for candor. Ah. Standing on the tip of a mountain singing out to the world. High-heeled shoes carry you to such warm, strong places you cannot help but want to go back. I reach inside and touch those places. Stroke them, lean on them. I pull up my black tights and put on my silk blouse. A blouse so thin only skin can see it. The blouse that tickles the callused tips of my nipples and rustles against the stubble on my chest. I swing my hands and move my hips to a rhythm dictated by high heels and silk garments. Then I am happy.

She's standing next to me now. Looking at the same shoes, perhaps.

"Aren't they gorgeous?" she says.

"The red ones?" I say.

"Gorgeous," she says.

I have memories. Nice childhood memories from a childhood I prefer to forget. My mother's dressing room with tall oak cupboards and a thick cream carpet. And the vanity table with the square leather-framed mirror and perfumes and light pink powder with soft brushes. And the wine-red Lancôme case with rectangles of blue, green, and brown eye shadow. When she was out, the room was mine. I could try on anything I liked. The tennis skirt with the pastel sunflowers and the skin-colored stockings that stroked my little pee-pee. I was in a void of evening gowns and soft shoes that were too big. And just right. For me. I would step out of the dressing room into the bedroom, throwing the skirt to the sides and spinning around to make it whirl around me. And the mink stole that even in summer was so cool I wanted to keep my cheek in it forever. I would wrap it around my shoulders and stand before the mirror. All dressed up.

At the vanity table I'd brush my cheeks gently with rouge and paint my eyes with blue shadow. I would screw the tip of the lipstick out of its tube, make an O shape with my lips, painting first the bottom then the top lip. Then I'd rub them together, back and forth, to spread the color evenly. Like my mother did before she and my father went dancing at The Room at the Top. I'd hold a tissue between my lips and press down and check what my kiss looked like. And the taste. The flavor that can't be compared to anything in the world. A taste that is nothing but itself.

Memories like these become immortal. That's when dead things stay alive inside. But like the dead, they haunt you. They come back to trouble you with unfinished business. They take you through labyrinths of mysteriously connected threads. Everything is joined to everything: the rouge to the mirror to the white skirt to the shoes in the window. And back to Dalia and the ballet classes I wanted to be a part of, and to her brother Ahron I loved so much I wished I was Dalia.

So? Buy the shoes, for God's sake! Easier dreamt than done. Believe me. It's not a question of money. And it's not a question of whether Leo would frown on it or not. He encourages me. I know he does. He brought me back a satin nightgown from his last trip to London. That's proof enough. He's a nice guy. My boyfriend. Leo. You'd like him. Imagine. Tall and dark with a beautiful chest, and a thick pair of hands with long, slim fingers. From the moment we met. Well, after the first few times. I told him: This is what I like. You like it, stay, you don't, don't. He said, you look good in that. Let's see you walk across the room.

Now I have my shoes made for me. So I try, as I must, standing here, to memorize their shape to tell Olga. Give me specifics, she'll say, or else you'll never get what you want. So I must remember the things that count. The size of the heel and the shape of the tip and whether the leather is suede or polished. I like the heels to be high enough so the ground seems softer, farther away. And the tips must be round. Olga says the rounder the tip the kinder the step. More subtle. It's her philosophy of footwear.

As for herself. She says if only she looked different she'd make her own shoes. What's the point, she says. If a person's fat and ugly, she says, who cares what they wear. Nobody notices. Unless they dress like thin people. Fat people who dress like thin people are different. Come in and sit down. Now imagine this. The Palace of Versailles boiled down to fit into one room. For her guests, a red velvet chaise lounge with a heavy wooden frame and one lace cushion. For herself, a high-backed chair where she strokes her Pekinese with one hand, ready to sketch with the other. Olga pours tea from the samovar she brought with her from Moscow. We suck on sugar crystals, and she says: Bring those shoes to life. Tell me everything. Which I do.

I have learned not to take the small details for granted. In the beginning I would say to Olga, put the glittery stars on this side of the heel, and make a rounded point. And back at the window the glitter would be on that side of the heel, and the point much pointier. I've learned to pay attention to what I must remember. I have no choice. I can't walk into a shoe store, dressed in a three-piece suit and leather briefcase, and ask the mouth with the wad of bubble gum, do you. Excuse me, do you have those red leather shoes, ahem, the ones in the window with the golden strips. Those ones. Do you have them in a size forty-four? Whoozitfor? Her nose is a raisin, and her eyes—narrow slits of suspicion.

People do that here. They don't mind asking who it's for, how much you earn, how much rent you pay, or what is it exactly the two of you do in bed? I just can't imagine! It's not that I mind, you see, they smile, it's just I can't think how you people can enjoy yourselves. If you want to fuck, the braver ones say, why not fuck the real thing. If they only knew.

Leo and I get our kicks out of imagining how the couple at the next table, the one with the steady jobs and the babysitter, how they'll react when they see us at home. Never mind in bed. Just walking around the house. Me in my tight skirt, stockings, and high-heeled shoes. Leo in his Levi's, white from wear around his beautiful thick cock, and his brown cowboy boots. And that white vest that hugs his wide chest tighter than I can. They'd flip. And if they came on Thursday nights, they wouldn't know what to do.

I love Thursday nights. Thursday is shaving day. I lie naked on the bathroom mat and Leo lathers me slowly, icing my chest like a birthday cake. His beautiful, caring muscular hands over my body. Then he takes the razor and goes gently across my skin, removing the bristles from my chest, circling my nipples, stopping to pinch them with the tips of his fingers. And like a magician, he uncovers me, wipes the foam off with a warm towel. Then he does my arms and my legs, taking care not to touch the sensitive flesh. Thoughts of his hands so close get me hard. Now? Leo says. Now, I say. So Leo sucks my cock until I come and I am drained and limp and ready to be fucked.

Leo lines my asshole with Johnson's baby lotion, straight from the pink plastic container, and then tickles the insides with the tips of his fingers. First one finger, then two, and then three, four, five. Opening me up wider and then wider and I want to swallow as much as I can to engulf that beautiful strong muscular hand that is all mine. He then takes his fist from my ass and lies down on top of me. Now that my ass is open he can jam his cock all the way in. Slide in and out. My muscles contracting to hold onto his cock and he goes in and out and in and out. He's on top of me and I push myself up onto all fours and he is holding his arms across my chest and kissing my neck and pulling at my nipples and he lets his hands wander across my smooth chest down to my cock and he plays with it until it's hard again and I can't tell anymore where the sensation is coming from nor what the sensation is and I want to forget myself. But I can't, for there are no words in that place of nothingness, in that void of pure pleasure. I pound my ass against his waist and take him in as much as I can. And when I'm about to come I push harder, wanting to be taken away, to disappear into his perfect body, into his solidness, into what I will never be. And then I am full.

And so we eat. Sometimes we go out and I'll wear my high heels and stroke the long straight hair that runs down my back, and make Leo want me. Want me, I say to him, tell me that you want me. Tell me that you'll die if you don't have me always. He does, because he does. And that's how we met. I was the one who did the seducing. At a Purim party two years ago. I wore my chiffon evening gown with an open back and a slit down the side. I wasn't shaving my legs then, so I had on my black stockings and the shoes I'd picked up that morning from Olga's. I was perfection, standing at the drinks table smoking a joint and pouring myself another Harvey Wallbanger.

He came from across the room. I'd noticed him before, but had kept his image to myself. He was the only one who hadn't dressed up. There were Queen Esthers and Hamans filling the place with screeching rattles. There was a pirate and her damsel in distress. An ugly duckling with the wings of a swan. Then Leo's green eyes were close to mine and I could smell the sweet taste of alcohol on his breath. A drink, I asked. Whiskey, he said. Nice, I thought.

We talked a little. He said he didn't really have a regular job at the moment. He painted houses, he said, did a bit of renovating. A bit of this and that. We danced together. He had his hands on my skin. I could feel his palms moving up my back and folding over my shoulders. Let's go now, he said.

I walk away from the window. Fixing my hard-on in my underpants. I could spit on the sidewalk if I wanted to. But I just keep walking. Floating almost. I have a picture in my mind and I'm taking it to Olga. I smile to myself at the memory of how Leo and I met. There have been several others like him. So I know it won't last forever. But I know that when it passes, the memory of it will remain. The feeling, that is. And that in itself is enough.

The Perfect One-Night Stand

Raven Gildea

It was almost the perfect one-night stand.

The trick to a one-night stand isn't finding the right person. Hell, almost anyone can be the right person for one night. The trick is knowing when to leave.

We met at a play party in a city where neither of us lived. I was going home the next day. We had no history, no friends in common, no expectations. Perfect.

He'd watched me top someone else earlier in the evening, and had concluded, I later learned, that I was competent and trustworthy. I sat resting after my scene, guzzling water and checking him out, and concluded that he was cute, boyish, and eager—in short, my type exactly.

When I asked him to do a Daddy/boy scene with me and he said yes, we had the world's shortest negotiation. "My asshole's off limits and I don't think I can take a whole fist," he said. I replied "Does that mean I get to fuck you?" and he said "Yes please!" Like I said, eager. My type.

We played in the main room of the party, and had quite an audience. Years later I still occasionally meet someone who tells me how much they enjoyed watching that scene. Not as much as I enjoyed it, though. He sucked cock like a champion, crawled across the floor with enthusiasm, took his beating like the good boy we both knew he was. To our mutual surprise, he also took my fist as if he'd been doing it for years. He came with a fountain of spray, standing before a mirror on shaky legs while I lay on the floor beneath him, my hand firmly embedded in his open, hungry cunt.

When we finally dusted ourselves off and began to notice the outside world, the party hosts were tidying up the room around us and politely clearing their throats, casting meaningful glances at the door. It was 3 a.m. My face hurt from hours of sustaining an ear-splitting grin.

We were careful not to make assumptions. We thanked each other for a memorable evening, discovered that I lived 200 and he 2,000 miles away, and said a fond good-bye. We did not exchange last names or contact information. I went back to the apartment where I was crashing and lay on the living room floor, my body buzzing and humming. I couldn't sleep, but it didn't matter. I had just had the perfect one-night stand.

The next morning I groggily walked to a nearby restaurant for breakfast, and there he was. He was just finishing a meal with two friends, who graciously excused themselves when he plopped himself down in my lap and showed no sign of following them out the door. Again, we were careful: obviously delighted to encounter each other again, but making no assumptions that further contact was expected. This time we spent enough time chatting to discover that we enjoyed talking as well as fucking. As we began to part ways, the gods wisely intervened and nudged one of us into cautiously broaching the subject of further contact. I will be eternally grateful that I left the restaurant with his e-mail address in my pocket.

We began to write. We discovered that despite living in different countries, more than half a continent apart, and despite the eight-year difference in our ages, we had similar class backgrounds and education, the same books on our shelves, the same lefty queer cultural references. A month later I was offered a friend's frequent flier miles, and used them to fly the boy out for a visit. At the end of our weekend together, I put him on the airplane home with a thoroughly explored asshole, a cutting on his chest, a green hanky in his pocket, and a collar encircling his throat.

The first year, we visited each other four times. I learned that he was a girl when he wasn't with me. Not just a girl, but a femme. Not just a femme, but a femme top. It turned out that the boy persona had been an experiment, just for the night. Having recently been dumped by her butch bottom lover, she had decided on a whim to attend that play party in boy drag, cruising for a butch top. She wanted to play, but needed it to be in a realm far distant from the source of her hurt. She'd had no idea that the boy would take on a life of his own, would demand his right to pursue a happy childhood. With each visit, the two of us watched this boy unfold into the joy of being cherished by a Daddy who fiercely loved him. He was part Muppet and part Tigger, a bouncy, humming boy who leapt out of bed in the morning to fetch my coffee, cheerily approached his lack of cooking skills by saying "Boss me around, Dad!" in the kitchen, and scandalized the postal carrier by mowing my lawn wearing only his combat boots, leather hot pants, and collar.

I got to meet the girl once, on the third visit. We'd arranged a butch/femme date, an oh-so-kinky game for two faggots like us. The Tigger/Muppet boy polished my boots, ironed my shirt, and disappeared upstairs, where he was transformed entirely. A boy went up, but twenty minutes later it was Annie Lennox who descended the staircase in a tight electric blue minidress and—be still my heart—white cotton panties.

The dress was a lovely match to my turquoise sharkskin suit. We went to a fancy bar in a fancy hotel, where I bought her drinks, lit her cigarettes, and fucked her silly in the bathroom. In the morning Annie Lennox was gone, and the boy was scurrying around my house, tidying up the debris from the night before. It was the perfect one-night stand.

The second year, we visited each other three times. My Internet café expenses were getting out of hand, so I acquired a beat-up old Macintosh so ancient that it didn't even have graphics on the screen. But it did have serviceable text-only e-mail access. Each time the boy came to visit, he dropped to his knees in the airport to receive my collar. At night we switched to his jammie collar, a rolled-up green hanky knotted around his neck. When he went back home, the jammie collar retained his smell. Months after he'd left, I could bury my face in it and be enveloped by the physical memory of holding him in my arms.

He was the best boy I'd ever had. He worked hard to please me, and he never let me doubt for a moment the joy he found in doing just that. He was also one of the smartest and most insightful people I'd ever met, and I learned to rely on his sound judgement. He saw me through no fewer than three major break ups, which I personally consider to be well above and beyond the call of duty. We had a running joke that there oughta be a Boy Scout badge for that. I knew I could safely sob in his arms about someone else without jeopardizing his heart or my credibility as his top, and believe me when I say that I know how rare that is.

The third year, we visited each other twice. Neither of us had much money for plane fare, and his teaching job gave him only a few small windows of vacation time sandwiched between grading the finals of one semester and starting to prepare for the next. We switched from e-mail to weekly phone calls. He met a girl, fell in love, and they bought a house together. I met her and liked her.

The fourth year, things began to go wrong. His relationship with his partner deteriorated to the point that I could clearly see it was abusive, but he didn't want to leave. Part of our agreement was that I didn't top him in his real life. What the girl did when the boy wasn't here with me was none of my business. But I loved that boy, and it hurt me to see him gradually compress himself into a smaller and smaller space, trying to please someone who could not be pleased. Trying to reassure someone who could not be reassured. Trying to placate someone who could not be placated. I told him that I thought the relationship wasn't good for him, and he agreed. I waited for him to decide what he would do about that. I waited a long time.

Looking back now, I realize that that is when my boy began to disappear. His partner said she accepted our relationship, but the boy was a threat to her. He was something that she couldn't control, something that didn't belong to her. He tried to give both of us what we needed. He tried so very hard. He forgot to ask himself what he needed. I think he forgot how.

The fifth year, our visits were different. We longed for each other, longed for the time and space to be together as Daddy and boy, but when he arrived he was unfocused, less present. He was trying so hard to hold everything together that he was unable to let go into submission. He'd been hurting so long that letting me hurt him wasn't fun anymore. I wanted my whip and my fist and my unconditional love to heal him, but I didn't know how. I think he needed to heal himself, and no matter how much I wanted to, I couldn't do it for him. He needed to take himself back, to belong to himself again. He couldn't do that while he still belonged to me.

He finally left her. He ran out of excuses, released his last shred of hope for a better future with her, and moved out of their house to begin a better future without her. When he came to see me, he brought an enormous rage and pain stuffed into the small space where his heart had once been. This time he didn't need a Daddy, and he didn't need a top. He needed a friend, and I did my best to be that for him. For three days we held each other and cried together. When he got home, he called to tell me that he needed time away, time to be responsible only to himself, time to get it together. He would call me in a few months.

I hurt. What he needed made perfect sense to me, and I hurt like hell. Knowing that this was for the best, that it couldn't be any other way, didn't make it feel fair. His ex had taken him away from himself, and she had taken him away from me as well. We talked on the phone about once every six weeks, and it slowly became apparent to both of us that the person I was talking with wasn't the boy I had loved for so long. It was the girl, the strong, sweet, smart, sexy girl who was slowly uncurling herself from the tiny dark lair where she had hidden, holding her breath, waiting for it to be safe to come out into the light. It became apparent that when next we visited, it would be she, and not the boy, who stepped off the plane.

There have been so many times that I haven't had a chance to say good-bye. There was the boy, years ago, who begged me to let him wear my collar home after a date, and then never called me again. That collar was metal, and locked: he had to have cut it off. I'll never understand why he didn't just come over and let me remove it properly. There was the lover who refused to acknowledge, even months after she'd stopped sleeping in my bed, that she had in fact left me. I've lost people I loved to illness, to accident, to suicide. I did AIDS work for ten years. I have learned to value closure, and I've learned that closure isn't always possible.

It's been nearly six years now, and the boy is gone. He left slowly, and he left quietly, but I don't think he's coming back. Not even to say good-bye. The girl who remains in his place is someone I love, someone I am grateful to have in my life, someone with whom I just may have a hot, long-lasting, butch/femme thang. Someone with whom I never doubt I will have a long, tender, fierce, and satisfying friendship. But my boy is gone, and I never got to say good-bye. For months I watched her pack up his things, send out cards reading "no forwarding address," let me know, as she discovered it herself, that he was going, going, too late, gone.

When I first noticed that it was happening, it didn't feel real. For months I kept waiting for the other shoe to drop. By the time I realized that it already had, it was gathering dust along with the green jammie collar that sits beside my bed, slowly losing the scent of passion, devotion, and submission.

Sometimes I wonder whether it might be possible to call forth the boy one last time, just for a few minutes, and have him kneel once more at my feet. I'd like to take a final look into his adoring boy eyes, wrap my Daddy arms around him, and pull his blond head against my belly. I'd like to take the collar off formally, even though I know that doing so would break my heart.

I'd like to say to him, "Thank you. Thank you for being such an amazing boy. Thank you for being mine. I am so grateful that the boy in her loved me. Thank you for giving me more than I'd ever expected. Thank you for taking such good care of me. Thank you for always being honest with me, even when you didn't know what to say. Thank you for a five-year, perfect, almost one-night stand."

Rebel Without a Cock
Cait

The bar was too loud. Or maybe I was just getting too old for bars. Hard to think that at thirty-five, I might be past the possibility of going out for a drink (and, with luck, a bit of something fun at the other end of the night with someone warm and wet), but one pays in one's dotage for the things one did in one's youth. In my case, playing bass in a blues band hadn't done my hearing any good, and I paid for it with a ringing that could really bother me if I let things get quiet around me. Self-perpetuating problem, that.

I could feel eyes turn to me as I came in, the automatic swivel of heads to check out the new meat. The eyes belonged to women, for the most part, the majority of the men in the bar quickly looking away when they saw a new competitor enter, with maybe a few lingering surreptitiously on me in the mirrors, and even one or two gazing with frank lust. The bar was a crossover hit, popular with gays, straights, bis, and probably folks who enjoyed varying other combinations too. I felt pretty easygoing about it, though I was pretty straight myself. Most of the patrons would have no problem with being turned down, and you didn't have to always tell them why, either, which suited me.

One—well, I've really got to say lady, rather than woman, because woman just doesn't fit—standing at the far end of the bar grabbed my attention, though I don't know if she noticed me right away. She was in animated conversation with a big butch dyke to her left, and she looked the part to grab the attention of any red-blooded butch who saw her. She was tall, perhaps even taller than me, if we got down to it, but in my boots, I always looked a bit more imposing than I might have otherwise.

She was really a full-on femme, but she did it in such a simple way: no hose, no heels, no big hair. The dress was simple, summer light, and she had a sheen of sweat showing between her breasts, glistening under the lights. It was entirely obvious from a fair distance that she wasn't wearing a bra, and her breasts, though perhaps small for a woman of her size, made my fingers twitch. A pair of sandals, her hair swept up in a couple of clips or something, keeping it off her face, a small bag for her necessaries, and out the door. Almost no makeup, save for an incredibly rich red lipstick, and lashes that looked so thick they had to be almost fake (they weren't, I found out; she was just lucky that way).

I got to the bar, ordered myself a beer, and leaned against the rail to survey the bar. I'd been almost staring at her, and it was good to look at someone else for a change. It wouldn't do to be too forward. I've long since learned that women respond best to a slow approach. It may not be what I'd have wanted, but if I wanted to get anywhere with her, it were best to remember it.

The place was swimming with people, the dancers steaming on the dance floor, open as it was to the patio. No doubt about whether I was going home alone tonight. One way or another, I'd be having break-fast with somebody tomorrow. The main question remaining was who that might be. My first survey had found a good few possibles, but my glance kept returning to the end of the bar.

She wasn't as young as I'd thought at first. She actually looked fairly close to my age, as I spent more time looking at her. The skin around her eyes was a little loose, maybe a little wrinkle starting, and she had laugh lines in her forehead. Her face was a little off-perfect, but beautiful in its way: she had a strong but not protrusive chin, her nose a little large for prime time. I was having an increasingly hard time (pun intended) keeping my eyes off her.

Worse yet, she was beginning to notice. She'd glanced my way in the mirror a few times, seeing my best out-for-a-night clothes: black jeans, black belt, white T-shirt, black vest. A bit James Dean, I know, but I'm not built all that wide, and I liked the way the T-shirt showed off my arms. I'd worked damned hard on those arms, and anything that showed them off was all right in my books. I wore a moustache and beard, too, but trimmed close around my mouth, and kept short. Buzz-cut and spiked hair completed the look, and the look got some looks. Even at thirty-five, I kept myself in noticeably good shape, without being muscle-bound, and a tight ass will always draw eyes.

The big dyke had moved on to easier prey. She'd obviously found no reciprocal interest in the lady, and like a good predator, given it up as a bad game.

I danced with a few possibles, but even the drunkest of them could tell my heart wasn't really in it. I was drawn to her, again and again. She danced, too, and with as many women as men.

I couldn't figure out the approach. She wasn't paying much attention to her dance partners, either. She looked almost bored with the whole thing, and I didn't want to waste my first try on a dance. A drink? Could I be more clichéd?

A rose seller came into the bar. For a moment, I wondered, but then the big dyke saved me: she stood near the lady, and caught the eye of the seller, but was favored only with an amused lifted eyebrow, and retreated once again.

She was prey, but untouchable. It was dazzling.

I'd always thought of myself as a similar sort of predator, and it was illuminating and not a little humbling to see the butch's defeat. I don't suppose I'd ever so closely watched the failure of one of my competitors. I'd never lacked for confidence before, but tonight I felt like the old lion of the pack, and it wasn't a pleasant sensation.

In a story, of course, this would be the point where the flash of inspiration would come to me, and I'd have the sudden idea of how to sweep her off her feet, and the rest of the story would tell you how we'd had incredible, mind-busting sex for forty days and forty nights.

In the real world, I flopped. I never even tried. I couldn't bring myself to try and fail, and the prospect of being seen to fail with this, this, this—was just overwhelming.

A little after midnight, she made some small joke to her current dancing partner, a suburban geek who was totally out of place, but whom she'd gone out of her way to be warm with. It was a piece of raw meat to us lions, of course; she'd given him more of her time and attention than anyone in the bar, and he was oblivious to the game going on around him. He was nothing, though, beneath our notice; only the prey held our eyes this night.

Many people went home alone that night, and probably never knew why. Wrote it down to luck, no doubt. We all have off nights.

It was Morrissey who said, "every day is like Sunday." Well, sang it, sort of. I'd never been a clock-watcher, but things couldn't have been more dull for us. September is a deadish time of year for travel, and though the airport was busy, it wasn't crazy like it can get at some times of the year. We actually had fairly regular downtime in the hangar, times when we weren't actively getting a plane turned around for the next flight.

I usually just left it at "I work for an airline" when my job came up. It was a lot more glamorous as a possibility than the reality: I fixed brakes. Now, it's a pretty important job, because there are really only two ways to stop aircraft on landing, and one of them was usually called "crashing." But it's not much of a thing to impress someone with, so I left it at "I work for an airline."

Eventually, of course, the end of the week came. Friday night, I played softball for the mechanics' team in an industrial league: a light bat, but a great glove at shortstop. I was oh-fer on the night, and made three errors. Couldn't keep my mind on the game. I had to buy a round after the game for taking the collar, but that was fair enough.

And so the next Saturday came, after about eight-and-a-half years. I'd overindulged in the postgame, uh, fête is probably too grand a word for the Oktoberfest Tavern get-together, and had a hangover that would probably have had a rhinoceros wishing he'd laid off the jeep bashing for a few days.

I was like a teenaged girl getting ready for the prom that afternoon. I must have dressed and undressed half a dozen times, and I don't have that extensive of a wardrobe. I finally settled on something a little softer than last week's look. I think I'd decided that this particular game was not going to be played by quite the same rules as I was used to, and that meant adapting to beat my competitors. The stone butch cowboy look hadn't done it. Tonight, I went with a denim shirt and a faded old pair of jeans, left the gel on the shelf, and I'd carefully nursed my beard into a respectable scruff across the bottom of my face, without it being shaggy.

I hadn't considered that she might not be there.

I usually arrived at ten, as I had the week before, but this week I couldn't wait. I ate dinner early, and sat fidgeting until I could convince myself that it was all right to go. That moment came at sundown; I figured dark was dark enough.

So there I was, standing at the bar, in the same place as she had stood the previous week, and staring at myself sweating in the mirror. I couldn't stop my palms from feeling greasy and hot and clammy all at the same time. I picked up the beer glass again, and it slipped from my hand.

Too much, I thought. This is too much, I can't stay here, I'm going to make an idiot of myself. I gripped the glass, drained it, and left.

Or started to, anyway. As I reached the door, I turned to the coat check to reclaim my union Windbreaker (hey, it's warm, and I'm proud to be a union man), and she turned away from the counter at the same time.

Shakespeare wrote in Romeo and Juliet (I'm not a high-tech mechanic because I'm dumb) that their eyes met, and they knew. I'd always thought it a sort of metaphor, that it wasn't really that instant.

I'd thought, to this point, of myself as the predator, and she as my prey. It was a comfortable self-image, and her eyes ripped it off my face as sharply as if she'd used claws. There was as much a predator in those eyes as in my own, and they were enjoying the dawning realization in mine as much as I'd ever enjoyed seeing someone close theirs in that impossible moment just before orgasm.

We faced each other from less than a couple of feet apart, so close as to be slightly unsettling. Our hands were both holding the plastic tags, and they clicked as we tried to avoid the collision. The sound broke the moment, and she laughed, quietly. Her voice sent a rush through me, Kathleen Turner and Eartha Kitt all rolled into one, and she saw the uncontrollable tics of it, and she laughed again.

"Going so early?"

And there wasn't a damned thing I could do to deny it. I'd got the tag out on my way to the counter, and you don't do that if you're staying (unless you're one of those geeks who leaves things in their jacket, and then you deserve what you get).

"Uh, I, uh, well, that is . . ." and of course my voice betrayed me; it sounded as stuck in high school as I felt, and I positively squeaked.

Once again, she caught me off-balance: "Well, perhaps next time." The smile alongside it this time was fond, and gentle, and strangely sympathetic to the effect she was having on me. As she walked past me, I caught the slightest hint of her scent, as her shoulder passed just under my nose in the crowded lobby. It wasn't perfume, nor even some bath oil, just the faintest hint of skin, and it nearly dropped me.

Shattered, it would have to be next week.

The previous week had passed in about eight-and-a-half years, and this week left me longing for those halcyon days of speedy passage of time.

Still, it was eventually left behind, and this time I just called in sick to the game on Friday. No way was I going to go out there and be even worse than last week. I couldn't afford the beer!

So I sat home Friday night, pretending to read.

Saturday night approached again, and this time I knew without hesitation what to wear. It was back to my armor, to what gave me confidence, my hunter's garb. James Dean only wished he wore it so well. I figured if I kept telling myself that enough, I may begin to believe it, but it was really fighting a losing battle. I was confused, adrift, unused to feeling like the prey, and not dealing with it at all well.

I managed to hold off until a full hour past sundown this time, but even so, she wasn't there. I hoped.

The big butch dyke was back, and she and I struck up a decent conversation about the chances for the Leafs this year, what did I think about them signing the new goalie, all that stuff. I got involved enough in the conversation that I only knew she was there when her drink hit the bar beside me.

Being caught off guard may have been the best thing that ever happened to me. I didn't have time to get worked into a lather. On the other hand, maybe not: "Do you come here often?" I winced.

She just laughed again.

"Well, I'm glad you said it," she said, "because now I know how silly I would have sounded saying it myself. Very kind of you to save me from that."

That was it for me. She could have asked me to hand over the keys to my beloved pickup, and I'd have giftwrapped them. And I never wrap anything.

"Can I buy you a—?"

She just raised an eyebrow. Her drink was untouched in front of her.

What next? "Look, I'm sorry, I seem to be saying the stupidest things, but I've got to be honest, you've got my head spinning so I can't remember my name." I was finding myself desperate to do something to keep her smiling.

"Colin, isn't it?"

I usually consider myself to be fairly quick off the mark, but my amazement must have shown on my face, and her smile was reassuring when she said "Local 3501?" My union jacket, embroidered, of course, with my name.

And it was then that I started to get that *2001* feeling, you know, the apes dancing around the monolith? This lady—for no other term could possibly apply, and I wasn't one for using it in general discourse—had enough interest in me that she'd noted my name last week. Maybe her parting line had meant more than I thought then, but I was still having a terrible time trying to adjust to the change in my status. Her hunt was gentle, but it was a hunt, and I was the game in this game.

We talked more easily then, of cabbages and kings, of sealing wax and strings, or so it seems to me when I look back to it. I couldn't tell you what I said that night for all the tea in China.

We moved outside, to the patio. It was considerably cooler, being late September now, and she pulled her sweater from around her waist to put it over her shoulders. It was much quieter on the patio, waiters circulating to take drink orders, the rose seller returning more than once.

She let me buy her a rose this time, but somehow it was only with her permission. This brought me up short for a moment, and she sensed it again. She read body language better than anyone I'd ever known; I could have no secrets from her. She said only, "Relax."

And I did. I didn't feel I had a choice, not through coercion, but through the fragility of what was happening here; a bridge between us spun of glass fibers, weak in their initial state but growing stronger with successive applications. Sorry—once an engineer, always an engineer, I guess.

"What do you do in the daytime, Colin?"

"I, uh, I work for an airline."

"Surely more than that, Colin. One doesn't find professional engineers behind the ticket counters?" Her fingers, long and strong, touched my pinkie, where the iron ring sat.

"I, well, I didn't like working in offices. I work on the braking systems for the aircraft, safety, inspection, all that stuff."

"Does it make you happy?" She wanted to know, honestly, and I could feel it. She had a remarkable knack for listening, putting in just enough questions to keep the conversation interesting.

I would have given her my kidney on the spot.

"It's all right. I'd rather be flying, but I haven't been able to afford lessons yet. Sometime." Her calmness was having an effect on me, outwardly; I felt more able to speak coherently. Inwardly, well, entropy increased.

"Don't let 'sometime' hold you back from what you need to do. I learned that lesson some years ago—sometimes you just have to go ahead and do what makes you happy. It's not easy to learn, we place such a high value on sacrifice as an ethos in this society."

All right, I know some of you are itching to look ahead to the good bits, so I'll skip ahead a bit. We talked all evening, and then we went to a doughnut shop and talked some more. There was more gray than black in the night sky when the cab finally stopped outside her apartment.

I offered her my hand, and my phone number. She grabbed the back of my neck, kissed me hard on the lips, and got out, leaving the door open. She walked to the front door of the building, unlocked the door, and turned, holding it open.

"Well?"

I looked at the cabbie, and he looked at me with a mixture of his cultural disapproval for what was about to happen, and envy that it couldn't be him. That was enough. I threw far too much money over the seat, leaped out, and tried not to run to the door.

For all my philosophizing about predator-prey relationships in bars, I don't really think of the women I sleep with as prey. I want it to be consensual; my function as a predator is to induce the consent. In this case, it was clearly more than consensual, and stunned as I was by the new status I found myself in (desired predator?), my body knew the answer.

Her apartment was like her, spare, perhaps underdecorated. Few photos of herself or family, very much a solitary person's place. It was neat, without being obsessively clean, today's newspapers on the coffee table in an obviously read state.

There were only four rooms to the place, a bathroom, a bedroom, and a living room–dining room combination that opened onto a kitchen. A small balcony was outside the sliding door she led me to, just one lounge chair taking up most of the available space. We watched the dawn together, she standing just in front of me, with my arm around her waist under her sweater, her head on my shoulder.

I could smell her hair, and it was making me crazy.

Inside again, we sat on the couch together in the growing light, watching the orange shapes crawl down the walls. She curled up against me, her body a warm presence under my arm. She wasn't wearing a bra again, and I could see down her shirt to the swell of her breasts. The skin was almost screaming to me to touch it, the pale softness that so rarely saw sun. I didn't dare, not knowing the rules of this new game, but wanting so much to play it.

Her ability to read me was undiminished by our utter lack of sleep; she knew. She turned to look me in the eyes, and brought my hand from her arm down to the space above and between her breasts, placing my palm flat there. She . . . swelled, drawing a breath so deep I was continually sure she couldn't possibly take any more, and then let it slowly ebb. Her eyes had closed as she breathed, but when she opened them, she seemed suddenly more open, and more scared. She looked away.

Her hand on mine became almost a painful grip, and then she laughed at herself as I gasped slightly, and released it. "Sorry," she said. "It's been . . . a long time since anyone touched me there."

My face gave me away again.

"You think I bring home just anyone? I haven't brought anyone here in four years."

I was chagrined. I opened my mouth to protest my innocence of any such thoughts, but closed it again when her eyes met mine. "My turn for an apology, perhaps?"

"Not to me," she said. "People go there for a reason, it's not unfair to assume that they may occasionally indulge."

"So—"

"Why haven't I? I like you. You're direct. Why haven't I? I haven't because I'm scared."

I misunderstood completely, of course.

"Hey, we don't have to do anything you don't want to do, you know, I'm really stuck on the whole consent thing, I don't want anyone doing anything they don't want—"

"Did you know you babble when you're worried?" She grinned. "Do you think you'd be here if I were scared of you? I've seen the way you look at me. You're—you'll think I'm a total narcissist for saying this, but you're interested in me. Not these, or this," she said, indicating what I'd originally been solely interested in. "In me. You want to know what I do, what I think, you're one of the best listeners I've ever known, and listen to me, now I'm babbling too!"

We laughed, together, and we both knew it was time.

She stood, and held out her hand to me. I took it, and rose to my feet, but I held back when she drew me toward the bedroom.

". . . ," I began, and then shook my head. "You know, I still don't know your name?"

"I'd noticed. I'd wondered when you would. Helen. Spare me the ship jokes." She held out her hand for the formal introduction.

I took it in mock solemnity, bowing over it, and murmuring something about how pleased I was to make her acquaintance.

She led off toward the bedroom again.

Again, I hesitated. I had to say, but it was the moment of terror. Often as not, this would work out just fine, but the stakes seemed much higher here.

"Helen." I choked on the next bit.

"Would you like to sit down again?" she said, making it rhetorical by doing so immediately.

I couldn't meet her eyes. At times like these, I felt the weight of the universe on my shoulders, the fear of her response.

"I need to tell you something about myself." God, I sounded like I had a contagious fatal illness. "I, well, I, uh . . . didn't always look like this."

"Is this a fashion confession, then? Should I wear a mink stole to hear it?" And I knew she knew, though not how, and I knew it would be all right.

"I wasn't . . . born male."

She said nothing, but her eyes (and only her eyes—her ability to read me was not reciprocated) smiled.

Out it all came in a great rush of words: "I realized when I was twenty-five that I wasn't ever going to be happy unless I did something about it. At first, I just crossdressed, but eventually went on to have some surgery. . . ." I couldn't say it, but waved my hand generally in the area of my chest. She reached out and placed her palm in the same spot on my chest where she'd placed my hand earlier.

There was no mistaking the warmth in her smile this time. She caught my chin in her hand, lifted my gaze to meet hers, and smiled brilliantly. She laughed.

Now, of all the responses I've had to this appallingly painful revelation, laughter is easily the last one I might have expected. I stiffened. You don't have to be born with masculine pride to suffer from it.

I stood, and strode to get my boots from the doorway. She looked stricken, and called out to me. I looked up, and she held up her hands and composed herself momentarily.

"Colin! Wait. I shouldn't have laughed, and I'm sorry. Please . . . make love with me?"

One boot half on is not the most dignified position to be in when this offer is made. I straightened as best I could, trying to surreptitiously lose the boot. "You mean it?"

She reached to the buttons of her blouse, and stared me in the eyes while she undid them. Her breasts were just as I'd imagined, smallish, but soft and crying out to be touched, and I struggled not to drool at the sight.

She walked toward me, undoing the top button of her jeans as she did. The zipper went next, and they slid smoothly down over her hips. She stood before me in nothing more than a pair of ordinary white panties, and I began to understand.

Dressed, she was a stunning woman. Undressed, her laughter's source became more clear. Her hips were narrower than I'd thought, and her shoulders broader. Her long, strong fingers, her lovely voice. And with a click, it all fell into place, and I laughed too.

"You—?" I couldn't say it, but pointed to her panties, and she nodded.

"You didn't?" She nodded, and the understanding was clear in her eyes. "Do you still want to—?"

I stepped closer, put my arms around her waist, and kissed her. She kept her eyes open—I'd never known anyone else who did that. I liked it, we looked into each other while we were locked together, and saw clearly.

I started to reach for her knees, to carry her, but she put out a hand and told me she weighed quite a bit more than it appeared, and it might be better if we just walked.

We walked, and she closed the door behind us. She held my eyes while she pulled my shirt up, and I raised my arms dutifully to let her take it off me. She stroked my chest, made a small pout at the scars of my mastectomies, but then kissed them too. My black jeans were button-down, and she knelt, enjoying undoing the buttons with her teeth. My knees nearly buckled when she got them open and hauled out my cock.

The mind is a powerful thing. In reality, that cock was just a piece of rubber, with no more feeling than a sausage. In my mind, when her hand closed around me, it fused with me, and became part of me, and I felt everything. When I looked down to find her licking the end, taking it in her mouth, I reached down to make her stop. I needed to get off my feet before they just gave up and went home for the night. I drew her to her feet, and kissed her again. I stepped out of my jeans and underwear, then led her to the bed.

Her turn to stop me. I was beginning to think that sex might be a bit complicated for us, each with our own neuroses. This one, however, was much more surprising to me than the last, in its own way.

She sat down on the bed beside me, and put her hand on my arm as I prepared to lie down.

"Colin, I . . . I've never . . . that is to say, this is the first . . . I mean, I've only ever, you know," and making a face, she made it clear what she meant by "only ever you know."

I was staggered. Scared. I'd never been someone's first.

"You don't want me, Helen, you can't—"

She put her hand over my mouth. "Please don't finish that sentence. I've never wanted anything more."

I started to lay her back on the bed, and she pulled her panties off. I was frankly curious, and her eyes were scared, but they said I could look. I did. Her pubic hair was soft, dark brown like her hair, with just a few grays scattered about. I reached out and touched the hair, and she gasped, her legs slamming together with an audible smack. I raised my eyebrows and looked at her over her knees.

"Sorry." Sheepish smile. "You're the only nonmedical person who's ever seen that. It's kind of an old reflex." She slowly opened her knees again for me, and I looked again.

It was incredible. If she hadn't told me, I'd have been hard-pressed to know from even a close look. Her labia were pink and full, and if her clit was a little larger than some, at least mine was bigger! I reached to touch her, to push the hair aside, let me see her clearly.

She was struggling with herself, but she was letting me look, and touch.

I stroked along the pinkness, and her whole body arched.

Her eyes were closed. I crawled up her body, and lay myself full-length by her side. My right leg was draped across hers, my hand tracing idle patterns on her belly, drawing ever nearer to her breasts. When I touched them, her eyes shot open, and she searched my eyes for a moment, reassuring herself it was safe.

She closed them again, and my hand moved to her areola. They weren't much darker than her pale skin, but they were large, and they crinkled beautifully when I stroked a ring around one. She was biting her lip now, and it was my turn to laugh. We were in an arena I knew, now, and pleasing women was something I'd become very, very good at.

"Something you're trying not to say?" I teased, knowing that it was all too easy for that bitten lip to turn into the letter f, and knowing she was struggling hard not to say it.

I reached a hand to stroke her neck. She jumped, but she let me, and her arms came up in goosebumps when I did. She had a small belly, and it shivered along with the rest of her, so I kissed it. Her navel was a small inny, and when I wet my finger and slid it just inside the rim she cried out a little. I settled on a course of teasing, wetting my fingers and putting them inside all the places I could find except the one she wanted most.

Her ear, her mouth, her armpit, the crack of her ass, I even fucked her toes with one finger for a moment. Her pale skin was flushed now, her breath shallow and rapid, and it was her turn to have the sweat running off her upper lip.

Finally, I cupped my palm, and placed it down on her mound. She smiled, and then moaned in frustration when I moved only my thumb and pinky finger, stroking the cleft of thigh and mound, but remaining still on her pussy itself.

My ring and index fingers gathered small clumps of pubic hair and tugged, gently pinching them against the middle finger. She could feel my finger just above her clit, and her hips wiggled to try and bring it closer.

I began to touch her labia, then, stroking them gently with a dry, soft touch, just to see more shivers.

"Damnit!" she said. "Haven't I waited long enough?"

I laughed this time, and so did she, and she blushed when she realized what she'd said. I began to stroke more urgently, and she put a hand on my arm to stop me. Her other arm reached into the night table drawer, and returned with a bottle of lube. "Sorry," she started to say, and I just looked at her. She nodded, closing her eyes. "Okay."

I got the lube into my right palm, and started rubbing it with the left to warm it. Now when I reached for her labia, the silky lube made it very easy to just slide gently inside, not far, just enough to find the entrance. I held my fingers there, just two of them, and looked at her. She looked stunned, shocked, pleased, overwhelmed, on the brink of tears.

I caressed her face, and she looked at me, and she nodded. "Please."

I pushed my fingers in more, and her mouth made an "o," and then I moved them back out and in again, and she let out a deep sigh. Her body relaxed onto my hand, and slowly I began to fuck her in earnest. She started to ride with it, her body moving, her back arching, her breath in time with the movement of my hand, and with a notable effort of will, she stopped me. I looked at her face, worried I might be hurting her, but she shook her head, and held out her arms to me.

It was time.

I lay in her arms for a while, but then rose to kneel between her legs. I didn't know who was more scared. The thought that I might hurt her was far larger in my mind than it had been ever before, and I could see the same fear in her eyes. She might be thirty-five, but in this case, she might as well be a virgin bride on her wedding night. She didn't know quite what to expect.

I lubed my cock, and then leaned forward over her, my hands to either side of her body. We looked into each other's eyes, and struck by the incongruousness of it all, we laughed again. And while we laughed, I entered her.

Her eyes looked like an anime heroine's, all whites, and her hands held my wrists in a strong grip. She may have been relaxed before, but in the event, she was squeezed up so tight now I couldn't possibly get

in. "Helen," I called softly, wanting to bring her back to safety and reality, "Helen, it's okay, I promise to do my very best not to hurt you.
If it hurts, we'll stop for a while, or as long as you want, okay? Let me
have my right hand now."

She was so wigged right now, she let my left go, but I wasn't about
to argue about it. I reached down between us, and stroked her clit
gently. She gasped, but began to relax, and as she did, I slid into her,
slowly at first, and then all the way in.

I looked at her again, and she was crying. And smiling. And then
laughing, and pushing, and kissing me and thrusting against me, and
I could feel the cock slamming against my pubic bone, and then her
pubic bone slamming against me, and just the look on her face
brought me to the boiling point, and she could see it in mine, and . . .

Well, I'd like to say that we both came then, but we didn't, and we
eventually drew apart, and I brought her finally to orgasm with one
thumb on her clit and three fingers inside her. Just watching her come
brought me off as well, the orgasm ripping up from a place I hadn't
found before.

Now, if this were a story, you would be waiting for a happy ending
or a sad ending, or some kind of resolution. The truth is, I don't know
yet. I am thinking of her as I tinker with the brakes on Monday morning, and even with the grease on my gloves, I can smell the scent of
her on my arm in front of my face.

And I'm going back tonight.

Tango
William Dean

It's Tango Tuesday at the Le Chat Noir, New Orleans. To cut the crowd into doers and watchers, Chris, the sometimes bartender, slips to the end of the room and pours a half shot from his private bottle behind the bar. He kicks it back then flicks a cheap Zippo and shoots a three-foot flame out of his mouth. The crowd gasps, shuffles, a few applaud as Chris quickly downs a big glass of milk to kill the kerosene taste. Then he's back scooting beers down the polished bartop and dipping shooters to the heavy drinkers.

Kutti Gray wants to be hanging from the ceiling fan; wants to be dragged along the floor by her tango-stepping partner for the night; wants to to feel good enough that dying would be a release into just one more place of ecstasy. She fingers the stud in her tongue—solid gold ball top, naturally—and makes "I-could-suck-your-cock-in-a-heartbeat" flirty eyes at Piedro beside her. She can't stand him; can't hardly bear to feel his fingers creep along her stockinged thigh, but—shit!—can he dance. She presses her legs together under the table and traps his fingers before he gets any higher.

"Take me dancing, bitch," she says with a flutter in her throat.

"The fuck? You hear any gotdamn music yet, Kutti?" Piedro waggles his head and nervously clanks his bling-blings—flaking gold-plate, naturally—like they're wind chimes.

"I want to be first on the floor. They're going to start now, look. Take me dancing." Kutti pushes his hand away then reaches between her thighs, under the thin leather skirt, to make sure her cock is still securely in place. Her nylon panties feel a little moist from sweat or maybe she's been dribbling precum. She's been feeling excited since the fire-eater show.

A heartbeat later the band is settling in on the tiny stage above the dance floor. The oldest, a dyke geezer with a faded gray ponytail, smoothes his blazer and pulls it taut enough so the audience can see his small breasts outlined against the cloth. He puckers his carmined lips a few times and leans back on the chair, fingers already assuming the talon shape of a string master. He rips a few sweet chords from the guitar then jumps into a driving flamenco thrum. He nods to the rest of the band. And it begins.

Already heated and humid, the Chat Noir's temperature is kicked up a bazillion degrees by the opening, a torrid tango number the regular crowd has heard over and over, but it never fails to get toes tapping, heads bobbing, and shoulders hunching up and down. It's sex music, pure and simple.

"I want to dance, dammit," Kutti urges. She can already feel her pierced nipples tingling as if the geezer bitch's strumming fingers were connected to the—gold, naturally—rings on her tiny tits. She suddenly sits still as she feels her flaccid cock twitch against her thigh. "Wait a minute," she whispers and slurps her rum and cola, letting the ice clink against her front teeth. She breathes deeply. When she feels her cock settle again, she stands. "Now," she breathes.

Piedro slouches to his feet, sniffs his fingers, scratches the flat expanse of his ass, and waddles across the floor like a hippo sliding into ooze. Kutti assumes the position: head tilted back, spine arched, one arm stretched long and bony to the front, the other tucked close, and falls into Piedro's experienced dancer embrace. It's as if she were suddenly engulfed in flab in movement. Piedro cocks his right foot high and begins sliding—impossibly sinous for his massive size—Kutti across the floor.

Kutti's ass is tingling already. *Fuck,* she thinks, *I am going to try this time; try not to get sucked in, sucked down, sucked along with this fat bastard's show,* but she can't help herself. When the music hits him, Piedro is all style. His Jell-O consistency hardens into whippy titanium; his size eleven feet become doves—delicate *palomas* in flight—never settling, but spinning, arcing, skidding along the polished floor. He whirls Kutti sharply; he uses her body like a bending, twanging fencing foil to parry off the other dancers. Kutti bites her lower lip and gets lost. Again.

Piedro uses his inescapable strength to throw her almost to the floor and then drags her—helpless—up his meaty thigh; she can feel his stubby cock imprisoned in the tight dark pants and her own responds, swelling and bobbing against the thin silk restraint of her panties. "Oh, it's good!" she murmurs as he lifts her. His eyes are drained of everything but the rhythm, the clicking beat. She wants to suck his whole face into her mouth and taste that blankness; eat his concentration. Just as her mouth gapes open—like a python to devour—he snaps her away from him, then back with a velocity that takes her breath away. He bends his knees and cheek to cheek they slink; their entwined hands a cutting prow through the other couples.

The music pauses—the old butch geezer's fingers frozen over the next driving thrum—and Piedro is an immobile wall which Kutti is sprawled against. She gulps air and squeezes her thighs together; her rigid cock, trapped at an angle, has escaped the leg of her panties; hot head burning and swollen against her leg; wet dribble feeling cool and odd. The drummer reenters the tango battle with a staccato roll of sticks to the taut pale skin of his drum and the world unfreezes. The rest becomes frenzy, becomes madness, becomes the tango penultimate. Kutti again thinks she wants to die now, right now, held like a rag doll in Piedro's rough hands.

Now the sweating starts and the couples on the floor begin to steam slightly under the spinning lights from above. A greenish face—pale as a vampire—slides past Piedro's shoulder and stares at Kutti with half-lidded eyes, immediately replaced by a whirling face that is male, no, female, then male, then female again. Kutti's eyes widen. It's the mirror of her/his soul, not confused, just dashing madly around and around in sex and sexless sweep. Kutti blinks, the face is gone, and Piedro cranks her arms like a windmill in a hurricane. "Fuck it!" Kutti whispers through gritted teeth. "I'm lost again."

At long last, the rum grabs her mind and Kutti slumps; she feels her cock evaporate and a cunt blossoms at the V of her legs. Piedro becomes the giant of all her remembered fairy tales, carrying her off—a forlorn princess—to his lair for unspeakable acts of thick-fingered fumbling and impossible fuckings. She imagines herself a sponge, nothing but holes, holes, holes filled, stuffed holes, holes plugged. Mouth, cunt, ass, grasping hands, between her toes, every cell of her ravished at once by the giant's massive cock. And then, the dream is splintered apart as she feels Piedro's tongue wallowing inside her mouth.

She bucks backward, stumbling out of his embrace. "What are you doing, you fat prick?!" Piedro stands rigid. His hands outstretched like Pavarotti delivering the perfect climax of his aria. The other couples laugh and stop their shuffling slinks to watch.

"I was almost there, goddamnit!" Kutti shrieks.

Piedro looks puzzled around himself; also like Pavarotti, he slips a handkerchief from his hip pocket and dabs the rain of sweat from his forehead. He permits himself to smile slowly. "The bitch is crazy for me," he murmurs politely and reaches a giant's paw down to adjust the small bulge at his crotch.

Kutti's hovering by the bar, watching Chris pouring Bacardi 151 Rum into her glass. She makes eye contact with him and looks deeply.

"Loved the fire act, cutie. It always makes me hot," she says with a little laugh.

Chris nods and stops pouring. "Me, too," he mumbles and grabs her money. "Thanks for the tip," he shoots over his shoulder as he moves away toward a pair of whispering women at the other end of the bar.

Kutti slouches her shoulders. She should have figured him for a pussy hound like every other bartender. She licks the rim of the glass and sucks down the rum, swaying slightly as the heat hits her throat.

"That was fucking rude," Piedro says behind her, his hands cupping her buttocks and squeezing.

"That's me, honey. I'm a rude slut and you knew I'm a rude slut, so what's your point?" Kutti spins slowly and brushes his hands away.

"I want it." Piedro frowns with a tilt to his head. "That's always my point."

Kutti shudders. She feels like the new rum is floating on a greasy pool of memory; all the slab-of-flesh horniness of Piedro bucking against her on the small bed in her small nights; all the reaching between her legs to guide his small cock into her ass; all the slobbery licks on the back of her neck. All the pearly drops—like black ink splashes—on her pillow from her melting mascara. All the penned-up feelings of womanhood pounded out of her by his urgent shouts: "Come with me!"

Piedro's hands come up and thud down on her shoulders. "Point taken?" He smooths a palm down the side of her face.

Kutti looks up at him. His face is red and round as a balloon.

She pouts. "Am I your slut?"

Piedro frowns and nods.

"Am I your whore?"

He nods again.

"What else?" Kutti waits.

Piedro looks aside and shrugs. "Whatever you want, you are. Okay? Are we done now? I want it."

"Well, maybe I want it, too. You ever think of that?" Kutti runs her finger around the bottom of her glass and then sucks the skin dry.

Piedro shrugs again, still looking away. A tear forms in his left eye and starts to slide down his plump cheek.

"Oh, for fuck's sake!" Kutti gathers up her purse and weaves toward the exit, closely followed by the now-smiling Piedro. Chris waves them good-bye.

"She's crazy about me." Piedro beams back.

They're silent on the walk back to Kutti's. Silent still, through the old wrought-iron gate to the courtyard. Silent across the worn, moonlight-splashed bricks; silent up the old staircase; silent through the door.

Piedro walks over and smooths the rumpled bedsheets, then with a loud creak sits on them. He runs his hands over his face roughly as if washing his features off, preparing an emptiness.

"Lipstick first," he says softly. "I like that part a lot."

Kutti grabs up things from the top of her old oak dresser, bundles them over and kneels in front of him. She sighs loudly—all the air in her lungs coming out at once—then inhales deeply. She can sense the sweet magnolia and stale perfume, the sweat of last night—almost the coming sweat of the rest of tonight, salty and sweet together. Her eyes drift up to Piedro's thick lips. And she begins to paint them with the bold, slick red of lipstick.

Piedro closes his eyes and relaxes his lips into pulp tubes resembling a smile. "I love you to make me a woman," he whispers.

"I know," Kutti answers, voice drifting back into herself with a hollow echo.

Dream Searching

Barbara Brown

"Hey sister, wanna grab a coffee?" she asks late one night after dinner and a film. Neither of us wants to go home, although I want to go home with her.

"Sure, but make mine mint tea, and I'm not your sister." We push our way into the crowded café.

"No prob," she replies, only about the tea. Her burly figure saunters toward the server, a number of eyes following.

"Milk in that, Carmen?" she calls from the counter. Eyes turn to me with disbelief.

"No," I answer, avoiding surprised expressions. Returning to their lattes, the murmur of conversation thickens. Our evening out will be old news in two days.

Sheena's powerful stature hunches in toward the cashier as she orders, laughing loudly with the ultragay skinny boy at the till. Her belly tightens with her laughter, showing muscle under a growing cover of fat. Her softened definition makes me want her that much more, teasing the sure fact that it won't happen.

We are the kind of friends where sexual attraction brings you together despite everything to the contrary. This is how it is between us . . . I like theatre and silent meditation and the sensual pleasures of eating fine food, all vegan. She listens to opera and 70s rock and orders pizza. She's butch and total woman. I'm something in between, neither butch nor femme, not quite woman or man. I am older, but only by a little. She wants kids. I do not. She's monogamous. Lesbian. I am not. She has a name for herself. I do not. It isn't a match and we know it. We are the kind of friends who eventually have to make a choice.

How long we'll be able to shift our patterns to fit each other hovers in my peripheral vision. To obscure my view, I don blinders like a horse who only has one destination. The attraction is that strong. And demanding. I want to reach the finish line, although I don't know exactly where it is. From my holding gate, one of those damn uncomfortable molded plastic chairs, I watch Sheena's body morph with her laughter, appreciative of the layers. She's put on weight since Darlene.

Sheena brings over our steaming drinks, carefully setting my steeping brew on the table. Her sleeveless T-shirt displays her tattooed arms. Lizards, snakes, and extinct birds wrap themselves around her heavy-set arms, ascending into hiding beneath the black cotton. I have never seen her chest or back tattoos although I often touch her as we say good-bye, hoping my hands will discern what lies under cover. She sniffs at my tea then curls her nose away from its swirling vapor. My hand, quick to wrap around the warm paper cup, grazes her retreating fingers. She grabs playfully at me, smiling. I smile back and we hold each other briefly with our gaze. She is the first to break it.

"How can you drink that stuff?" she grimaces.

"I like it."

"You're missing taste buds, girl."

"You're missing taste." I let the "girl" go.

"Ouch," she retaliates, taking victim position for her own benefit, only slightly wounded from our word parley.

"I don't want to go home tonight, Sheena. I hate my apartment. It feels empty since Selma left," I move us to shared territory, lost love.

"Selma left more than a year ago. Get over it." Perhaps the word-jab wounding is bigger than I realized. Our jockeying often takes us deep into each other's soft spots, deeper than we recognize until it is too late.

"A year isn't long after what Selma and I had," I defend myself.

"What Selma and you had was boring and bitter. You just managed to sustain it for a long time."

"Well, the sex was good. And frequent."

"Wish I could say the same thing."

"Forget her. Darlene was one confused puppy. She just didn't know what she wanted. That's not your fault."

"Darlene stole my heart." I can't reply. Her voice is dripping with defeat, sadness, anger, and total confusion. Sheena sounds younger than her twenty-seven years. Much younger.

Silence falls between us as, in her mind, she conjures some scenario of Darlene that I'm sure is mostly fantasy, leaving me alone at the table with her. I sit with the silence until I see Sheena receding even farther into some distant past. If I let her go there she won't find her way out for days. Her moods come and go, and when they are here, she isn't. Reaching out to bring Sheena back from her private journey, my elbow knocks over the carefully placed tea, spilling it in her direction.

"Ow!"

"Sorry, sorry." With ineffectively thin paper napkins I mop at the stream pouring across the table and into her lap. I am relieved she has returned.

"Come on, let's get you home. Here, stuff these down your jeans." I hand her a wad of the flimsy things hastily grabbed from the coil-sprung dispenser.

"Sure, like I want to pack in public. I don't think so."

"You'd look good," I tease, touching her, firmness palpable through the thinning, worn shirt. She hesitates from walking out of the coffee shop, letting my hand linger on her back. I resist pressing my whole body against her.

"I'll leave that up to you," she says.

"Let's go." I push her gently toward the door.

Hailing a cab, I stuff her, wet jeaned and grumpy, into the back seat and slide in beside her. Sheena throws her reptilian arm across the back of the cab seat. While ruffling my wild-man-of-Borneo hair into further disarray, she wipes a square of fog from her window to look out. Her hand stays entwined in my hair.

"What do you think of these?" she strides out, fashion model in red-checked pajama bottoms and a cotton tank top. Her nipples are dark under the white shirt, her tattoos an indiscernible mass of color covering her entire torso. Her pajama bottoms pull tightly around her quads, following the contours of her hips and butt. I've never seen her this stripped down.

"Think of what?" I ask.

"The jammies. Darlene gave them to me the day before she left. This is the first time I've worn them."

"They look good on you. Darlene obviously had *some* sense."

"Yeah, just not enough."

"I wonder what she'd say if she knew *I* was the one getting the fashion show out of her gift?"

"She'd probably be relieved . . . think it was fine for her to go off fucking someone else. And a boy, no less."

"Who cares, boy or girl? She left." Sheena sits on the sofa next to me. A great auk spreads its tiny wings across her forearm in an aborted attempt to fly. There is no ocean for it to swim away. The warmth of her painted skin is close enough for me to feel.

"Want to watch a movie?" she asks, although we've already been out to one earlier.

"No. I should go home."

"You said you didn't want to. Why don't you stay?"

"Where would I sleep?"

"Here on the couch. Or with me. It'd be okay. We're friends."

"I don't have pajamas."

"I'll lend you some," she says, moving quickly to retrieve a pair of loose boxer shorts and one of her many black T-shirts. "How about these?" she dangles them out the bedroom door for me to inspect.

"I guess I'm staying."

"Great. A pajama party."

"So much for your butch status. You are way too gleeful." I change and we slide into her queen-sized bed, both careful to stay on our own side. Part way through the video, I fall asleep snuggling my pillow, dreaming.

Tucking me into bed, my mother arranges the blankets around me, stroking turbulent hair from my face. It's so peaceful all I want to do is curl up and sleep, sleep, sleep, until . . . oh God, no. She is holding a set of plastic pastel-colored curlers in her other hand, futilely attempting to hide them. There is utter disgust on her face as she twirls my unruly locks. I swat her hand away.

And actually hit something.

"What?" I jerk awake to Sheena rolling away.

"It's nothing," Sheena mutters, seeming half asleep herself. "Go back to dreaming, Carmen."

Morning arrives quickly. Groggily I bring myself out of the land of sleeping, trying to make sense of where I am. The first reminder is Darlene's gift, disheveled and exposing a slip of skin on Sheena's back. Old stone steps majestically lead out of her pajama bottoms. I imagine an ancient city sprawling across her ribs and shoulders, a city inhabited by the creatures of her arms. The insistent yearning to touch these stones, feel their cool welcome, draws my hand onto her skin. Touching her directly for the first time is delicious. She rolls toward me allowing my arms to wrap around her and discover more skin. My hand explores the cityscape as I stroke her back, fingers wandering through empty streets of ruins.

"Do you think we should do this?" I ask.

"We'll be okay," she responds as she takes off my shirt.

When I reciprocate, she whispers, "The shirt stays on."

I concede to her direction with disappointment. It isn't the first, or the last, time I allow her to tell me what to do.

"Pants stay on. Don't touch down there. We don't kiss." I close my eyes by choice. With rules established, we grab at each other as if this will change our reality, bridge the difference between us. My mouth takes her neck as my nails scratch deep into her back. She pulls my loaned clothes off immediately, cupping between my legs, palm pressing into my mound.

"Our bodies look hot together," she murmurs, my eyes still closed. I imagine my white skin against her tattooed arms, her sturdy body next to my much softer form. She tells me she likes how I move.

"We move well together," I say, but she ignores my words and my body stiffens in response to the disregard. There is no *we* here.

Sheena and I spend the morning in bed, searching for the right ways, the right words to touch each other, but don't find them. I cum only with effort as my mind jumps between Sheena, Selma, and last night's dream. Sheena doesn't even get close to orgasm. Exhausted from our attempt we sleep again. I feel chilled as I tentatively reenter the dream world.

Tug. Tug. A flightless bird tries braiding my hair into one thick plait, tiny feathers woven in.

Midafternoon releases us from the bed. Our conversation starts and stops, stumbling toward inarticulateness. Agitation urges me to leave. I desperately want the empty apartment I couldn't face last night, but take no action toward leaving. Under the agitation is a seed of hope. Its planting is keeping me here.

"I've got to go to my mom's soon," she says.

"Babysitting again?"

"Yup."

"Who's she out with tonight?"

"I don't know. I can't keep track."

"You're dedicated."

"I'm stupid. But if I don't go . . ." her voice drifts off into dangerous territory.

"Why don't you leave her to do it? They're not your kids. It's not your responsibility," I say. Sheena's three younger sisters see more of Sheena than of their mother. Her mother likes to fuck too much, Sheena says. Her mother likes to drink too much, I say. Sheena's older brother left before he was sixteen. He is the lucky one who got away.

"Butt out, Carmen. It's not your business."

I shut up. I am in no position to judge. Family ties baffle me. My best attempt to make things better on the parental home front has been absenteeism. It's not that they did much, or at least, not much one could call them on. They didn't understand me and my queer ways. It was painful enough. I wasn't the ideal daughter—how could I be? What I wore, what I ate, who I slept with was all suspect. My sister got the coveted role of "perfect one" and with it, the little bit of love there was to be had. I was tired of the raised eyebrows when I entered a room and the glaring silence that followed everything I said, so I stopped going home. All I left behind was a lot of aggravation, similar enough to the agitation I am feeling now watching Sheena pack up her stuff without speaking. My parents were relieved to see me go.

Sheena walks out while I am in the bathroom, slowly putting myself together. I am staring into the mirror with incredulousness that this morning's romp is all there is. I am trying to gather the courage to talk to her.

"Just drop the key back through the mail slot when you leave," she calls as she goes. "I'll see you later."

She disappears. For a long time. I phone and leave her messages, but they are not returned. When I go out, I look for her, but she isn't around. All our trying is over, but it is not finished. Once I stop looking, there she is.

As soon as I walk up the stairs of the club I see her, leaning against a dingy wooden pole surveying the dance floor. I beeline for the bar, lingering in the shadows. Sheena eye cruises until she decides on her pick for the night. I have seen her do this before. Following her perusal of the crowd, I try to determine before she does who will be the lucky one tonight.

In the year since our encounter she's lost some weight, spiked her hair. Her shoulders seem wider, firmer, with the slim waist below. The Laughing Owl still follows an undulating path across her deltoid. She cuts a look across the room and catches me peering at her. The dark of the smoky bar hasn't shielded me. Having her stone grey eyes on me summons the brief encounter with her ancient city and a door clicking closed as I examine my own reflection. The hurt of her sudden departure makes me want to storm out, head high, now that she has seen me. Simultaneously I consider ignoring her, unwilling to let her presence derail me from an evening of pleasure seeking. But her presence makes me weak-kneed all over again, longing to unravel whatever this pull is. The time apart has changed very little. She is staring at me and my bottle is empty. I have to do something. I meet her straight on, walking up to her, holding her stare.

"Hi. It's been a while. How ya doing?"

"Shit. But what do you care?"

"Tell me or don't. Whatever." I glance at the dance floor, absently.

"Rebecca left. It didn't work out. She went back to Jay." Rebecca—her lover less than a week after we'd slept together. I'd heard. I haven't been with anyone since.

"Sorry to hear it."

"How is it I end up here every fucking time?" The anger in her voice is tangible, her last year's confusion submerged by it. I don't answer. There's a lull where her attention wanders away from me and the bar.

"Hey?" I say, laying my hand on her arm.

She shakes her head, returning, and asks, "Wanna dance?"

"Sure."

We ease our way onto the crowded dance floor and slide into each other's rhythm, the sexual tension strong as ever. Avoiding conversation and eye contact, hips glued together, we move. The music fades into the background, inconsequential and absolutely necessary. Her strong hands run the length of my back over and over, pulling at my tightly wrapped tensor. Occasionally she lets her hands rest on my hips as my bulging groin taunts her. I sink my fingers into the front of her shirt worried I can't keep myself upright, making sure she doesn't leave again. We stay like this until last call.

As the crowd thins and waitstaff clean up around us, Sheena says, "Let's go."

I know exactly where we are heading. Her apartment, the same one, is close. We walk in silence, not touching, the space between us necessary for us to decide. Memories of our morning together and of our parting flood me, but don't stop me. What am I looking for? I can't answer my own question.

As we enter the apartment lobby she asks, "Are you sure?"

"Yes." I reply with certainty as the elevator doors open and invite us in.

Before the doors are closed, she throws me up against the wall. Sheena holds me there for a moment, the cool of the metal handrail on my back, her breath hot on my cheek. Locked in a challenge to see if either of us will look away, my aching body opens to her. She kisses me with such force that my head falls until I hit the wall and stop. I kiss her as fiercely, her power giving way to me momentarily. The elevator doors open and we exit quietly, walking the long corridor to her apartment. She is clutching my hand as she struggles with her keys. I stroke her neck, colored flames riding the pulsing veins. My longing for her has drenched my underwear. I am anticipating the moment she discovers my wet, free-flowing adoration.

In her room, she moves slowly, methodically. She turns on the small bedside lamp. A dark blue scarf thrown purposefully across its shade barely allows the light to touch us. She shuts the door, goes to her closet, and brings out a briefcase, laying it beside the bed.

"What's in there?"

"Things to make you feel good," she says, and proceeds to undress me gently, carefully, leaving the soft gel dick between my legs. She folds my smoke-filled clothes and rests them on her chair. For a second time I allow her to undress me, although this time, my eyes are wide open. Swiftly, she picks me up, lays me on her bed and drops the full weight of her clothed body on mine.

"Are you still sure?" she asks.

"Yes," I smile, touching her silky-skinned cheek, hot from the summer's sun. "But I want to see you naked."

Without a word of agreement or protest, she begins slowly stroking me, touching every inch of my body. Her hands, large and soft, discover nooks and crannies, each dip and curve, every bump, scar, and callous of my body. With each caress, I let myself go, allowing her to become my whole world until I can no longer move, immobilized by pure physical pleasure.

She stops. She lets me linger untouched in the blue haze while she, standing, opens the briefcase and pulls out three things—her strap-on, the biggest dildo I've ever seen, and a whip. The bluing light flickers across the ceiling, captivating, before she flips me on my belly and begins talking.

"Put your ass in the air, cunt."

Her harsh words startle me after the sweetness of her touch, but I am not surprised. I do as I am told.

"Spread your legs farther apart. I want to look at you." My labia hang open between leather straps, swollen and wet in the dark blue light.

"I hate you," she growls, as she brings the whip down on my back with enough force to smart but not enough to bring blood. My welting skin is stinging with desire.

"Every single fucking bitch I love has gone and left me. Little whores," she mumbles. Another crack of her whip, this time only nearing my body, the rush of air cooling on my legs. The sound is enough to make my body tense. My legs are shaking from holding my ass so high. I don't know where we are heading.

She must see my body falter, feel my shift in attention, because she puts down the whip and whispers, "Except you, I suppose. I left you."

I turn to see her face, but the light behind offers only a silhouette.

"You needed to leave. I couldn't be what you wanted and you couldn't live with less. It was okay."

With those words, permission granted, she plunges her cock inside me, pushing as far into me as she can. The violent penetration makes me gasp, my arms give out, and I fall face down on the bed. She hesitates for a moment, the shift in position unnerving her. I can feel her drawing away.

"You can keep going," I say. I don't want this to end. Not again.

Her absence is brief as she hears the urgency in the words. Something clicks in.

"Carmen, you're not a 'cunt,' are you?"

"No. I'm not."

And with that, she rides me from behind slowly, a constant wave of motion as she enters me, then pulls out and enters me again. Her hand reaches forward and wraps itself around my shoulder. She begins pulling me into her, the rhythm of her hips shifting only in speed. Her breathing becomes ragged. Small noises sounding like a dog left too long in its kennel come from behind me. I want to see her but know if I look, if she is seen in this state, she will not continue. I close my eyes and imagine her.

Her movements become faster, her fingers dig into the muscles of my shoulder, deeply enough to leave bruises. Her whimpering sounds become louder. I begin rocking my body in response, the timing flawless between us. I lose track of her grunting as the walls of my insides turn to fire like the flames on her throat. All I want is for her to continue, to push harder, deeper. I begin ramming my butt up against her, desperate to release her passion and step over the edge, my edge, into oblivion.

"Fuck me," slips out of my mouth, and she responds by pulling me so close that there is no room for air between us. My hands run up the headboard in front of me. I am almost sitting straight up, my back to her, her in me. With a few quick, hard thrusts she cums, crying out. We wilt onto the bed, too exhausted to untangle ourselves.

When I wake, she has tidied the sheets around us and laid me on my back. Her head is resting on my chest. Her unclothed body curls around mine. My erect nipple hovers in her drowsy, open mouth and her back lays bare before me. Unhurriedly, I stroke Sheena's naked skin, feel loosened muscles rippling beneath my touch. The imagined exploration through ruins of ancient days fades with the truth exposed. The stone steps lead not to a city but to a sky filled with a moon eclipsing the sun. The darkened orb swells with each deep, sleeping breath she takes. Haloing rays of sunlight cast shadows across the steps below, and above, ignite the blaze. Everything, the Great Auk, the Laughing Owl, the steps, the sky, is consumed by her flaming fire. There are dried tearstains rolling down my breast.

The Fury Factory

Jason Rubis

All right. Here we go.

The back is a narrow length of white skin, crazy with freckles. The hips aren't overly wide and the ass isn't much to talk about, but if you were here you'd want it. Shoulders bunched and sullen, hung with a mess of red-blonde hair, wiry and frazzled looking from too much primping, too many back-and-forth dye jobs. Still, sun gets on it from the window and makes it shine.

One leg—and it's a long one—lifts and slides a knee onto a chair, displaying a dirty sole with monkey toes. Now the face, turning slowly for maximum effect and glaring over the shoulder. Slight traces of last night's makeup. And oh, that pout.

"Don't these fools realize I'm a *star*?"

"Some people," I tell her, "weren't raised right." I have no clue who she's talking about. Probably someone who approached her at the club last night, after I left. The pageant is big news down here. It's attracted dozens of afficianados and curiosity seekers, all wanting to chat up the girls or just get a closer look at them. Not all of them are polite.

"I don't want to talk about it." She jerks her face back to the window, her attention turned firmly to Bigger Things. "Oh, those *fools,*" she whispers, as a parting shot.

She loves all of this, the clubs (assholes and all), the excitement of a new city, the prospect of getting on stage. She's twenty-five years old.

I light my last cigarette. It tastes pretty bad. My head is screaming for coffee, but I know better than to call room service when Ginger (what she's calling herself at the moment) started the day loudly declaring that she's too fat (!) and hungover to eat.

I could walk across the room and put my arms around her. There's part of me likes that idea very much. I could let one hand fall and caress what's on the other side of her ass, see what happens. My stomach gets tight, thinking about that.

She woke me up last night at 4 a.m., slamming the door and falling face first into the pillow beside mine. She let me wrap an arm around her and bury my face in her hair, but it was like every other time. Like doing it—or trying to—through a pane of glass. I angled my knees up into the backs of hers, let my belly warm her back, my breath at the nape of her neck. Like she was my baby. But you can't fuck a baby.

"I *hope* you're going to empty that ashtray when you're done," she sniffs, not looking at me. "It's so tacky when you leave it all *full* like you do."

"I'm sorry," I say, inclining my head a little, with as much irony as I think might actually get through to her. "I'll try to do better."

"*I'm* going to take a shower," she informs me, stalking over to the bathroom door. "Then I'm going to the pool."

"I'll meet you there. I'm going to head out, take a little walk." I'm thinking about the continental breakfast they're going to serve in the lobby. Coffee, lots of it. Hot and black.

"Don't be long," she says nervously, lingering at the door. "We'll go together when you get back." Same old story. She won't go anywhere alone—the pool, a club, a bookstore. But once she's safely installed and holding court, I'll be left to wander.

I nod, and she disappears into the bathroom. The shower comes on seconds later, filling the room with the rattle of water on plastic and porcelain and her chest. I stub out my cigarette and leave without emptying the ashtray.

To hell with it.

"No, you can't slide down that slide," Miss Girl tells me. She's followed me into the little playground the hotel has for the guests' kids. I'm sitting crouched on the sliding-board's edge; Miss Girl is standing beside me, looking incredibly out of place in her tight red dress, shoes clutched mock indignantly to one hip. Noon sun has bleached the slide and swing sets and the playground's ankle-deep layer of sand an unbearable, blistering white. No kids around just now. The heat is inescapable; Miss Girl has her feet thrust beneath the sand as a kind of halfway measure. I can see her toes wiggling smugly under the blanket of white grit.

I'm feeling argumentative for some reason. I squint up at Miss Girl and hold up a finger. "Number one: what makes you think I have any intention of sliding down this thing? Number two: if I did have any intention of doing it, why *shouldn't* I?"

"Because that slide is for children," Miss Girl sniffs. "A grown man shouldn't be sliding down no kiddy slides, *you* know that."

Miss Girl is called Miss Girl, I think, chiefly because if she were called Miss Thing (and I believe she was, early in her career), everyone would think she was a joke. I only met her last night, but I can tell you already Miss Girl is no dummy. She's as lean as Ginger, but considerably older. Too, Ginger's body still has some faint suggestion, here and there, of softness. You wouldn't dare call it baby fat, but it's there.

Age has leached all the softness out of Miss Girl's frame. Her fingers especially are like leathery claws; a dark, oily brown, tipped with ruby, constantly snapping and gesturing. Even her hair looks hard. But her eyes, under the brim of her big, floppy sun hat, are amazing; they're abundantly lashed and evil.

"And you ain't no child, are you?" she says, smiling just a little.

I get up laughing, patting her shoulder as I move gently past her. I like Miss Girl, but she's dangerous. They're all dangerous.

"Oh, I know where *you're* going," Miss Girl says, slipping into step beside me.

"Yeah? Where?" I ask, keeping my eyes averted like I'm afraid she could put a spell on me.

"You're going to that heathen," Miss Girl says. "That beast. That *other* queen of yours."

I know she's talking about Ginger, lying out by the pool, risking sunstroke so the other guests—mostly vacationing suburbanites at this time of day—can get a good gawk at her.

"*Other* queen?" I say, a laugh edging out of my voice. "How many do I have?"

"Some men like to play little games," Miss Girl informs me. I can hear her smile. "Some men like to be coaxed." Her hand slides over my ass and I rise up comically on my toes, scooting forward out of her reach.

We're out by the pool now, weaving our way between meandering lines of buff, bored-looking men and women. I'm moving faster, keeping two or three steps ahead of Miss Girl. The quicker I get to Ginger, the quicker Miss Girl will back off. Maybe.

"It only takes time, baby," Miss Girl says behind me. "I know what you *really* want."

"I'm glad someone does," I tell her. And there's Ginger, finally. She spots me the same time I spot her, sprawled on a beach chair beside the glassy blue smear of pool. Someone thin and blonde and out of it is sitting on the concrete beside her.

"Kevin!" Ginger shouts, leaning forward and gesturing at me like I'm a waiter. "Kevin, I have made a *decision*!"

"And what's that?" I ask. There's not another chair near her so I sink down to a squat on the unoccupied side of hers.

"My *name*. I'm going to change it. Well, not change *it*, but change the spelling. J-I-N-J-U-R, like General Jinjur in the Oz books. Do you like it?"

"It's fabulous," I say, then wince a little. I can never say "fabulous," so that it sounds natural or enthusiastic. Out of my mouth, it always sounds like I'm making fun of you. Things could get ugly now. But Ginger is too busy preening over her latest career decision to even notice.

"Who's this?" I ask, pointing at the nodding blonde.

"That's Lovedonna." Ginger snickers. "She's here for the show too."

"Lovedonna" isn't her real name, of course. Ginger likes to give people names. But the blonde answers to it readily enough, jerking her head up and smiling deliriously. She's slightly older than Ginger, wearing a pale blue T-shirt over a tight bikini bottom. Whatever she's on, it isn't hormones. A faint but noticeable stubble colors her jaw, and her eyebrows are heavy and werewolfish, dark under her spiky, bottle-blonde hair. She's pretty, though. She *oohs* at me, reaching an overlarge, blue-nailed hand out across Ginger's legs to stroke my cheek.

"That child is on *drugs,*" Miss Girl says severely. She's positioned herself off to one side of us, waiting for an opportunity to make her presence known. "I do not *associate* with drug fiends."

I flick my eyes cautiously over the other guests. All we need is for some bitchy vacationing *hausfrau* to overhear Miss Girl and scream for the cops. But the other guests (platoons of them, lying out on all sides of us) are too interested in their tans, or planning how they're going to score themselves that night. Still, I need to shut Miss Girl up, at least for a while.

"Let's get some champagne," I say loudly, getting up. "How about it?"

Miss Girl purrs approvingly. "You talked me into it," Ginger says promptly, pushing her shades down and sinking back into her chair's cushions. "Good stuff now, not that crap you usually get."

I nab one of the passing waiters and order four glasses.

"Another thing I've decided," Ginger announces, not to anyone in particular, "is my company's name." The company is a long-standing fantasy of Ginger's, the venture (apart from her career in show business, of course) that will allow her to quit her job at the costume store and spend every day shopping and drinking. The company has at various points been a boutique, a restaurant, a modeling agency, and a hotel that caters exclusively to rock stars and famous artists.

"I'm going to call it the 'Factory.' Isn't that *perfect?*"

"I think that name's been taken," I say carefully.

"I'll use it anyway. What are they going to do, *sue* me?"

"Factory," Lovedonna says, drawing circles on her palm. "F-f-factory. *Fuck* factory. Fur factory. Fury factory." She giggles loudly and swats her thigh.

"That's right, Lovedonna," Ginger says comfortably.

"Heathens," Miss Girl snorts, in an ecstasy of jealousy.

The champagne comes, the waiter looking so snotty that I casually overtip him, just to see his eyebrows shoot up into his hairline. What the hell, the magazine's paying for it.

"Maybe you *should* call it the 'Fury Factory,'" I say, raising my glass and looking at the sun through the bubbles. "The bunch of you are like furies. Snakes for hair. Sprung from the blood of a dead god. Pursuing guilty men to the ends of the earth." After all my previous caution, I'm risking a monumental tantrum from all three of them. Sometimes I just can't help myself.

Ginger, however, remains cool. "I already have a name for my company. Thank you. But I'll consider it. Thank you," she says, sipping her champagne with butterfly delicacy.

"What do you mean *snakes* for hair?" Miss Girl demands.

Lovedonna drinks her champagne like it's soda pop, then crawls over to me, her lips parted and drawn up in an idiotic smile. She hooks an arm around me and draws my face close to hers, then kisses me loudly. For some reason, I let her. Ginger ignores her, but Miss Girl makes a strangled, unbelieving noise.

"I'm gonna be inna show," Lovedonna tells me, kissing me again, hard so our teeth click together. She smells like sweat and something sticky sweet, like cotton candy half melted in the sun. "I'm going to get up and sing. I'm beautiful. Don't you think I'm beautiful?"

"Sure you are," I say, stroking her shoulder. No way they're going to allow this poor thing on stage. I know the MC, a savage bitch from New York, and apparently a friend of Miss Girl's (Miss Girl, as she told me last night, never gets around to performing herself, but she's friends with *everybody*). Even if Lovedonna manages to get cleaned up and fabulous by showtime, Miss Girl will have whispered in the MC's ear long before then. Of course, she may not have any real intention of being in the pageant. She may have just wandered onto the hotel's grounds; she may have been brought here by whatever Daddy is keeping her supplied with happy candy. It may just be a fantasy, like Ginger's company. Who am I to start playing realist?

"I come up all the way from Nashville," she says. "I'm going to *sing*. What are you?"

"I'm a journalist," I tell her. "I'm here to write about the pageant. I brought my friend. She's going to be in it, too." I feel compelled to point out Ginger's presence, out of some half-assed kind of loyalty. Waste of time. And the words sound increasingly unreal to me, in any case. The champagne isn't sitting well in my stomach and the sun is slowly roasting my head. I put my glass down.

"Look at *her*," Miss Girl says suddenly, contemptuously. A tall Latina queen is sashaying across the pool area, plainly reveling in the way the other guests' eyes are devouring her. The afternoon is getting on. The girls here for the pageant will start taking over the pool in a little while, getting some relaxation in before it's time to start seriously primping. Dozens of them, showing themselves off, running the waiters ragged demanding champagne and vodka.

"This feels good," Lovedonna tells me, clumsily massaging my chest. "Doesn't it? You have a room? You have someplace we can go?"

I look at Ginger; she lies unmoving, her sunglassed face impassive. Somewhere behind us Miss Girl is fuming and muttering, slowly withdrawing to someplace where she's *appreciated*.

Lovedonna takes my hand and pushes it between her legs. I give her an obliging squeeze before taking my hand back. I'm decided now, but we can't do it out here, for Christ's sake. "Come on," I tell her, taking her hand. She'll want money afterward, probably, or maybe not. Maybe she's just horny, like me.

"Gentle," Lovedonna burbles, looking at my fingers gripping hers. She pronounces it *jennel*. She lifts my hand to her mouth and half kisses, half licks it. "You're gentle, you're nice, I'm gonna *like* you."

"Going up to the room for a minute," I tell Ginger. She pulls her shades down and regards me.

"Ooo, Kevin's got a girlfriend," she chants. The shades go up again. "Change the sheets when you're done," she says, grandly flipping one finger at us. Out here, surrounded by colleagues and admirers and enemies, she doesn't need me. The next time I'll see her, she'll be hurricaning around the room, getting ready, insecure and crazy, demanding the odd hug or reassurance. Or maybe she'll be on stage by then, pouting and strutting and synching, receiving the crowd's squeals and catcalls with a regal grace while I stand in the crowd drinking bourbon and planning my article, mentally listing tasteful synonyms for *transgendered*. Either way, she'll be the only one in the world who knows how truly beautiful she is.

Lovedonna is on me as soon as the elevator doors close. It takes me a minute to realize it, but I've started kissing her as hard as she's kissing me, groping and rubbing. Her belly is smooth and hard under her T-shirt, and she's got one leg raised, trying to lock it around both of mine. She gets hold of my left wrist and pins it up over my head with a surprising strength. Too late to be frightened, and anyway, I'm not. No wall of glass here, nothing to hold me back.

I'm bumping my hips against hers, my whole brain's down there now. "My man," she says, and says it again, over and over, growling and insistent: "My man, *my* man, my *man,* my man, my man."

She licks my throat like there's something sweet there. "Are you going to stay with me? 'Cause I love you? 'Cause you're my man? Huh? Huh?"

And I'm saying yes, yes, yes honey, because there's a whole eight floors before I lay her down and get inside her, and (so like Jinjur now), I find I have to say *something,* anything to make my own voice heard.

Bridges

James Williams

Forty years of being a bum had made Bridges a pro. Even in winter he could find a drink and a place to sleep. But winter down by the docks at 3 a.m. when it rained was not the place for a pro. Certainly not an old pro.

It was the rain that had finally driven him to the subway. He had ducked under the turnstile and caught the first train out, uptown. He remembered as far as Times Square, then he had slept.

Now iron wheels ground along on iron tracks tucked tight between damp stone walls in the dark. The train shrieked through the tunnel like a string of huge tin cans dragged over boulders and spikes by some monster child. Bridges slumped down in his hard pink plastic seat and wrapped his arms around himself, trying to keep warm. He wondered which part of the city he was under.

The door at the far end of the car opened to a loud clatter of wheels. The torso of a man stacked up on a rolling board slid into the car. The man was dressed in a ragged red flannel shirt whose grimy ends were stuck haphazardly beneath the stump of his body. His face was streaked with dirt and a scar ran down one cheek to his scabrous lips. A dented metal cup hung from a splintered broom handle that rose crookedly up from the front of his board like a broken finger. The man leaned forward and placed his enormous hairy hands on the floor of the car and pulled himself forward. "Please," he said. "Please."

Bridges cowered. For all his years on the skids he thought the man horrid, obscene. A pretty girl, too young to be a woman, wearing a bright green coat opened her black leather purse and took out some change. When she placed the coins in the man's cup she looked him in the eyes, expecting nothing.

"Thank you. Bless you," he whimpered.

"You're welcome," she said. "Bless you too." And she smiled.

The man on the board rolled through the car collecting money in his cup. Bridges was the last person he came to. The man stopped in front of him and looked up.

"I don't have any money," Bridges said.

The man said nothing.

"I don't have any money," Bridges said again. "Look." He emptied his pockets: some dirty tissues and a pencil stub, lint, a Lifesaver. The man continued to look at him.

"Hey, listen, you've got more money in your cup than I've had in years. You should be giving me something." He pulled his pockets inside out for the man to see and an unexpected quarter fell to the floor with a dull clink. Bridges watched the coin roll with the rocking of the train until it came to rest directly in front of the man's board. Bridges looked at the man, whose expression had not changed.

Bridges shrugged his shoulders. "I didn't think I had it. Go on. Take it. You can have it." He bent down and picked up the quarter. He was about to drop it in the cup when the man shook his head.

"No," he said.

"Go on," Bridges urged, "take it. I'd have given it to you right off if I knew I had it."

"Don't want it."

Bridges looked at the money and looked in the cup where several dollars worth of coins nestled together like eggs in a nest. He looked back at the man whose expression still had not changed.

"Please open the door for me," the man said. "I can't reach."

"Sure," said Bridges. "You sure you don't want the money?"

The man said nothing. Bridges put the quarter back in his coat pocket and stood up and opened the door between the cars. The noise of the train grew louder. The man looked out toward the next car, whose door was closed. He looked back at Bridges. Bridges stepped out between the cars and slid the second door open, straddling the cars and keeping the first door open with his foot.

"I can't cross between the cars," the man said. "My wheels get stuck."

"What do you want me to do?" Bridges asked.

"Pick me up."

Bridges hesitated. "Wait till the train stops."

"It's easy," the man said. "Pick me up so I can reach the crossbars. I'll hold on while you move my board. Then you just set me down on the board again."

Bridges looked past the loose chains that swayed between the cars with the rhythm of the wheels. The tunnel walls sped by. "All right," he said.

He bent down to the man. Ozone from the tracks mingled in his nose with the man's old sweat and something else vaguely medicinal. Specks of soot kicked up by the train wheels stung his cheeks and eyes. He squinted and set his lips and clenched his arms around the torso.

The man was unexpectedly heavy. Under the best conditions Bridges wasn't sure he could lift him. But standing on the lip of the moving car—

"Count to three," the man said. "When you say 'three' I'll jump."

Jump? Bridges began to strain.

"Count to three."

Bridges grunted. "One. Two. Three."

And the man did jump. Abruptly he became lighter, and Bridges lifted him off his board and turned to face the following car. Slowly, to keep his balance, but as fast as he could, he moved the man toward the crossbars flanking the opposite doorway. To reach them Bridges had to step across the empty space that slid between the cars. As he put his first foot down he felt the man begin to slip from his grasp. "No!" he shouted, and flung the man forward.

The man cried out in pain and the bottom of his shirt shook loose and for a moment Bridges could see the reddened fish-white skin that was the end of his body. But his hands gripped the bars and he clung to them while the tunnel wind whipped the red cloth about his missing hips.

Bridges grabbed the board and set it in the mouth of the car. He gripped the man under his arms from behind and half lifted, half threw him down to his board. The man gasped and his eyes watered.

Gingerly he placed his hands on the floor and adjusted himself on the board. He took some quick, shallow breaths and then, without looking back, tucked his shirttails under him and pulled himself forward and away. The door between them slid closed. Wan light filled the tunnel. The train slowed and stopped.

Bridges didn't move until the train did. Then he felt he couldn't wait. He climbed the thin chains that had just begun to sway again and leapt off the train onto the end of the station platform. He lay where he fell while the sound of the train died away. The dull click of thrown switches and the faraway rumble of other trains in other tunnels drifted up to him. He got to his knees and looked at his hands. They were covered with blood. From where he knelt he could see the door to the men's room. It was padlocked.

Outside the rain had stopped, but the air was still wet and the streetlights seemed to emerge through a patina of frost against a black and colorless, textureless background. Bridges didn't recognize the corner. He looked down the street wondering what there was in that direction. Then he looked up the street and saw the girl in the green coat. She was standing at a bus stop watching him. He turned in the other direction.

"Wait," the girl called.

Bridges paused. He didn't want to talk to the girl. He only wanted to find a dry doorway to sleep in until it grew light enough to panhandle carfare back down to the docks. He turned and faced her anyway.

She looked down and toyed with her purse for a few seconds. When she looked back up she said, "You're a little bloody."

"Many people make that mistake," Bridges said. "Actually I'm a little drunk."

"What happened?"

"I fell."

"Where?"

"On the subway platform. I think I skinned my hand."

"You should wash the cuts."

Bridges looked at the dirty rainwater trickling down the gutter. "With what?"

"What? Water. And soap."

Bridges grinned at her. "I think I left them back at my hotel."

"Come here. Let me see your hands."

Bridges did as he was told. She took his hands in hers and examined them. Up close she wasn't quite as young as he had thought. Young, but a woman, not a girl. She looked tired, despite her careful hair and expensive coat.

"You didn't cut your hands," she said. "This isn't your blood."

Bridges looked at his hands and saw that there was blood on his shirt as well.

A bus appeared out of the mist with a ghostly hiss.

"Come back to my place," the girl said. "I have a couch you can sleep on, and you can have a wash."

Bridges peered at her. "Why?"

She shrugged. "What difference does it make?"

Suddenly Bridges felt exhausted. She was right, he decided. It didn't make any difference. A couch, a doorway, washed, not washed. He climbed on the bus and she followed, paying his fare.

She was a prostitute, she said: a high-class escort who turned tricks by appointment with executives and diplomats. She was employed by an agency in midtown. She said she was very well-paid.

"You must be awfully," he searched for the word, "professional."

"Sometimes."

"Were you working tonight?"

She turned to the window. "Oh, yes," she said to the glass.

"You don't sound as if you liked it much."

She smiled thinly and drew a Happy Face on the foggy pane. "Sometimes yes and sometimes no. Tonight—no."

"Is it so hard?"

"The hours are short and the money is long. It isn't like walking the streets. But after a thousand strangers have come and gone you get driven down inside. Or you become the stranger, and he isn't really there at all. I used to pretend I was screwing myself. But then I started to disappear as well."

She wiped out the Happy Face with her fist, opening a hole in the steam on the window that let the night come through. "Tonight I had an old boyfriend," she said. "He didn't recognize me. He didn't know who I was."

Her apartment was high above the Hudson, which slid like a silver worm through a crack in the earth below. He stood at her window swaddled in towels and watched the far-off water wend its way to parts of the city he knew best. Far away, on a night like this one, he'd squat beneath the West Side Highway and keep warm by holding his hands above a trash fire. Winter would go and he'd have survived again.

Light filled the room and he saw himself reflected in her window: younger than he'd looked in years, the muscles in his bare arm defined by the shadows they made. Then he saw her in the same glass standing in the bathroom doorway with the light bright all around her. She was naked. One arm was raised and her hand rested high on the door jamb. Her body looked as young as he had thought she was when he saw her on the train. He didn't know what she expected him to do, so he continued to stare at her image as if looking out the window.

"The way you live," she started, "are you lonely?"

Bridges began to sweat and cursed the rain that drove him from the docks. "I don't know," he said. "I never think about it."

"Are you lonely tonight?"

He faced her. "I want to go home," he said.

"Your clothes are all wet. I washed them. You'll have to wait until they dry."

"I've worn wet clothes before."

She let her hand fall down from the jamb, slow and white. She walked toward him like a guilty child, head down, watching her feet cross the thick beige carpet. She took a last step and placed her foot, very lightly, on his own. Her fingers climbed his chest and hooked the top of his towel. She tugged gently till it fell away, and turned her face up to his. "Please stay. We've both had hard nights."

Sometime in the dark he woke and listened to her breathe beside him. She breathed more like a man than like a woman, the sounds deep and sonorous as the air left her body. Her arm, when he touched it, felt strong like a man's arm too. Bridges fell asleep again and after a long time he began to dream. He dreamed that it was morning, and that he awakened and cooked himself some eggs, and made toast, and a pot of coffee. He dreamed that he ate, and washed the dishes, and went into the bathroom where he saw his tattered clothes, dry and wrinkled, hanging on a rope above the bathtub. He dreamed that he looked at them with a kind of fondness, and that he carefully washed his face and patted it dry with a thick towel, and put on eye shadow, mascara, eyebrow pencil, rouge, and lipstick. He dreamed that he put on a pair of brightly colored underpants cut very low, and a skimpy, sheer brassiere. He dreamed that he put on a blouse of dove-grey silk, with a matching scarf he tied into a bow around his neck. He dreamed he put on a garter belt, and rolled a pair of stockings up from his toes to his thighs, and hooked them to the belt. He dreamed he put on an ivory-colored skirt, and that the zipper almost snagged. He dreamed he put on a pair of dark gray shoes with short heels. He dreamed he slung a black leather purse over his shoulder, and took a bright green coat in his arm. He dreamed that as he looked out the window a brilliant day had already begun. He dreamed he looked at the bed and saw among the rumpled sheets a middle-aged man, half bald and gone mostly gray, asleep with his arms around a pillow. And he dreamed that on the street, walking to the bus, he put the green coat on and put his hands in its pockets and found, in one of them, a quarter, which he placed in the tin cup of a blind man selling pencils in the sun.

In That Country

Ann Regentin

"Hello," she said as he stood on her doorstep, trying not to gape. Rick was expecting something different, he wasn't totally sure what, but not a woman, especially not a woman in blue jeans and an ordinary blouse. "Mr. Turner?" she asked. He nodded stupidly. "I'm Laura Worthington. Come in. Can I get you something to drink?"

"Um . . . a Coke. If you have it." He didn't drink while he was working, a rule he was sorely tempted to break.

"Sure," she said, and she led him into the living room, offered him a chair, and went into the kitchen.

He sat, looked around. The room looked like it had been decorated by an ordinary woman with ordinary tastes, neither too feminine nor too masculine. The colors were dusty shades, the sort of blues and greens and pinks you see at twilight, colors that had names he would never remember and the patterns were comfortable and homey. The curtains were open, there were halogen torchieres casting light at the ceiling, a reading lamp by the couch; on a coffee table were a framed photograph of two men with a dog and a child's drawing. A local paper lay folded beside them. Nothing, absolutely nothing out of the ordinary.

She came back in carrying two glasses. The Coke in his sputtered a bit around the ice, stinging his nose as he drank. This had been a bad idea, this whole thing had been a bad idea.

"How can I help you?" she asked.

Her voice was a woman's voice, not a falsetto or even a tenor but a sweet, husky alto. "Laura Worthington?" he asked, just to make sure.

"Yes," she said, smiling. "Were you expecting someone butcher?"

"I . . . I didn't know what to expect," he said, thrown by confusion into honesty. "This is new territory for me."

"It's new territory for most," she said kindly. "Where do you want me to start?"

"Let's start at the beginning," he said, taking the recorder out of his pocket and switching it on. "I'm going to state for the record that the magazine has agreed to preserve your anonymity by publishing no names, photographs, or other pertinent details without your permission, and I will do my best to see to it that you are not misrepresented in any way." That was better. Routine anchored him. "So let's start at the beginning," he said again. "When did you know that you were different?"

"That I was a girl?" she asked, smiling. "I must have been about six or seven. That was when my little sister was born and I fell in love with her, not just her but her things, too. She had all of these pretty dresses, these dolls, and I couldn't keep my hands off them. I loved them. It was like coming home, you know?" She grinned. "I kept stealing one of Sarah's baby dolls. In retrospect, it was this horrible little thing; it had a cry like a mechanical cat, but I loved it to death. I brushed its hair, changed its diapers, gave it its bottle. All secretly, of course. My parents would have hit the ceiling if they found out."

"Did they find out?"

"About the doll? No. But my dad caught me putting on makeup one day and damned near broke his hand on my butt."

"How old were you then?"

"About eleven."

"Your parents weren't supportive?"

"It's a rare set of parents who are, and I was named Lawrence Robert Soffield Junior. Men who name their sons after themselves don't tend to take it well when the kid wears lipstick and signs his name 'Laura'."

No, Rick thought, *they wouldn't.* For that matter, how would he handle it if it were his kid? Probably not much better. "What was school like?" he asked.

"Not too bad in grade school. There were bullies, but there were always bullies. It started getting ugly in junior high."

"What was it like?"

She made a face. "Think about it for a minute. By then, I knew what I was, I mean, I knew I was a girl and I was expected to shower in the boys' locker room. Gym was hell. I had to dress in drag just to get along and I never quite passed. The shape of my body didn't really hide who I was and I didn't want it to. I just wanted to be myself and there was no place for that. There was a handful of boys who used to kick the shit out of me whenever they could, just for the heck of it. I was overweight, too, partly from stress but partly because I just did not want a male body. I hated it. It was hell. I couldn't wait to get out."

Rick took another drink of his Coke, remembering a boy in his class, not the most macho kid on the block, a bit heavy, with bottle-bottomed glasses. He hadn't thrown a punch, but he hadn't been kind, either. He winced inwardly. "How about high school?"

"I didn't go," she said.

"Why not?"

"My dad kicked me out of the house when I was fourteen."

He knew that most transgendered kids had it rough, but it was different seeing it up close like this, in a real person. "What happened?"

"The short version is that he came home early from work and found me in a dress. I used to wear girls' clothes after school, when my parents weren't home. My sister never told on me. I don't think she understood, but we got along okay. But then Dad came home and found me, and that was that. He booted me out with nothing but the clothes on my back."

"What did you do then?" Rick asked, shocked. Fourteen? Jesus! Fourteen was still a child.

"I peddled my ass," she said bluntly. "I didn't really have a choice. Come winter, I ended up in a shelter, where one of the caseworkers took me under his wing. He got me into a group home, kept an eye on me, and gave me periodic pep talks and tongue lashings. He probably saved my life." Laura gestured toward the photograph. "That's him with his partner."

"He was gay?" Rick asked, startled.

She smiled. "He is gay, yes."

Rick cringed inside at the thought of a gay man working with troubled youth, then stopped himself. Dammit, he thought he could handle this! He thought he'd be okay with it. He knew better than to think that way.

"No," Laura said suddenly, "he didn't."

"What?" Rick asked, startled.

"He didn't take advantage of me. Not only is he not a pedophile, he's gay. The last person he'd want to sleep with is a girl."

"Why did he help you?"

"He liked me," Laura said, and he saw the fidgeting of an ex-smoker under stress, the twitching fingers, shifting body. She picked up her glass, sipped from it; he saw a lemon slice floating on the ice as she set it back down. "He understood better than most. His partner is a drag queen."

Rick glanced at the picture. Now that he knew, he thought he could see it, but then he realized that only one of the two was a drag queen and he had no idea which it was. His head was starting to hurt. "What happened after the shelter?" Time to get this back on track.

"I went into a group home for queer kids."

"How was that?"

"How do you think? Nobody raves about life in a group home. There were a ton of rules, most of them designed to make us feel as abnormal and oppressed as possible. When I was seventeen, I became an emancipated minor. I changed my name legally as soon as I could. With Don's help, I got my GED and got into community college. I went from there to get a BSN."

"That's right," he said, back on something like normal territory. "You're a nurse."

"Yes. I'm a pediatric nurse."

Whoops! His throat closed. "Pediatrics?"

"I love children."

Part of his mind screamed at the idea. Another part looked at the woman sitting across from him on the couch. No one could possibly know. If he had passed her on the street, he would have given her a second glance but only because she was beautiful. She didn't look like a guy playing dress up.

"This is my own face," she said, "the face I was born with."

He knew that many transsexuals had facial reconstructive surgery. He looked more closely at Laura, trying to see it, but all he saw were the faces of men he'd known, guys with pointed chins, smaller noses, fuller lips, less brow. On Laura, it seemed that they were all put together in a face that might be, maybe male. Or not. A face that could go either way.

"Take a look," she said, handing him a small photo album.

It was Lawrence Robert Soffield Jr., the child. He looked like a pretty normal kid, maybe a haunted kid, but a kid all the same. As the photos showed the boy growing up, Rick thought he could see it, in the hair worn a bit long, almost feminine shirts, the extra weight. Lawrence almost never smiled. He glanced up at the woman on the couch. She radiated confidence. He looked back at the boy. The pictures stopped abruptly at junior high. Apparently, group homes didn't do photographs. "What all have you had done?" he asked.

"I've had breast augmentation surgery," she said. "That was nice, because it meant I could lose some weight."

Her breasts were marvelous under the shirt, a C-cup, he thought. He wondered if she had scars.

"I've had electrolysis on my face and body," she said, "except for the hair on my pubic bone. I don't have to shave at all now, not even my legs. I also had my Adam's apple removed when I had my breasts done. I take hormones, of course. But that's it. My face and the hair on my head are all my own." The pride in her voice was unmistakable.

He looked hard at her, thought he saw a faint scar at her throat. It made a remarkable difference. "The rest?" he asked.

"I haven't made up my mind," she said. "My partner and I have been talking about it for a while. I could do it. I've been living in role, as they say, for my entire adult life, but I'm also a nurse and I know exactly what the surgery involves. I'm not very happy with some of it. It reconstructs the female genitalia pretty well, but I'm not convinced that it reconstructs female sexuality adequately at all. I'm talking to a surgeon about maybe trying something new, seeing if we can go partway instead of doing a complete reassignment. I'd like to keep my sex drive, which means keeping my testicles, but I'd like it if they weren't visible. I'm also not sure about certain aspects of complete reconstruction. Sexual response isn't as reliable as I'd like." She smiled. "I'm not quite happy with my body, but I can afford to wait. The thing that I would most like to end is ejaculation."

"But wouldn't that stop you from having orgasms?" he asked, stunned.

"No," she said. "Male bodies can have orgasms without ejaculating. I've learned how, but it takes a lot of work. When I'm with my partner, I don't want to pay that much attention to myself. I like to be more focused on her."

Her. That's right, Laura was a lesbian. Suddenly the whole thing seemed like a waste, a farce. If she was attracted to women, why bother with the surgery?

"I'm not a man," she said. "I'm a woman. I just want my body to match up. Is that so unreasonable?"

"Your partner," he said, trying to keep his voice level. "How does she feel about it?"

"She accepts me. She loves me as I am, loves what I am becoming. I couldn't ask for more."

Rick's mind was racing, imagining the two in bed. A lesbian with a cock, those perfect breasts and a cock. Jesus Christ! Pictures flooded his mind of Laura with a woman, any woman, fucking her, and his own cock began to twitch in response. He took a sip of his now-watery Coke, trying to get a handle on it before he ended up with a monster woody.

Laura sighed. "All right. You have your interview, I think. I know why I was tapped for this. I'm a happy, well-adjusted transgendered woman who is contemplating additional surgery. It's all there. I'm happy. I'm well-adjusted. I'm contemplating. Unless there's something else you need?"

"Why?" he asked, his mouth dry in spite of the glass at his elbow. "I mean . . . why?"

"Because I'm a woman," she said, and he heard anger in her voice for the first time. "Do you think I enjoyed getting beaten up in school? Do you think I liked being kicked out of the house? Do you think I liked being fucked by a lot of sick jerks? Do you think group homes are fun or that it's easy being an emancipated minor? No. Surgery isn't fun. Electrolysis isn't anything to write home about, either, and it had to be done twice in some places. I wouldn't do this if I didn't have a pretty compelling reason, don't you think? Ask yourself: Are you a straight man or are you a lesbian? There's a world of difference, believe me."

Rick was silent, mostly out of shock. This wasn't what he had expected at all. Sure, he'd done his homework, he always did, but he hadn't expected this. Deep inside, he had expected a caricature, or maybe he'd wanted one. He'd wanted it to be a farce. He hadn't wanted Laura to be a woman.

"Do you think I can read your mind?" Laura asked.

He blushed red with shame, then with fury. He knew that she could.

"I know all the questions you won't ask because they're the ones guys always ask, usually the same guys who would have pummeled me as a kid. You're a professional so you're being polite, but I know what you're thinking because I can see it all over your face. You're disgusted with me at the same time that you're titillated by the whole thing." He started to voice a denial, but she cut him off. "Yes, you are! As soon as I started talking about the details of the surgery, you started getting hot. It happens all the time."

Rick burned, but he had one last question, not for the record. "Do you really want them to cut off your . . . ?"

"Penis?" She spat the word out. "Why not? What good has it ever done me? It's a big lie and always has been."

"But what about sex?" he asked, unable now to shut himself up.

"I have never used it the way you do," she said. "When I make love to my partner, it is always as a woman. When she wants something thick inside her, I use a vibrator or if the mood is just right, my hand. That's all."

Rick's mind churned, turning in on itself, Jesus Christ, what was this? What was she? He wanted to run, get as far away from it as he could, and he was sick at his own revulsion. She wasn't hurting anyone. If anything, she was the one who was hurt, treated like shit for no good reason by a society that turned its back on people like her. He knew that there were transgendered people throughout history, that some cultures had found places for them where they could live if not in honor, then at least in safety. He saw the monstrous injustice of it, but he also saw in himself a primal terror of anything that summoned the X chromosome that lay sleeping beside his Y. Laura was his greatest secret fear made flesh.

At the same time, he was hit by a tidal wave of desire. He wanted to see it. A thousand glimpses of "tranny porn" flashed through his head, the voice of a man in front of a bar in New Orleans yelling "Boys will be girls!" into the crowd to entice customers. He glanced at Laura's crotch, but her jeans were too comfortable. If she had a cock, it was well hidden.

"You want to see it?" Laura asked.

He bit his lips together. He would not say it.

"Well?" Not a question or a demand, but an accusation.

His head nodded without his consent.

She rose from the couch, kicked off her sandals, unbuttoned her shirt and let it drop, then reached back and unhooked her bra. It fell away to reveal a pair of stunning breasts, round and perfect. If there were scars, they were well-hidden and those nipples, those nipples couldn't possibly be male. He stared, wracked with self-loathing, hating his own desire that pushed shamelessly against his zipper. Her eyes flashed, then she dropped her jeans.

She wore tight black spandex and beneath it, the outlines of her cock and balls were clear. When she pulled her panties down, they sprang free, not hard, not even getting hard, merely unconstricted. She stepped out of her underwear and held her hands behind her back, letting him look. She showed no sign of arousal, only anger, maybe a masculine anger, but maybe a feminine anger, a woman pushed beyond endurance. Women had displayed their bodies in protest for centuries, an act of defiance and even violence in its own way, and in Laura was a rage that went back almost to birth. She knew him better than he did himself, and she had every reason to despise what she saw.

It was too much. He took a deep breath, swallowed the last of his Coke, cursing his shaking hands, his traitor penis. "Thank you," he said as steadily as he could.

"You're welcome," she said, her voice cool and sharp as frost.

"I have to go."

"All right," she said, still chilly. "Call if you need anything else." It was almost a dare.

"Thanks."

He nearly forgot his recorder. She handed it to him, ostentatiously clicking the off button.

He fled. About halfway home, he called his wife and begged off dinner, saying that he would be very late. He had nowhere else to go, but he wasn't ready for his family, not just yet, so he drove through a maze of back roads, going nowhere, thinking nothing.

As his cock deflated, his brain started to function again. He should talk to her. He should scrap the tape and do the interview all over again. If he could bear to face her. He rewound for a few seconds, hit play, and hit stop right away, burning again, hearing the thick heat in his own voice. Laura was right. It turned him on. Why? He wasn't sure, but he would have to get a handle on it if he was going to write this piece. Then again, maybe he shouldn't write the piece. Maybe he should pass it on to someone else. He could, but suddenly he didn't want to, he wanted to talk to these people, see what their lives were like, see if he could make sense of it in a way that other people would understand. That was his job, telling other people's stories. He was good at it, damned good.

But he wasn't this good. When he had taken on the assignment, he'd thought himself so cool and cosmopolitan, but when confronted with his first male-to-female transsexual, he had fallen apart, behaved like a trailer park reject with a penchant for cheap kink. He thought of his son, whom he had stopped short of naming Rick Jr., but for whom he had so many dreams. Could he handle this? Could he handle his son coming to him in a dress one day and asking to be called Danielle? Could he support him through the surgery that Laura was contemplating? He wanted to think he could, but he knew it wasn't true. He needed his son to be a man for the same reasons he needed to be a man, reasons he could not put a name to but that filled him with terror all the same if he stopped too long to ask questions. He'd call his editor, let this one go. It wouldn't be good for his career, but going back to Laura, filling in the missing pieces, would be worse. His mind made up, he turned around and went straight for home.

The house was dark except for the nightlights, a steady, guiding glow near the baseboards. He went to his office without turning anything else on and popped the tape out of the recorder, tossing it onto his desk. Then he changed his mind and put it on top of the highest bookshelf, where even the cleaning lady never dusted. His balls ached a bit, and he sat down in his chair and unzipped his fly. His cock responded promptly to his firm hand and trailing thoughts, mostly of a new intern at the magazine, his latest favorite bit of mental adultery. She was pretty, smiley, with long black hair that shone like obsidian. In his mind, he had her face down on a desk, her skirt hiked up around her waist and all of that gorgeous hair flowing through his fingers as he plowed into her from behind and he sighed, reaching for some tissues. Soon, yes. Very soon.

But when the moment came, it was Laura he saw, not angry as she had been but soft and sweet. And hard. He saw her hard and his hand was full of her, it wasn't him coming it was her, no ejaculating just as she wanted it, a woman's come, and he was holding her as she shook, telling her how beautiful she was. He came to a place where the boundaries and barriers had collapsed, no checkpoints, no passports needed, where the man he knew himself to be could embrace the woman Laura knew herself to be without fear or contradiction. In that country he had nothing left to defend and he could lay down his arms. It was so intense it almost hurt and he had to bite his lip to stop his groans.

It was past midnight before he dried his eyes and crawled into bed with his wife.

Finger

Greg Wharton

I awake abruptly, jumping up as if from a bad dream. My hand grabs at the side of the bathtub. I'm lying inside, naked but for my boxers that are twisted uncomfortably around my balls. I fight the urge to throw up, and wonder whose bathtub I'm in, and why I'm missing most of my clothes.

My head throbs as I try to lift myself up. Once sitting, I contemplate lying back down now that the pain in my head has risen a few notches. I remember having drinks at Harry's bar, yes drinks, and there was a broad. I bought her a drink and told her she looked like Lana Turner. She was . . . oh, the urge to vomit comes again, and I lean over the edge of the tub and gag. Nothing but bile. Just a little bile.

"You look like Lana Turner."

"Oh, you sweet talker. You're smooth, aren't you? Buy me a drink, honey. My name's Edie, but I like Lana. Call me Lana."

"Well, Edie, ah, Lana—"

"You know, honey, things aren't always as they seem."

I lay my head against the cool porcelain and close my eyes. We'd gone back to her apartment for a nightcap. This must be her apartment, but where was she? She was beautiful . . . I think. I have a foggy

memory of her sitting on the edge of the bed, rolling down her stockings . . . yes, beautiful. That's the last thing I can remember.

"Damn, Lana, you're beautiful."

*She puts an old record on the turntable, then sits on the edge of the bed seduc-
ing me with her eyes as she slowly peels the stockings down her long smooth legs.
With a curling finger she signals for me to join her. I sit my drink on the bedside table and walk to her—my cock throbbing against the inside of my now too
tight pants—in response to her invitation.*

*"You know, baby, I think I owe you some payback for all the sweet talk and
the drinks."*

*She licks her ruby red lips with her tongue as she slowly unbuckles my belt,
unzips me, and frees my anxious member. I moan in disbelief at my luck as
Lana wraps her mouth around my hard cock and Johnny Cash sings how it
burns, burns, burns . . .*

Okay, no time like the present, I think. I stand up and step out of the
bathtub I've made a bed. My legs feel as if they're having a hard time
supporting my weight. I step over my puddle of bile and lean against
the sink. My reflection scares me. I have bruises all over my cheeks
and my right eye is swollen shut. Shit! I've got to remember what
happened after I nailed the broad.

I shuffle to the toilet, lift the seat, and piss for what seems like an
unusually long time. My balls feel heavy and ache. I look around the
dingy bathroom, flick off the last couple drips of urine, and flush.

There's no medicine cabinet, just a cracked mirror held onto the
wall with nails. One after another I open the drawers below the sink in
search of aspirin. Finding none, I decide what I really need is more of
what got me here. A good shot or two of bourbon, and if I can find my
lady friend maybe a little more loving. An explanation would help.

I grab some toilet paper and blow my nose hard, ratcheting the pain in my head even higher. I toss it toward the trash can, but miss. When I pick it up and toss it again at the target, I see it. A finger.

A finger!

There's a fucking finger wrapped in bloody toilet paper in the trash can!

Panicking, I back up and try to catch my breath before I scream. What happened last night? I sit down on the edge of the tub and start to cry. What fucking happened? I check to make sure all my fingers are still attached, then rest my head in my hands and stare at my feet on the cold white tile of the bathroom.

I had drinks at Harry's. I make friends with a beautiful babe who I share more drinks with. She invites me back to her apartment for a nightcap, we hit it off, I bang her, maybe, and . . . then what?

"Oh, careful Lana! You gotta slow down or you're gonna make me explode. Damn girl!"

I pull myself from her mouth with a pop and back up. I'm standing in the middle of her bedroom with my cock bouncing up and down ready to shoot, my pants in a wad at my ankles.

She kneels at the edge of the bed, reaches back and unzips her red velvet dress. It falls from her shoulders and she catches it, teasing me, slowly uncovering her lovely small breasts one at a time. I let out a growl, and decide to get ready for the fuck of my life!

I trip over my own feet getting to the chair, and settle for the carpeted floor, where I fumble with my shoelaces. "You know, baby, sometimes what you least expect can be exactly what you want the most."

Lana stretches out those long legs and gingerly steps off the bed. She takes a deep breath and lets the dress fall. My eyes nearly pop from my head as it billows in slow motion down to her feet. Her tiny nipples harden as she steps out of her black lace panties, one smooth leg at a time, and her thick red cock—red as the dress at her feet, as red as the lipstick from her lips now smeared on my own cock—bounces free.

I suddenly remember her boyfriend storming into the room, and he was pissed. He started yelling at her, calling her a cunt, and she was bawling like a baby. He kept shaking his finger at her, his ring finger. His ring finger! I run to the trash can and look in at the finger.

Yes, the finger has a ring still intact. Holy Jesus, have I done it now! If I could just piece a little more together to know how the husband lost the finger. I stand, go to the sink and turn on the water. I splash my face, and swish my mouth out. I don't dry off, just run my hands through my hair and stare at my face. The skin beneath my eyes is swollen and blood vessels blossom across my nose and cheeks. I look tired. So tired. And scared.

I decide to be brave.

"Surprise!"

I am speechless. I've gotten in some trouble with drink in the past, but this definitely takes the cake. Oh, but is she lovely. I slowly stroke my cock as the truth sinks in.

The front door bangs shut, and I don't even have time to react before the heavy stomping footsteps bring a very large, very angry man into the room. Shit, I still have my pants wrapped around my ankles!

His face is red with rage—as red as Lana's thick cock, as red as the dress at Lana's feet, as red as the lipstick from Lana's lips now smeared on my own cock. He looks like he's going to explode!

"You slut! You fucking cunt! Who is this faggot?"

Faggot? "You know Lana, I think—"

"Lana? Edie, you cunt!"

He takes three quick steps past me and slaps Lana hard across her cheek, knocking her down onto the bed. Blood spurts from her nose and open mouth and she looks up at him like a cornered animal.

He turns back to me and lunges. I try to get up but my pants trip me again, putting my face just where I assume he wants it, right in line with the steel toe of his big boot.

Lana is sobbing, half her body hanging off the bed, black mascara tears mixing with the blood, her shriveled cock laying limp against one leg. He storms out of the room after kicking me again, this time right in my balls. My senses all scream at the same time, and I curl into a fetal position.

He returns with what look to be gardening shears, and I start screaming bloody murder.

"Not you, faggot! Shut up! Edie, I'm tired of this! I'm so fucking tired! Why do you do this to me? Why do you always do this to me? I love you so much—"

The shot makes me jump up and back, and I have just enough time to see him fall to his knees before Lana takes aim and fires her gun at him again, his chest exploding, covering me in thick red viscera. And I pass out.

Be brave!

If I get out of this mess, I promise to lay off the drink for a while. God, please, let them both be alive!

I open the door, and on very shaky legs, go in search of Lana and her fingerless boyfriend.

Small Considerations

R. Gay

I have a constant craving for my best friend, Blake. Under normal circumstances, I would covet his soon-to-be ex-wife. Yet he is so indescribable that I find myself, awake at night, imagining what it would feel like for him to rub his salt-and-pepper beard against my navel. But I can't let myself cross that line. It is too complicated. Masculinity gets in the way . . . his, and mine. Such a small consideration, he always tells me. Not small enough, I reply.

His shoulders . . . they're broad, the muscles tight and sinewy. His legs render me speechless. Strong, lean, tanned to the hem of his shorts and disturbingly pale just above there. And when he crosses his legs, I can see the muscles of his thighs flexing beneath his slacks. He runs, eight miles a day. The best time to get thinking done, he says. I prefer to think within the comfort of my couch. A cigarette helps the effort. We have little in common beyond our mutual attraction. At the same time, we have a lot in common, but I rarely allow myself to see that.

Blake has the kind of body I've always wanted. In my mind, I have dissected the most enviable parts of his anatomy. Half of one of my bathroom walls is covered in black-and-white collage of the person I have become. His arms, another guy's torso, and the calves of that Dutch model, my cunt the only body part I really want to keep. I've carefully pasted all these body parts together, and the resulting image looks exactly how I sometimes feel, scattered, incongruous, awkward.

At times, I think that Blake knows more about me than I know of myself. We met seven years ago, during our senior year in college as we turned in our theses. Mine was a wordy treatise on gender and lesbian identity in mainstream films. His was an exposition of deception and betrayal in Hamlet. Standing in front of our advisor's door, we quickly exchanged documents, scanned, and muttered the requisite approval. Later, I found him at the water fountain, letting the thick stream of water splash across his eyes. And I felt an uncomfortable twinge between my thighs as he stood, turned toward me, and smiled. It was a slow, almost lazy smile crawling from the center of his lips to the corners, until his mouth opened widely enough for me to see and instantly adore a charmingly imperfect set of teeth.

We went out for drinks that night to celebrate the end, or perhaps it was the beginning of something . . . neither of us were certain. We told each other almost everything about our lives. At some point, he covered my hand with his, and I didn't move away. I just slid my fingers between his, and held on. He hated poetry and trusted in the superiority of women and understood why Raymond Carver is brilliant. He believed in music as the closest he'll ever get to God and he believed in the necessity of soul mates and he didn't even blink when I explained that I was a raging feminist lesbian type person out to deconstruct notions of gender. In fact, he wanted me to tell him more. I tried, but could only get so far, because I didn't quite have all the answers, myself, particularly when I found myself squeezing his hand tighter, locking my ankles around his, wondering what it would be like to take him home and continue the conversation over breakfast. And as we exchanged phone numbers somewhere between nightfall and dawn, he told me I was not quite. Not quite what, I asked nervously, cracking my knuckles as he rubbed his chin slowly. I'm not sure yet, but I'll let you know, he finally answered. When I walked home, those words kept bouncing around my mouth as I muttered them repeatedly. And I was scared. In a few hours, he had managed to put into words what it had taken me twenty-two years to voice.

We've seriously crossed the line once, Blake and I. Three months ago, he needed a ride home from the airport so I offered to be his chauffeur for the evening. And when I saw him standing in the baggage claim, watching the same green suitcase traveling around and around the carousel, I was in awe of his profile. I could see the gentle creases in his forehead, the sharp slant of his nose, beard neatly trimmed. I hid behind a bank of phones, watching as he twisted his wedding ring and shifted his weight from foot to foot, and concluded that it was his overt masculinity that kept me silent and hidden.

When he turned toward the exit, I stepped from behind the phones and smiled. He waved me over and I jogged toward him. He stretched his arms outward and it only seemed natural to bury my face against his armpit as his arms wrapped around me. I could smell sweat, the lingering scent of cigars and deodorant, his cologne. His beard tickled my forehead, and before I could stop myself, I raised my head, he leaned down, and brushed his lips so lightly against mine that my back arched and I clasped my hand around the back of his neck, kissing him in an entirely inappropriate manner.

I pulled away first. I had to. Because if I didn't, I would have to admit certain things about myself, and so would he. Welcome home, I whispered. He brushed his thumb across my chin, and stared at me. I have to go to the bathroom, he said gruffly, and I nodded, following. As we stepped into the last stall, my throat tightened, and I shoved my hands in my pockets to stop the trembling. He set his briefcase down and leaned back against the wall. I felt an overwhelming need to say something, but the silence between us was so fragile that I was afraid that my words would create something irreversible. He began loosening his tie, but I shook my head, took my hands out of my pockets, and carefully untied the loose knot, letting his tie dangle about his neck. Slowly, I began unbuttoning his shirt. I love the feel of his shirts, sharp, almost slick against my fingers, as if they are made of some mystical material, not a cotton-polyester blend.

He rested his hands against my shoulders, curling his fingers into my back as I pulled his shirt apart and began kissing the dark base of his throat, the muscled arcs just below his nipples. I was intimately aware of his wedding ring pressing through the thin material of my sweater, but I chose to ignore it. The ability to commit adultery was another one of those things I don't care to admit about myself. But then I told myself that they were separated, soon to be divorced. Adultery was a small consideration under such circumstances. Tentatively, I let my tongue slip past my lips, drawing a thin line of saliva between his nipples. I was fascinated by them, light brown, thick and hard, swelling as I flicked my tongue against them then suckled them into my mouth, my lips pressed against his chest. I heard a groan circling in his throat, and I placed two fingers against his lips. His hands slid lower, to the empty space where my breasts used to be. I instinctively leaned into him, but then pulled away. I was not ready for him to touch me there, and I don't think he was either.

Let me touch you, he said softly. I shook my head, sliding to my knees, as I traced the muscles of his stomach with my tongue, letting my tongue play briefly inside his navel. Inhaling deeply, I pressed my forehead against the cool brass of his belt buckle, enjoying the quivering sensation of his cock beneath his slacks, against my cheek. He had no way of knowing how much I fetishized this very act of dropping to my knees before him. I have imagined the possibilities so many times in so many different ways that I closed my eyes as I loosened his belt buckle and undid his slacks, pulling them around his knees. I licked my lips and moaned softly as he pressed his fingers against my scalp. Holding his cock in one hand, I brushed my lips across the head, but then I stopped, and pounded my fist against the tiled floor. I can't do this, I said, staring at the toilet. I expected him to curse, shove me away, but he nodded and began straightening his clothes. Later, in the car, my sweaty palm gripping the emergency brake, he covered my hand with his, brushing his fingertips across my knuckles until we pulled into his driveway. I stared out the window as he gathered his things, but before I pulled away, he said, You think too much. I have to, I answered, thinking how weak those words sounded.

We haven't discussed it since, but when I see his lips, I remember and I hope he does too. We've been avoiding each other lately, communicating rather cryptically, through postcards, sending and receiving up to three or four a day. The lady at the card store thinks that I have a paramour in some far-flung corner of the world. Every morning, she smiles and shows me what's new, asks about my paramour, tells me that its nice to see a young person keeping the art of manual correspondence alive. It would take too much effort to explain that I am sending these cards to a man who lives seven miles away from me. And it would take too much effort to explain why I'm more comfortable filling postcards with tiny print rather than picking up the phone, or meeting him for lunch. Some days, there aren't enough postcards in the world to tell Blake all the things I need to say. And I wrote that earlier today, on one of my cards. But then I tore it, and flushed the brightly colored shreds of paper down the toilet.

Instead, I will send him two cards, hoping he'll read them in the correct order, explaining my well-thought-out plan for killing a co-worker, and the mailman who feels the need to read Blake's postcards before dropping them in the mailbox. I caught him today, because I was home early from work, so this message is in part for him. These mundane details will mask my loneliness, my hunger, my doubts, my fears.

My life is so full of irony these days that I can almost laugh about it all. I've put so much time, energy, and money into reassembling myself that I have lost sight of what it is that I am looking for. I do not want to want this man or any man for that matter. But God do I want Blake. And I constantly berate myself for that want. Why put myself through all these changes, only to end up with a man? It seems like I'm taking two steps forward, five steps back. But then I tell myself that it is not about whom I want to be with, but who I want to be. And then I imagine the expressions on my friends' faces were I to tell them that I am in love with a man—the chagrin, the shock, their open disgust in the face of my betrayal to the Cause. I will send a third postcard to Blake today, explaining all of this to him. I need him to understand what I cannot understand myself. And then I will wait until tomorrow's mail arrives, and pray that he writes back. Because if he doesn't . . .

The night before his wedding, Blake and I went to the seediest bar we could find, Jake's Bait, Tackle, and Beer, and slapped a hundred dollar bill down on the bar. Keep the beer and whiskey flowing, we told the bemused bartender, who crumpled the money and tossed it into the cash register. We smoked cigars, chastised ourselves for a general lack of imagination, and rocking back and forth on his stool, Blake sulked about his impending nuptials.

"It should be you and I tomorrow," he slurred.

I laughed, taking a shot of whiskey, as I twirled myself around on my barstool.

"Never let liquor speak for you," I told him.

He set his mug down and planted his hands on the sides of my stool. "I'm speaking for myself here. I want to be with you, marry you, whatever."

I crossed my eyes and tried to focus. "Barefoot and pregnant has never been my color."

"I don't need you barefoot and pregnant, although, you have delightful toes."

"Blake, just stop," I told him. "Nothing good can come of this conversation."

"We will not know that until we have this conversation."

"I don't do men. I don't know how to explain that in simpler terms."

Blake began tracing watermarks on the bar. "That's rather hypocritical, don't you think?"

"Come again?"

"You're all hung up on my—as it were, when in the grand scheme of things, it's a minor detail."

"That's easy for you to say. You know what you are."

"I know what you are too."

"I'm a little more complicated than not quite . . ."

Blake chuckled. "You remember that?"

I nodded. "I do."

"Have you ever considered that I welcome those complications?"

"You're straight."

"Not quite."

"And I'm not."

"Really?"

"You're too clever," I whispered.

"I'm not trying to be."

"You aren't ready for me."

Blake slammed the palm of his hand against the bar, and I jerked my head upward. "You do that all the time, you know . . . deciding how other people feel, what other people want."

"I'm making a decision for me. Respect that."

"If you let me in, just once, I might surprise you."

"That's a chance I'm not willing to take. I like things as is."

Blake rubbed his forehead. "And you can watch me marry someone else tomorrow?"

I wanted to cry. I wanted to let him in. I wanted to grab his hand, and run out of that shit hole, and drive all night to Vegas. I could feel my heart falling apart, ripping at the seams and floating away from my center, at the thought of him, in a somber tuxedo saying I do to someone else. But I was equally terrified by the thought of me, standing across from him in a tuxedo of my own, two hundred guests staring at us, murmuring in confusion. "I don't have a choice," I finally replied.

Blake took another sip of beer. Patting my back, he said, "You're a better man than me."

In that moment, I wished I could record those words. And in that moment, I knew that I would always be in love with Blake, even if I couldn't allow myself to be with him. I wanted to steal away to the parking lot, and slide into the back seat of his car with him. I wanted to fumble with his clothes, just to feel the smooth of his skin against my hands. I wanted to straddle his lap, ignoring the roof of the car putting pressure on my neck and the bright street lamp exposing us to passersby. I would ride his muscled thigh, and grasp the thin of his neck skin between my teeth. I would circle the base of his cock with my fingers, and move him inside of me. I would kiss him the way I've never dared to kiss anyone, tasting whiskey and cigars on his breath, and my head would swim and I would feel slightly nauseous. But I would hear him moan, and press himself against me, and raise his hips to fill me. Nothing else would matter.

I want to write this on a postcard as well. I want to tell him that I'm ready. But a man can only be patient for so long. It's probably too late for us. The postcard I'm writing is full, and now I'm filling page after page of my favorite notebook, with a letter that can never end because I am putting to paper my every thought. There's a knock on the door, and sighing, I remove my glasses, push my chair away from the desk, and drag my feet to the front door. I'm not expecting anyone, so I am irritated. I peer through the eyehole, and bang my forehead against the door. Blake is standing on my front porch. Wincing, I open the door, and he hands me a stack of postcards.

"It would cost me a fortune to send you all these," he says. "So I am delivering them in person."

He looks tired, worried. It is an expression I have seen on his face once before. For my twenty-sixth birthday, I treated myself to a mastectomy. I never wanted to completely alter my body. But I needed something more streamlined . . . more masculine than the soft curves of my chest. So I went through a year of therapy and warned all the people in my life of my decision. It was Blake who took me to the hospital. I wanted to go alone, but he insisted. And afterward, when I was groggy and high on opiates, the nurses told me that Blake had spent the entire time pacing the waiting room, harassing anyone in a medical uniform for information. I tried to laugh, but the throbbing beneath my stitches forced me to smile instead, so hard, that my cheeks ached. I heard a light knock on the doorframe and Blake stepped into my room, hesitating.

"You can come in," I said hoarsely.

He cracked his jaw and approached the bed. As he sat down, he covered my right hand with both of his, and the one thing I remember is how large his hands were, and how small and pale mine was. His hands were warm, and I could imagine our hands melding together. I could feel his pulse against my thumb. I wanted him to hold my hand forever . . . hold all of me between his hands. He surveyed my body anxiously, his eyes lingering on my chest. "How are you feeling?"

I raised my left hand limply. "Couldn't be better."

He squeezed my hand tighter. "Are you sure?"

"I hurt, Blake. I hurt everywhere, but I've never felt this good."

He exhaled one silent sob, resting his head on the edge of the bed. "I've never been so scared."

"It's a routine surgery. Women have been rearranging their chests for years."

"You're not just any woman," he said wryly.

I turned, staring out the small window. "Truer words."

"Never spoken."

"How long can you stay?" I asked.

"Forever?"

"But seriously."

"I'm not leaving until you do."

My heart pounded, so hard, I feared that my stitches would tear. "You shouldn't say things like that."

He drew a finger along my jawline. "Today, you don't make the rules."

I tried to protest, but I was so tired and sore that I nodded, and let my eyes fall shut.

Eight weeks later, I felt confident enough to face the world. I had needed time to learn how to live in my new and not quite body. I invited Blake over for dinner, and I wore a form-fitting white T-shirt, jeans, my feet bare. When I passed by the mirror and saw the outline of my new body, I giggled aloud. It was an odd thing, finally being able to recognize myself in my reflection. When he hugged me, and I could feel his body against mine with nothing in between, I shivered so hard my toes curled.

"I've missed you so goddamned much. You look fantastic," he said, and I could feel his beard tickling my ear. It was a curious sensation that traveled along my earlobe, down the side of my neck into the pit of my chest. We held each other for too long, as we often do, and blushing, I pulled him into the kitchen, taking the bottle of wine he handed me. He sat at the table, stretching his legs, and I bit my lower lip, looking away. "Can I see?" he asked shyly.

"See what?"

"Your body. I want to see your body."

I shook my head, concentrating on the stew I was preparing. "What you see is what you get."

He smiled softly. "I will wait."

I reached across the stove and turned the fire down. "No one can wait forever."

"I can."

I clenched my fingers into a tight fist. "You don't have a choice."

Blake stood and crossed the short distance between us. He brushed his lips across the back of my neck and slid his hands down my arms. I wanted to let myself fall into him, move to the side, have him take me against the cabinets, my forehead held to the ceramic counter, as I screamed his name and all the nasty things I wanted . . . needed him to do to me. "What's stopping us now?" he demanded.

"The same things that have always stopped us."

He stepped back, and sat down. "Right. How dare I forget."

I began ladling stew into two bowls. "You're angry."

"I'm frustrated."

My gums hummed with tension. "I'm sorry."

He sighed. "I know you are. And I do not want to pressure you or create more crap in your life, but frankly this all pisses me off. I do not know how to make myself into someone you can want."

But you are the person I want, I could have, should have said. "You can't."

"So you don't want to be a woman, or a man, but you have to be with a woman and not a man? It makes no sense."

"I don't expect you to understand. It makes sense in my head." I was intimately aware of the coarse denim against my thighs.

"Can I crawl in there for a few hours?"

"I wish you could. I want you to," I said, cursing inwardly at the slip.

"Aha! Progress."

"Don't read into that, Blake," I said sharply, setting his stew before him.

He pursed his lips and nodded. "Smells good."

I wanted to sit on his lap, wrap my arms around his neck, and drink wine until we stumbled into my bed and simply slept, together. I wanted us to feed each other and feed upon each other. But I took my bowl, and sat across from him, moving pieces of celery around with the edge of my spoon. He caught my eyes, once, and I tried to share with him all my thoughts. I tried to hand him the key to deciphering my desire with that one look. He cocked his head to the side, as if the message he received was incomplete. And it probably was.

Looking at his hands, I notice that his wedding ring is missing, the only remaining evidence a pale band of flesh. I rub my eyes and take the postcards. Blake has very neat handwriting. Each letter is small and deliberate, making complete words elegant. Part of me wants him to leave, so I can soak in my bathtub, carefully poring over each note. But a bigger part of me wants him to stay so I can give him the pages and pages I have spent all day writing. We go into my office, and he sits on the futon. I can hear the sound of his knees cracking.

"I've got something for you too," I stutter. He arches his eyebrows as I hand him three postcards and my notebook.

He pats the empty space next to him. "Let's read together."

It is the little gestures like this that make me love this man so much. The way the word together sounds so natural coming out of his mouth, as if it is the way we have always been meant to be. I swallow, hard, and sit, close enough that our arms brush. We are silent for what seems like hours. I try and memorize each message, as if these postcards will fade away the moment I set them down. I wonder if he is doing the same. He moves his lips when he reads and I am comforted by the hushed sound. Finally, he sets my notebook down and turns to me. It is darker outside but I can see arcs of tears resting on his lower eyelids.

"I don't know what to say," he says.

My heart falls. "I've shared too little, too late."

"Not at all."

"I didn't realize I said that aloud. I guess I don't know what to say either."

Blake gently caresses my face, and I lean into him tentatively resting my hand against his thigh. "Seven years is a long time to wait," he whispers.

"It had to be this way."

"I understand that."

I let the postcards fall to the floor, and we watch as they float midair and then scatter across the room. I inhale deeply and grab my inner lip between my teeth. Straddling his legs, I place my thumbs against his forehead and drag them along the contours of his face; the sharp of his cheekbones, his jawbone, the deep cleft in his chin, finally resting the pads of my fingertips against his upper eyelids.

"You act like this is the first time you've ever seen my face," he tells me.

"It is."

He nods knowingly, and I move my hands to his shoulders. Inching forward, I press my forehead against his and he wraps his lips around mine, pulling them into his mouth. I can feel his tongue moving across the thin ridges of my lips. I part my lips. I want to feel his tongue with mine. The muscles of his stomach tense against my chest, and his hand slides down my back, grabbing a handful of my T-shirt. I am nervous. My hands tremble as I slide my fingers across his cheeks, trace his earlobes, and slide them beneath the collar of his shirt. His skin is warm, slightly damp. I can tell that he smoked a cigar earlier as the stain of tobacco rolls down my throat. I clench my thighs around his, and deliberately pull his shirt apart, the buttons flying in every direction.

Blake's hands are under my T-shirt now, fingers crawling along my spine. I tense and my breath quickens as he wraps his hands around my ribcage, his thumbs arching upwards toward my chest. I can hear the sound of his thumbnails against my nipple rings. And then he hooks his thumbs inside the rings, gently tugging them away from my chest. I kiss him harder. My lips hurt as I try to pull his mouth into mine.

"I want to see your body."

I circle his wrists with my hands and pull them away from me. His lips stop moving, and his eyes are haunting, the crest of disappointment almost spilling out of him.

"I need this," he says hoarsely.

I need it too, but I do not say this. Instead, I ignore the butterflies in my stomach and the doubts in my mind, and pull my shirt over my head, throwing it to the side. Blake's shoulders slump with relief. I sit perfectly still. He pushes me backwards and I plant my hands against the thick futon mattress, my back sharply arched. No one has ever seen me like this, and if I think too much, I will simply pass out. I do not know how to make myself comfortable with such exposure. He kisses my shoulders and rubs his cheek across my breastbone. For moments, we sit like that, my breathing ragged, his calm . . . steady. He is waiting for me, and before I can stop myself, I can feel a tear trickling down my cheek, falling onto his face. Blake wipes the tear with one finger, brings that finger to his mouth to taste. He stares at my chest long and hard, then slowly, so slowly its almost painful, he feels along the thin scars on the underside of where my breasts used to be. It is as if he is creating a memory of my flesh. Blake leans down, brushing his lips, tracing with his tongue, the map he has drawn with his fingers. I shiver, and my skin tingles beneath his mouth. He draws his tongue upward flicking the tip against my right nipple, then my left. As he pulls my nipples into his mouth, sucking hard, almost violently, I can hear his teeth clacking against my rings. It is a sound I have imagined countless times.

I slide my fingers through his hair, clenching them into tight fists, thrusting my chest into his mouth. The crotch of my jeans is soaked. I tell myself that I should feel betrayed by my body, but I don't. I welcome this wetness. I want us to drown in it. My clit throbs and suddenly, I need to feel his body with my mouth. I slam him against the back of the futon, and desperately bite his throat, scrape my teeth down to his navel, and lower, moving to the floor. Quickly, I undo his slacks, and pull them off. His cock is thick and hard, red. I slide my tongue from between my lips and circle the tip, letting my tongue dip inside the wet slit. He tastes salty, a little sour, and I groan, loudly. I explore every inch of his surface with my lips and my tongue, sliding one hand around to grab hold of his ass as I take his balls into my other hand, enjoying the warm weight of them. The pale skin of his upper thighs are stretched taut. I want to swallow him whole, so I relax the muscles of my throat, wrap my lips around the head of his cock, and lower my mouth until I can feel hair against lips. I struggle to breathe but I tighten my cheeks. As if he is finally able to decipher my desire, he gently places his hands against the back of my head, and guides me along his rigid length.

I squeeze his balls between my fingers, harder, as he shoves his hips toward me. He holds my head more firmly, and my mouth now feels raw. My lungs are burning, and I feel as if my chest might explode. But then Blake stills me and his cock falls out of my mouth. I look up at him, confused. He pushes me to the floor and removes my jeans. I can feel postcards sticking to my sweaty skin. He moves to mount me, but I shake my head, and roll onto my hands and knees, spreading my thighs, my ass high in the air. His hands start from my shoulders, move down my back, again slowly, as he creates another memory. I can feel his shaft against my ass cheeks, throbbing, insistent. Blake's hands pass over my ass, and I rear against him, then freeze, as his fingers dance along my wet inner thighs, my pussy lips. His tongue tastes the small of my back, the dark shadow just above my ass. He flicks just one finger against my clit, and I hear a sound that I cannot recognize until I realize that it is me.

"You are stunning," he whispers, letting one finger slide inside my cunt.

I clench myself around him and spread my thighs wider. A creature inside of me begins to beg, pant, plead for him to treat me like his slut, his whore, his bitch boy. And I realize that I can say these things to him, because he understands. He removes his finger from my cunt and slides it into my mouth. I suck eagerly, tasting me, his cock, his cigars. I reach through my legs for his cock, pulling the head to my ass. I need him to take me like this. I need him to be the first. I hear him rustling with his pants, then foil ripping, latex rolling. He dips two fingers inside my cunt, then smears my juice against the wrinkles of my asshole. Carefully, he places the tip of his cock against me and moves slightly. I gasp. My thighs quiver and I scrape the floor with my fingernails.

"Take me," is all I can say. "Just fucking take me."

He grunts and slides his cock, inch by inch, into my ass. I spasm around him. I feel stretched . . . torn. I cannot control anything. He pulls back, and it feels like all of my internal organs will come pouring out of my body. Sharp twinges of pleasure spiral directly from my ass to my cunt. He slides forward again . . . deeper. He holds my body between his hands and begins a sensual cadence of his hips, slapping against mine, then emptiness, then his body pressed against mine again. My face is burning. My clit is burning. And then he is thrusting into me hard. I fall to my elbows. My ass grips him tightly. Up until now, he has been controlled, but now, I can feel the frenzy in his skin. He is telling me he loves me. His right hand slides around my torso, over my mound to my most sensitive place, and he presses with two fingers, circling with each thrust of his cock. I have no experience in my life to compare this to. I begin shaking uncontrollably. I am unable to form words. Instead harsh, guttural sounds fall from my mouth. There is a tiny part of me that wants to wrench myself away. Run somewhere. Hide. So I tell him not to stop. I tell him to fuck me harder. I slam my body against his. His other hand is on the back of my neck. He holds my head to the floor. I open my eyes, and I can see our reflection in the glass of a painting resting against the wall. I like the look of us.

I can no longer keep myself tight around his shaft. As I loosen, widen to him, he is fucking me faster. There is no more rhythm between us. We are reaching for something. I am really crying now and I have no idea when this flood of tears started. I think he is crying too. My body shudders, just once, and then I feel my skin crawling as if it is trying to escape my bones. With a scream, I come and with a final thrust, he falls on top of me. There is a wet, sucking sound as his chest heaves against my back. We don't have the energy to move, but eventually, his body drifts to the side, and I wrap myself around him.

My jaw is tight as I try to speak, but I need to fill the silence between us, find something to hold on to. "I don't know what to say."

"You don't have to say anything," he says, kissing the top of my head.

"I'm still not quite . . ."

"Neither am I."

I try to smile, but I am too tired. "I made you wait so long."

He is quiet for a moment, then brushes his nose across mine. "That is but a small consideration."

I look over his shoulder at our reflection in the painting. I still like the look of us.

Twist

Helena Settimana

Rain. A high view of a busy street—revealing umbrellas open against the onslaught. It's downtown Vancouver in winter—alpine scenery and dismal English weather. The view moves inside a hotel room, turns back, looking out though a pattern of drops on glass that makes the classical façade of the adjacent Vancouver Art Gallery seem to melt on the street below. A sidewalk artist's work dissolves into puddles of abstract color on the gray pavement.

A man is speaking and as he speaks a new scene is revealed . . .

"Being a bellhop's got its charms. I get good tips, sometimes I meet a famous person, get invited to parties for laughs, sometimes take a chance and get lucky and once, I got a call as a player for a ball-busting freak fuck that ended when someone died—you'll know the story—but I've got my version. Wanna hear about it?" He looks around, vacant, lost. "Buy me a drink, buddy—I'll tell you. I need to get this offa my chest." His hands drum the tabletop.

The setting is a bar—smoky, filled with raucous voices, thumping music, neon—dilute in the gloom—occasional flashes of strobe. The speaker smokes nervously. He's in his thirties, short-short hair, groomed beard, pinched, pale face. He's saying, "This guy came in from LA. Made out he was some sort of movie bigshot. Not a star, right?—more of a 'player,' you know? Skinny. Dressed like a gangster in this narrow charcoal suit and black shirt. Shaved head, café au lait skin, with this tat of a bull's-eye on the back of his skull. Tossed his keys to the valet, tossed the bags to me. I took him through the lobby.

"There was this gorgeous hot tamale doing a decent Nina Simone set. I usually don't pay much attention to the lounge but I remember *her*. She was singing 'Don't Smoke in Bed.' Did a good job, almost sobbing it out. Sex standing up. Made me smile—the song that is. She wasn't my type, being a dame, but that voice—man oh man, like Glenlivet and a nice, thick Havana. I asked the guy if he thought she was hot. 'She's pretty,' he said, and looked away, scanning the audience. Apparently she wasn't his type either . . .

"I thought *he* was cute, though. I helped the guy with his bags, wondering if I could help him with *his* bag, if you know what I mean. Thought it was an idle daydream. He had a nice face, basket, and that full, high ass—the bubble butt of all bubble butts. Sort of slight build, five-ten or so which was okay from where I was standing. He had a funny, reedy voice. It was weird, but I thought he was cool in a kind of androgynous way. So sue me. We went up the elevator and he asked me, 'Where does a guy go for fun in this town?' 'What kinda fun?' I ask.

"'Companionship, meet new friends, solve the world's problems,' says he.

"'That depends on the kind of companionship and problems,' I go.

"So he looked at me for a sec.

"'You know what I mean. Where do *you* go?'

"Ah . . . so now I know I've been made. So I told him about this place and so he asks me how to get here, and I tell him and we go to his room and he opens the door and I drop his bags inside and turn to go and he flips me ten bucks—a greenback no less, and says, 'Thanks for the tip.' I figured he's not going to ask me to stay any longer so I touch my hat and say thanks too—and out of the room I walk. I'm telling myself *fuggedaboudit*. I did for a while."

"You're funny," says the listener. "I thought only people in Mickey Spillane stories talked like you." He placed a hand on the speaker's knee.

"I'm not laughing. You gonna listen?" He pried the wandering hand off and replaced it on the bar. "I took the guy a tray of sandwiches, 'round midnight. He'd been into the bar fridge and looked kinda fucked up—crazy around the eyes. I got wondering if he'd met the pharmacologists from Hastings. Eh, eh, y'know? I turn to go, finning his tip. 'When are you off work?' he asks, and I tell him, 'In an hour,' and he says, 'Why don't you come back here and keep me company for a while?' He's sitting in one of those green velvet chairs all sprawled out, on display. 'It'll save me a trip downtown.' He looked at me hard, and I said, 'Yeah, sure, why not.' I get a hard-on that's tough to hide for the next hour.

"So I goes up to his room about one thirty. The door opens and I slip into the room. It's almost dark inside—and he offers me a drink—Scotch. I down it in a gulp. I go over to the window and look out. Icy rain makes hard little ticking noises on the glass like sand's being thrown against it. Then he comes up behind me. Puts a hand on my shoulder. Fast. No waiting. I turn around. We're necking hard, in front of the window.

"I was holding his face in my hands. He had the smoothest skin I ever felt on a man and just a bit of stubble on his chin. It was weird, I tell you. I felt his chest, his arms—smooth muscles, toned. . . . Flip me a smoke, sunshine, I'm outta them . . ."

The listener shakes out a du Maurier, and offers a light and while the bellhop talks, the scene plays out in his head:

The guy from LA fondles the bellhop's hard-on and unzips it, pulls it out, twists it in his long, tapered hands. LA sinks to his knees. His mouth stretches and pulls, his jaw disappearing into his neck. *Cocksucker.* He's on his knees on the plush carpet, huge mouth, lips pulled back over shiny white teeth scraping the roll of skin collaring the head of the bellhop's cock, bobbing from his fly. LA pulls the bellhop's pants down and is rewarded by fingers gripping his bald pate. He stands up, spins the bellhop around to face the window, pulls the drapes open just a bit more and presses his face down so that his cheek rests on the sill, the bellhop's head and neck bent like a broken puppet. Bends him over. Another zip. The bellhop tries to feel the man's cock; has his hands shoved away. Is told, "Get off!" The LA man fingers the bellhop's ass. A digit sinks in, deep. The bellhop's pants are around his ankles, and he's moaning. Sound of latex snapping. Something hard, hot, and massive is knocking at the bellhop's ass, slipping between his cheeks. Man bites his neck, reaches around and grabs him, pumps him while jamming his cock to the hilt. The bellhop comes, shooting his load on the glass. LA zips before the bellhop catches his breath and turns around—moves away as he tries to touch him. Nina sings "Mood Indigo," somewhere in the dark . . .

"You're making me horny," says the listener. "Don't stop." His hand creeps off of the bar, down, down . . .

The speaker blinks, "I came so hard it hurt. I didn't even see his cock. He kept telling me to 'twist on it,' in this raw, hissy voice. I could feel his balls slap my ass, but he pinned my hands, and then it was over. Then he says to me, 'Finish your drink and just leave. Wash up at home. Here's fifty for your trouble.' His voice sounded shrill, bitchy. It shouldn't have mattered, since I got off on it and I didn't expect to be sent flowers, but *holy shit*. He sat and just stared at me until I pulled up my pants and left that room feeling like a cheap whore. *Sonofabitch*.

"He turned up a couple of times that week—once right here. I looked over and he was up at the bar over there with his hand on this little guy's ass talking really intently. I started to check him out, looking to see if he had a different MO, but no. That kind of pissed me off—part of me had hoped I had got something original from the experience. Aw Christ, I guess I did, but not in the way I meant, not the way I thought."

He lit his borrowed cigarette, and his hand shook just a little . . .

"He was feeling up this guy and then they both moved to the back of the bar. I went down to check them out. Same thing—the little guy he was hustling drops his drawers, and our man from LA pins down his hands and slips it to him hard. I swear he was even telling him to 'twist on it.' Then he just walks away, smirking."

"No shit? And when was the last time you saw him?" asks the listener, a shifting shadow, barely visible.

"I got a call asking for some more booze because his bar fridge had run dry. Christ, it was eleven o'clock in the morning! I tried to get someone else to take it up, but we were kind of busy with checkouts, so I wound up taking it myself. I knocked and called 'room service,' but there was a 'do not disturb' sign on the door and some sounds coming from inside letting me know that he meant it. I didn't know who was getting screwed but there was a helluva racket coming from in there. The sound made me hard, though, and I wondered if it'd go down before I had to return to the lobby . . . I figured security would be by to tell them to can it pretty soon. As I turned the corner I spotted a room being cleaned—but the maid was just standing in front of the window with her mouth open and I knew she could see them, I just knew it. She crossed herself about forty times, swear to God. I went and looked over her shoulder."

He laughs briefly and then gets really sober looking and goes on. His listener shifts in his seat while the scene again comes to life:

The man from LA is staring at his partner's ball sac, making a good show of feeling himself up through his own trousers. His cock strains down the inside of his left thigh. He's still mostly dressed. The other man is dancing in the dull gray light dribbling through the window. LA sits in a chair, calls him over—runs his hands all over him, feeling him like he would any renter, sucks each ball in turn, swallows his head. The man starts to moan, then shout. LA works his well-worn groove—up against the glass, sweat smearing, pushing hard, ripping though his fuck's solid need with a well-oiled thrust and the man yells with every stroke. The guy at the end of the cock is flailing, trying to reach around and rip the clothes from his top. They don't see the Filipina maid saying her Hail Marys across the courtyard. But the maid does see what happens next and what happens next is unbelievable. The glass gives way. She sees the glass shatter outward and the unnamed bottom's flailing tumble into the damp morning and the camellia-like bloom that spreads out from his head on the slick walkway below. LA guy's got his hands on his head, wheeling in a circle in front of the window like an erratic compass, cock bobbing, still hard.

The bellhop pauses for a second. "Poor bastard died, of course—fell six stories. The cops came in an army and there was a zillion questions asked and of course, that guy from LA was taken downtown and then it all came out . . ."

He leaned forward, hands gripping his glass.

"You remember the story—you have to. It was in the papers—one of those bizarre incidents the tabloids love. No one, not a single one of us, and especially not I, ever would have guessed that bastard was a fish with a goddam rubber cock. . . *Shit*. Not in a million years. Apart from the cops, I just never ever told anyone that I knew her let alone fucked her—or rather that she fucked me. I never saw or felt any tits. She had a cock. I *felt* that! What does that make me, huh? I tell you— a chump, that's what. A chump straight outta Main Street Palooka- ville. A freakin' woman, *man* . . . Just goes to show that you . . ."

He stared into the smoky bar, into the neon-rimmed shadows. His audience of one says quietly, "I have a real one," but it's as if the speaker has gone stone deaf.

"Toss me another smoke, eh? I gotta go buy me some more."

Overboard
Kai Bayley

We spent too much money on women and vodka.

Most nights we alternated between two bars. His favorite spot was The Hatter, so named because all of its patrons were crazy as loons. I liked to hit the Outside Inn, the seedy gay bar on the edge of town, barely still inside the city limits. We each had a surprising amount of luck at either place, but I couldn't let him have his way every time.

Jonas and I were often mistaken for brothers. He pulled his black hair back into a neat ponytail; mine was buzzed short, sharp enough to cut with. Each of us had eyes so dark they often seemed black, turning from soulful to predatory in no more than a blink. Straight white teeth, mine a gift from nature, his a result of years of orthodontia; a little too much hip, a curse of nature for me, a motorcycle accident for him. Both of us wondered what the fuck we were doing in Florida.

A few other notable things Jonas and I had in common: an 8¾-inch dick, and an uncontrollable weakness for redheads. Real, or from a bottle, it didn't really matter. Women who dye their hair red are choosing what they want, and either way they are wild in the sack.

Tonight we weren't in the mood for the same old hairdos and halter tops, and were driving around town in my beat-up blue Mazda looking for a fresh façade. The conversation had turned to what we do in the sack. Men seem to be obsessed with two women screwing, and I had taken it on as my personal crusade to educate them on the differences between "porn lesbians" and "real lesbians." I was horrified when he shared with me "The Blueprint for Sex." This was something he had read about in an old porno mag and had adopted as his approach to sex. Step 1 was showering a woman with compliments, Step 2 was kissing, Step 3 was fondling her titties, and so on. I was shocked into silence, too appalled at the idea to even begin to attack it.

With a hoot of laughter Jonas grabbed the "oh shit" handle and demanded that I turn right immediately. The tires squealed as I slid into the gravel parking lot of a place I'd never been to before. The flickering neon sign proclaimed the place to be "The Captain's Mast." My chuckles merged with his; ending the conversation was a relief and I was excited to explore this new joint. A few nights ago, suffering from a bad case of the bed spins, we had proclaimed my bed a ship sailing the treacherous Sea of Pussy. It was a twin-masted ship with sheets for sails billowing around our cocks.

This had to be an omen.

Everything in Florida is decorated in a nautical theme right down to the fast-food restaurants. The minute we stepped inside the joint I was ready to nominate the place for some "Pride of Florida" award—if there was such a thing. There were round windows meant to look like portholes, and canvas or rope covered every available surface. I wouldn't be surprised if the john offered canvas squares instead of toilet paper. Even the shelves were made from planks balanced on rope knots.

"What'll it be, mateys?" I turned to place our customary drink order and could hardly contain the snort of laughter that started in my chest and threatened to burst right through my nose. Behind the bar an old scab missing most of his front teeth was looking at me with a dead serious expression on his face, waiting for my response. The wrinkles on his face disappeared underneath an authentic-looking eye patch. The front of his blue shirt was damp from wiping out the glasses but I could still read the embroidered letters that spelled out Richard. Was this place for real?

A hush had fallen over the patrons sitting at the bar, and I was still sober enough to realize that I better do some sweet talkin', and fast.

"I thought you was my long-lost granddaddy there for a minute," I said, pulling a slow drawl out of my bag of tricks and hoping I was speaking the right dialect of 'good ol' boy'. "He went out for a cold one back in 1976 and never did come home. Bein' as how your eyes are blue and his were black I don't suppose you could be him. Ever go by the name of Teddy?" I waited, wishing like hell that this routine would keep me out of whatever trap I had been about to fall into.

"Nah," he replied after a moment.

"Could I trouble you for a couple of beers?" I asked.

Jonas arched one eyebrow at me in surprise, but didn't say a word. I had never ordered anything but vodka tonic before; thank God his thick head finally stopped his big mouth from saying anything. Faster than the Virgin Mary could say "no," two bottles appeared in front of us. I left some bills on the bar and retreated with Jonas and the beer to an empty set of chairs in the corner.

"Right now he thinks I'm a man, and I think we better make sure it stays that way." I gave him by way of explanation. I didn't think he could grasp the intricacies of our current situation, and I just wanted him to keep his mouth shut. Just then a blonde woman clad in the dive-bar uniform of leather and denim walked in. Sensing that I needed a little cheering up, Jonas tipped his bottle in her direction and asked me "bottle or birth?"

Usually this was my favorite game. Since starting it a month ago, I was holding strong at 100 percent accuracy. I would tell him whether or not a woman's hair color was natural, then it was up to him to find a way to see her pubic hair and find out for sure. One girl had been completely bald down there, but given my past accuracy he had been willing to call that one a win. Only once had I asked him how he got into their pants to find out. He had replied with a wink and said, "I'll tell you my secret if you tell me yours." I didn't have the heart to tell him that growing up with a Grandma who did hair would enable you to spot a bottle job even across a smoky bar.

"Bottle." I said with a total lack of enthusiasm, "Man, even you can tell that one. You want in her pants or somethin'?"

"Nope," he said. "Just bored."

"Well, finish your beer, we're leavin' after this one anyway."

He tilted the bottle and drank what was left in a few bobs of his Adam's apple. Pushing back his bar stool he said, "Fine with me, let me hit the john first."

Briefly I watched his broken amble toward the back of the bar before returning my attention to the beer at hand. Finding this place had been an omen all right, but a bad one. The downward spiral of my mood swing was interrupted by the clank of beer bottles on the table. Not two bottles, but three.

"Man I thought you had agreed . . ." my sentence trailed off as I laid my eyes on the little redhead hanging on his arm. I picked up my jaw and my sentence and continued, ". . . to let me buy this round."

She was everything we loved about women rolled into a petite ball of energy. Her green eyes and red-orange hair fairly crackled with it. Probably no more than five-three with bare feet, her black heels brought the top of her head even with my nose. Her shapely calves gave way to ample thighs proudly and fully displayed by a black mini-skirt. The lack of pantyhose gave her away as a native, but I was willing to forgive her anything as my eyes traveled her rounded hips and made way to a slender waist. I judged her bra size to be a healthy C-cup and was willing to bet my ass against a football that her nipples were the palest shade of pink. What we had here was a genuine red-head, with a sprinkle of freckles to prove it. I hopped up quickly to offer her my seat as Jonas began the introductions.

"Melissa, I'd like you to meet my good friend Ahab." His thumb jutted in my general direction, but his eyes never left her face. "Ahab, this beautiful woman is Melissa."

I moved to kiss her left hand, lingering just a moment. I paused partly to inhale the subtle lilac scent of a warm summer night back home, but also to sneak a chance at composing myself. It wasn't really a surprise that Jonas introduced me under a hideously fake name—he did that often enough. No, I had about swallowed my tongue when he came up with the name of the captain from *Moby Dick*. Hell, up until this point I was about convinced that he couldn't read.

We slid into an easy conversation about hurricanes, tourists, and pool hustlers, and then we moved the little party to an empty pool table to smack around a few balls. Jonas and I showed her that we both knew how to handle a big stick, and Melissa returned the demonstration. Sliding that pole around in her hands had both of us adjusting uncomfortable places under the buttons of our jeans, and the way she licked her perfect cocksucking lips while she concentrated had me about ready to tumble her behind the building.

Beer descended around us like a glacier effect creating mountains of brown bottles in its wake. It was my shot, a beautiful bank shot I had practiced for hours in my parents' basement. I could feel that eight ball in the pocket just as sure as I could feel my own balls through the pockets of my jeans. I drew a bead on the target, testing the force of the shot with my hands. I pulled back the cue, driving it home, just as Melissa hollered out "Hey Dickey One-Eye, can we get another round over here!"

It was a dirty trick. She knew it was a dirty trick, but you could hardly tell that behind the wide-eyed innocent gaze she aimed my way. The heavy clink of the cue ball falling into the corner pocket was the sound of me kissing ten bucks good-bye. I could barely hear it above the din of conversation around us, and I just breathed a sigh of relief that it wasn't my ass I was kissing good-bye.

"Dickey" delivered three more of the same and settled a kiss on Melissa's cheek with that sagging mouth of his. She planted a kiss in the crevices of his face, "Thanks, Pawpaw; love you." Turning back to us she flashed a dazzling smile and said, "This round's on me," as she tucked the ten from the table into his gnarled hand. I'd been conned, but Melissa made it feel good, like I was part of an inside joke instead of the butt of one.

As I tipped back the bottle Dickey had delivered I started thinking about how there was only so much a person could drink without needing to go to the bathroom, and that created a problem for me. Neither option afforded an easy out, so I mostly tried to avoid public bathrooms at all costs. Jonas had hit his groove, and was lining up shot after shot. No matter how hard I tried to gain his attention, his eyes never met mine. He had been known to avoid me when he was having a good time, and I suspected that was the case here. Selfish bastard.

I was surprised to feel Melissa's hand on my shoulder, pulling my ear down to her mouth. "Could you take me to the bathroom? I'm not sure I can make it by myself." A grin started at my right ear and stretched on its tiptoes across my face until it brushed the left one. That was an invitation if I'd ever heard one. I offered my arm like a good escort, and was rewarded with her arm twining around mine. We slowly made our way across the bar, Melissa using the precisely placed steps of an aware but inebriated person. I deposited her at the door marked "Mermaids" with a deep bow, and leaned against the wall with my arms crossed prepared to wait for the return trip. She latched on to the front of my shirt and half pulled, half fell with me into the bathroom.

Inside the small room she immediately straightened, once again the confident woman balanced perfectly on the precipice of those heels. Hiking her miniskirt up around her hips she crouched over the toilet seat, offering me a glimpse of closely trimmed red hair. She went about her business like it was an everyday occurrence for her to have an audience. Hell, for all I knew, it was. Right then all I could focus on was the fact that she wasn't wearing any panties. God I love dirty girls.

"Yer turn," she announced, pulling her skirt back down around her thighs with a shimmy of her hands and hips. Uncomfortable with the position I was in, I stood there immobile. I really did have to go pretty badly, but we hadn't had our "little talk" yet. She looked at me with clear eyes; any pretense of intoxication was gone. "You may have the guys out there fooled, but I know why you haven't been to the bathroom yet tonight."

She made it a point to turn her back and study her nails. Not liking the alternatives, and suffering from a nagging cramp in my lower back, I took my turn. The relief was damn near better than an orgasm and I'll admit that I groaned just a bit from the pleasure of it. With a jangle of buckles and snaps I tucked my cock back into my shorts and adjusted it to ride in the right place. I hit the handle with the heel of my boot, destroying all the evidence.

Melissa turned and stepped up to me, running the palms of her hands up my chest and behind my neck until they met again to stroke my hair. Dipping my head at the insistence of her hands, our lips brushed, met, and held. It was the sweetest, most sexy kiss in my whole life. Just two sets of lips greeting each other like new friends yet old lovers.

She pulled back slowly to break the kiss. Once separated it was still a few seconds before her eyes opened. She fiddled with a string hanging from a button on my shirt, her eyes riveted to that spot. Still unable to meet my stare she quietly asked, "What's your name, Ahab?"

"Jo. Actually, Josephine. Kinda old fashioned but it shortens up nicely. Gets kinda confusing when I hang around Jonas. He pretty much gives me a new name every night, but I don't really mind." I caught myself in that awful habit of talking too much when I get nervous. "Does it really matter?"

"Must be terrible not to truly have an identity of your own." She finally looked up, mischief chasing sadness from the green pools of her eyes. "Besides, I make it a practice to always know what name to moan. Hey, are you about ready to get out of this place yet?"

Was I ever! We stumbled out of the bathroom in a good imitation of two drunken people who'd engaged in some heavy petting. Melissa jumped on my back and rode me all the way back to the pool table, biting and sucking on my neck. Hoots and catcalls followed our progress; I'm guessing now that her ass was probably hanging out the bottom of her miniskirt. Back at the table Melissa rubbed her ass against the front of Jonas's jeans as she passed him. "You know," she absently said to herself, "I'm not really sure which one of you I'd like to fuck tonight."

"Who said you had to pick just one?" This from the man who had told me not long ago that although we had a good time together it would be weird if anything happened between us. At the time I had looked at him like he'd grown a third head and ignored him, irritated that he would even think anything *could* happen. Bastard thought he was irresistible to anyone born with woman parts, and no matter how many times I tried to explain to him how I was different than that, he never seemed to get it. I was one of the guys to him only as long as I was wearing a man on the outside. Now we both pretended that the conversation had never happened. The aging barfly that had targeted Jonas while we were gone took this as her cue to leave. Leaving seemed like a good plan, and soon we stepped out into the clean night air.

"It isn't really his name," she stated, seemingly out of nowhere. I tensed, remembering our bathroom conversation and having no idea where she was taking this thing. "My grandpa's name is really Michael O'Shea." I relaxed, realizing at that moment how much I dreaded confronting Jonas with anything. As I saw it, the less we talked about "Josephine" the better off we were. He'd asked me once

if I'd ever had dick, and I shrugged and said "I've got one every day."
That had been the end of that type of conversation.

Melissa continued with her story, "Till the moment she died my
grandma swore he was a one-eyed dickey chasing her night and day.
He really fell apart when she passed away. The family thought he'd
lost his last marbles when he announced he was opening a bar. He
used the money from her life insurance policy to create this bar and
persona. Says he feels close to her here, sleeps here most nights too.
He makes most of his regulars call him Dickey, but it's a privilege to
be earned."

"That's real sad about your grandma," Jonas said as he trapped her
body between his and my car. He nuzzled her neck as I smiled sympa-
thetically at her. Seems I wasn't the only one with a tendency to ram-
ble when nervous. She accepted my empathy with a smile of her own
before laying her head back and surrendering to him. Not one to be
left out of the action, I joined in, searching for a mouthful of my own.
It wasn't hard to find, and soon the parking lot was filled with the
sounds of our sucking and groaning. He and I were startled from our
pursuits when our hands met under her skirt.

"Um, guys? Think we could go somewhere else?" Melissa breathed
the words, taking advantage of our distraction to redirect us.

We jumped into the car, eager to be on our way. She straddled him
in the passenger seat and I jammed the car in reverse, envious of his
position. The tires spun in the gravel and I realized quickly that I
better straighten up. The last thing I wanted was to see a cop's cher-
ries flashing in the rearview instead of the show that was unfolding in
front of me.

Their mouths locked together in a heated battle of lips and
tongues. Jonas's hands roamed her body over the barrier of cloth as
she ground her clit against the bulge in his jeans. He pushed a single
finger inside of her cunt from behind, then pulled it out and rubbed it
on her lips. His tongue traced the wet path his finger had left, then
followed it up with another hard kiss. Again he dipped inside her, but
this time he reached over and touched his finger to my tongue. We all
moaned at once, a chorus of shared pleasure. I sucked his finger clean

of even the barest hint of the taste of her. Thank God we were only six minutes away from home.

I pulled into the parking lot of the apartment complex where he and I had been staying. I could barely pay attention long enough to throw the car in neutral and pull the parking brake. I had been patient long enough, now it was my turn. Still riding Jonas, Melissa leaned over to kiss me. It was nothing like our first kiss had been. There was a wild promise of what was still to come mingled with the musky taste of her. Bracing a hand on each of our shoulders, she moved to put one knee between each set of our legs.

Kicking aside the remains of fast-food dinners and empty cigarette packs in the floorboard, Jonas spread his feet apart to make room for her knee to sink into the gray bucket seat. Yellow cardboard trees that hung from my mirror and had once offered a vaguely vanilla scent now swirled around her head like a bizarre chain of daisies as she straddled the air between us. Both of us instinctually lent a stabilizing hand underneath the closest thigh; I'd thought only high school cheerleaders could perform a stunt like this one. Jonas and I sent each other questioning looks through the veil of hair that hung between us. Never the type to let an opportunity pass us by, we each took advantage of the body parts closest to us. Lowering her hips slightly, she rubbed her clit against the bulbous blue plastic gearshift. Darting another quick glance at Jonas, I saw the same incredulous look that was plastered on my face.

Moving again, she positioned the knob of the stick shift until it parted her pussy lips. Out of the corner of my eye I saw his head move, seeking my attention. Holy shit; if she's doing what I think she's doing I don't give a shit what he's thinking. Sure enough, she slowly began lowering her weight onto the knob. She gasped, snapping her head up to look straight at me. In the weak glow of the streetlight filtering through the window I could see that her pupils had dilated until there was barely a hint of color rimming the black circles. Melissa eased down again, this time taking the entire grip inside her. The slow pace she chose was making me impatient with need. I watched her drive that knob into her over and over, imaging all the time that it was my cock driving into her. I released the seat belt holding me back and reached between her legs with my left hand to massage her clit, matching the speed she had set.

Her stare seemed glazed and sightless, and small mewling sounds were coming from the back of her throat. They quickly turned to moans; then staccato screams that punctuated each lunge.

"Ah, ah, ah, ah," they crashed together into a long wail, "Aaahhhhhh!" I could see the muscles in her stomach contracting with the ferocity of her orgasm. Her thigh trembled under my hand. A nearby porch light clicked on and I saw the green and white checked curtains sway in the living room of a neighbor's apartment.

"Help her up, slowly, slowly, that's it," I instructed Jonas, afraid she might collapse. She rested on his lap with her head tucked under his chin, flyaway bits of hair clung to his stubble. I got out of the car and opened the passenger door, pushing a sweat-dampened strand behind her ear. I carried her to the safety of the shadowy doorway; Jonas followed slowly, sifting through the change and wrappers in his pockets for the keys.

Closing the door against the prying eyes of open windows left us fumbling in the dark. Ashtrays and knickknacks were casualties in the battle for illumination, but we finally found the lamp when I knocked it over with Melissa's dangling foot. After navigating our way to the bedroom, I laid her gently on the bed, hardly able to coax her into letting go of me. I couldn't resist tasting her satisfied smile.

Jonas and I worked together, slowly removing her clothes. We licked and sucked each creamy inch of skin as it became exposed. I was very pleased to discover that I had been right about the color of her nipples, and I rewarded myself with a leisurely exploration of the sensitive crest and the flawless white flesh surrounding it. Fascinated, I used long licks and warm breath to tease the skin into a puckered point. Jonas mimicked my technique on the other side, and when our eyes met, we each pulled a nipple deep into our mouth.

Melissa groaned and her back arched, skin separating forcefully from the crisp sheet. She was saying something that might have been, "Nothing like it," but I couldn't quite make out the words. She had one arm wrapped around each head suckling her, forcing our faces hard against her breasts. I was seeing stars, drowning in her pleasure.

With every gasp I struggled for air, inhaling more of her into me. At the point where I truly believed I might pass out, she suddenly released us both, each of us falling backward, shuddering with every breath.

Jonas was the first to move, making his way down the plain of her stomach until his tongue pushed between her thighs; Step 5 in his "Blueprint for Sex." I moved up her neck to nibble on her soft earlobe. I kissed her again, capturing her bottom lip with my teeth and outlining its shape with my tongue. She unbuttoned my shirt, pushing the fabric down my shoulders. A ribbed white undershirt still hid the bindings that crushed my small chest into a more acceptable shape. I was relieved that she didn't make any gestures toward removing it; she sensed the imaginary line there that I didn't want her to cross. She did move her hand lower, cupping my cock through my jeans. Buttons popped free at her insistence and finally my dick sprung loose from its cage. It jumped up against my stomach and I could feel that it was warmed from the heat of my body.

She hauled me up by my balls, eager to wrap her lips around as much of it as she could. On my knees I hovered over her mouth, watching her tongue tease the head of my dick. She grabbed my ass and slowly forced inch after inch into her hot mouth. Once I was buried halfway in, I pulled out and started another slow plunge between her lips. The hand on my ass had a different idea and pressed me to a faster pace. Her other hand snaked around to push the base of my cock into my clit with every thrust.

I watched those lips stretch to devour me as I gave myself over to fucking her face. I was turning inside out, all my blood and emotion screaming their way through my body toward one goal, and my cock was a compass pointing out the right direction. I wanted to reward her, show my appreciation for her amazing mouth, but my cum pounded furiously at the solid cock, desperate to leave my burning body but unable to escape through the shaft.

Jonas tapped me on the side; he was ready for a taste of the action I was getting. I was ready for a taste of an entirely different nature. I wanted to taste her excitement, her pleasure—not just set up a wet place for my dick.

I watched him strip, hating him for the easy masculinity he carelessly wore. I hated him for the muscles that naturally developed in all the right places, for his hard edges and the crisp hair that grew on them. I took it all out on her cunt. The hate, the love, the envy, and the kinship; I poured them over her clit with my mouth, pressed it inside her with my hands. The taste of bitterness faded and was replaced with her cum, coating the inside of my mouth and running down my chin.

I pushed away, away from the pouting cunt lips, away from her altogether. She was making it all too easy. Like a good southern belle, she was taking everything into her and promising that tomorrow would be a different day. Jonas saw his chance and took the position between her legs. He eased inside her like he eased through life, setting the pace he thought he deserved. I wanted to pummel him—plunge a knife into his chest in the same rhythm that he impaled her. I stood to the side of the bed rubbing my dick and watching him fuck her. His beer-numbed dick would last forever and I just didn't think I could take it anymore. He couldn't even feel a sensation I would give my right arm to experience even once. I didn't want to be him; God knows he's shown me enough ways to appreciate not being a man if it means being like him. But watching him fuck her was like watching a three-year-old demolish a finely crafted antique violin.

"Kiss," Melissa demanded and I moved to comply. Her hand rested on my chest, stopping the descent of my mouth to hers. "Not me, him."

Anger crawled across my skin, igniting in my face. My eyes flashed like the end of a double-barreled shotgun. "C'mon," she pleaded, her hand still on my chest, "it makes me hot thinking about two guys getting it on."

Grudgingly we submit to her. At first only managing a dry peck, we were motivated by her laughter to try a little harder. His mouth was strange to me, larger and more aggressive than I was used to. He won the first round when I tilted my head the direction he wanted for the kiss. Dammit, I didn't want to give an inch. I did have one advantage, though—I was still standing. Straightening my back without breaking contact, I forced his head back into a submissive position. I grabbed his chin to hold it still as I pulled away.

His hands wrapped around my arms like a vise and he brought my lips to his for a bruising assault masquerading as a kiss. When I refused to open my mouth to him he cupped layers of fabric where a breast should be and grazed the pad of his thumb over a nonexistent nipple. That was the final indignity, and I broke his hold to leave the room. He'd never even taken his dick out of her, and had resumed pumping her before I made it through the door.

I closed the bathroom door behind me and gripped the countertop trying to regain control. Splashing water on my face my mind raced, desperate for a plan. Drops fell from my spiked lashes and chin as I contemplated my reflection. Fuck him.

Standing in the bedroom doorway I watched him pound her. It was like I had never even left the room; he was still pumping at the same speed as before. Judging from the lack of expression on her face, I didn't think she was getting much out of it. I would've thought even he would be bored with it by now. Careful not to touch anything with my closed fists, I made my way across the room. He didn't even notice me.

Slathering handfuls of petroleum jelly all over my cock, I walked up behind his thrusting ass. Placing greasy hands on his hips I crammed my dick into his asshole. Fueled by anger and humiliation I found the strength to push to the hilt into his virgin ass. He froze mid-thrust with a loud grunt. "Let me show you how it's done, fuck-boy," I hissed into his ear. Twisting his nipples with my slick fingers, my cock retreated an inch then slowly slid back in. I buried my face between his shoulder blades and concentrated on the dance of our hips. Tentatively at first, then with more enthusiasm he picked up on the gyrating rhythm and mimicked it with his own thrusts.

Melissa was the first to cum, screaming her approval. She clutched me, her nails biting into my skin, drawing me closer to him—urging us not to stop. The bed shifted slightly when she slid out from under him, but that didn't interrupt the cadence of our marching thrusts. The rustle of sorting clothes barely registered in my brain; her screams had released the knot in my gut, freeing me to let my own cum build. The soft click of the closing door released him.

The presence of her cunt had helped make it all okay at first, a familiar pleasure—not forbidden. But nothing had changed when she left, his thrusts were still moving to meet my cock. Leaning our weight back, I continued to fuck him slowly with shallow plunges, his heavy balls swinging between my legs. I could feel the weight of them slapping against me while I fucked him, as if they were my own. We rocked on our knees, his muscular legs framed mine and the bristles of hair chaffed—the prickly tips of feathers floating across skin.

Leaving one arm clenched around his chest, I moved my right hand to grasp his thick dick. It was everything I imagined jacking myself off could be. My lubed hand slid easily down the shaft, then back up to corkscrew the head. Gripping it tightly I could feel the throb in that cock matching the pulse in my clenched jaw. Every thrust into his ass was like thrusting into my hand. He reached back; callused hands grabbed my hips pulling me harder into his surprisingly soft ass, ready for rougher play.

Clamping down on his shoulder with my free hand, I used him for leverage to better meet his demands. As fast as I could feed it to him he swallowed me. Our bodies slammed together, filling the air with heavy grunts. I was falling. Falling into the mattress that sagged beneath our kneeling weight, falling into the hole I had pushed open, now sucking me in. I pounded that dick meat, feverishly matching the pace he set for our sweating bodies. The pitch of his moans sharpened and rose into a keening as his head fell back against my shoulder. With one last lunge I plowed deep into him, growling against his ear as I came; warm liquid gushed thickly between my fingers. I held on tightly as we convulsed, relaxing only when the shuddering subsided. We collapsed into a heap on the bed, my arms wrapped around him and a tangle of hairy legs.

Propping up on one elbow I watch him sleep. Moonlit softness hardens into sunlit angles. Time dries my fingers and I gently rub them together, the scent and texture foreign, unwelcome.

I mourn the loss that daylight brings.

Josephine
Linda Rosenkrans

There was something about her I couldn't quite put my finger on. Something I admired, perhaps an unconscious longing I hadn't yet fulfilled in my own life. Whatever it was, she intrigued me.

I was stuck in the six-o'clock traffic in West Hollywood on the Santa Monica Boulevard pondering over the decision to switch to the straight life and try a "man" on for size. Lesbian sex had become a monotonous chore for me, I mean, just how many licks with chicks was it going to take to make my cherry pop? Ten years, and still no rocky mountain thunder like I'd read about in the lezzy mags, and certainly no spontaneous combustion like I'd seen in the girl on dildo-demonstration porno flicks. I've tried every dick imposter imaginable, but I still couldn't take a strap-on very seriously without secretly laughing to myself and feeling a little resentful at the same time. Come on now, just whom do those rug munchers think that they're fooling anyway? Ribbed and slightly curved at the top, plastic dildos are an insult to mankind—they give the regular-Joe-just-trying-to-get-laid-schmo a bad name. "Oh, but they're better than the real thing." Says the never-had-a-man-before dyke with a rubber dick. Bullshit! Kinda like "The size doesn't matter" lie, which I think the hetero women came up with to make the puny pricks of this world feel better. Ha! Okay, so I haven't had a lot of men in my lifetime either, maybe less than a handful and no thunder to brag about to my quidnunc cunts afterward, but the few I have had to compare from, believe you me, size did make a difference. Yessirree-Bob it did! A small wanker is like the tampon commercial claims, "So comfortable you don't even know it's there." I gave up on men after the fact that I couldn't find one who knew how to use his equipment properly. I shouldn't have to give a man a list of instructions on how to use his poker correctly—"Ah, the hole is right here mister, in the middle, no, that's my pubic bone you dork! Honestly, hun, it's a no brainer! Just stick it in, move it back and forth, good boy! Now grunt like a pig!" Apparently that was too much to ask for, so I switched to electrical devices. I remember the first time I tried it, I was laying on the floor, spread-eagle, with this motionless instrument up my twat, holding the directions to the Babalu Buzzer with one hand while trying to get the vibrator to work with the other. "Requires batteries," the instructions read. "Turn the knob at the bottom for results." Oh, dah. I get up from my gynecological position, put batteries in, get situated spread-eagle again, turn the switch on, and holy shit, I thought my vee gee was going to shake off! I think I purchased the boy toy vibe by mistake! Okay, so the big, black, plastic, buzzy thingy activated multiple skyrocket orgasms, but it was too fast, too mechanical, and too impersonal, not to mention that it took an hour for the feeling to come back in my puss! At that point I just gave up on all men or any phallic object that even resembled a male, cucumbers included, and became a lesbian. I'm an all-or-nothing kind of a chick like that. I'd like to tell you dear reader that that was that, but nooo—I'm far too complex of a woman. That's just too simple for me. I have to make things complicated in my life, add a little drama to spice things up a bit. I mean, simultaneously slurping the honeysuckle for orgasm was okay for a while, but now, of course, I'm getting bored with that too! Now this vaginatarian is craving meat once again. What's a girl to do? I'll tell ya what's a girl to do, seek out and overwhelm a zesty chorizo with my fleshy clamp, that's what!

Suddenly, I was feeling trapped, claustrophobic; I had to get out of this traffic! I felt a panic attack coming on, and feeling dizzy I pulled into a retro-cool café on Santa Monica Boulevard and Gardener Street. I ordered my comfort food, french fries with a side order of blue cheese. I took a booth in the back. It was a typical 50s cafe, gray-and-white-checkered floor, with mini jukeboxes on the tables. Adjacent to the restaurant was a little outside patio, covered with a red and white beach cabana, surrounded by baby palm trees on all sides. It reminded me of being at a mini vacation villa. *Perfect,* I thought to myself. *I needed a vacation from the rush-hour traffic, and this place was just the ticket.*

A man walked in with a guitar strapped behind his shoulder; he wandered aimlessly up and down the aisle. Finally, he took the booth next to mine. He sat there staring at nothing. Maybe stuck in a mushroom thought trying to figure out what to order—"Let's see, umm, should I have mushrooms or mushrooms? I think I'll have some mushrooms, oh, and could I have some mushrooms on the side?" He gets up and leaves. I get busy eating my french fries—twenty li'l bluecheese-dipped penises anticipating the arrival of my mouth. The restaurant door shut; I looked up to a sexy blonde woman standing at the counter taking her order. She took a seat on one of the bright red, cushy bar stools by the window. What a delicious dish! Maybe I'm not over women after all. I watched her every move for about ten minutes. She turned her head my way, catching me in the act of staring at her. My face grew hot with embarrassment. She smiled at me, flipping her pink feather boa across her beautiful, Audrey-Hepburn-long neck. She fiddled with her silky platinum hair, twisting it around her fingers and revealing the yin and yang contrast of black underneath.

"Would you like to join me?"

A butterfly twittered inside my stomach. I turned around to see if she was talking to someone else. The booth behind me was vacant. When I turned back around she was pointing her two fingers at me like a cheerleader.

"Yes, honey child, *you.*"

I sat there speechless.

"All right sugar, if you're not going to come to me, I guess I'm going to have to come to you."

She walked over to my table and sat down in the booth facing me, the air redolent with the intoxicating scent of patchouli.

"Hi. My name is Josephine."

She held out her hand, and when I reached out to shake it, she grasped mine and kissed the top of it. Chills ran down my spine.

"And your name is?"

"Oh," I said nervously, looking down at her fancy shoes, "Kate."

Her shoes were the most exquisite pair of pink furry stilettos I had ever seen in my life. They riveted me, teasing my sexual senses in a way I had never quite experienced before. I felt my box get hot. I had a curious notion to remove her shoe and rub the pink softness against my clit, inserting the heel in and out of my vagina. My reactions felt weird to me. I never understood the whole fetish thing, thought it was a subject reserved for perverts, sexual deviants, or the kind of stuff you'd see in an odd porn movie titled, *Pappa Pee Pee Pumps Pink Pumps.* And here I was, miss priss, yearning to fuck her shoe. My devout Catholic grandmother would roll over in her grave, rise from the dead, and die again if she knew of my distorted sexual thoughts. Hmm, fucking a shoe, would that be considered a sin? Probably if I coveted my neighbor's shoe or committed adultery with my neighbor's wife's shoe. Shoe fucking in and of itself should be okay. The Bible doesn't say anything about fornicating with a shoe as far as I know, so I think I should be all right. I think she picked up on my thoughts, because I felt the furry stiletto slide up my leg. I looked into her sultry, foxlike eyes, then down just a bit to the subtle parting of her luscious lips.

"I live just in back of here, would you like to come over where we can get to know each other a little better?" she said.

When I woke up this morning I hadn't planned on picking up any pussy today, swore to myself that last night's one-night stand would be my last one-night stand; I was through with the plush bunny for good! However, tee hee, I was wet with delight, and decided I would try again tomorrow to look for an elongated, three-dimensional. As for now, I couldn't pass up this heavenly opportunity. It was as if God had put her in front of me to test my will. You know, it always seems like just as I finally make the decision to quit whatever it is I might be quitting at the time, the pill, pie, or potty hole becomes readily available to me. And there she was, this sexy, scrumptious thang, waiting for me to eat her up. Fuck it; I'm going for it!

"Yes."

She grabbed my hand, her fingers were long and slender, yet worn and callused, especially on the fingertips. Judging by the size of her big, broad shoulders, I figured she must do some kind of manual labor. Perhaps a plumber or one of those monster garage, auto-mechanic-type gals I'd seen on the Discovery Channel recently. Yummy, the thought made me drip. In any event she must work with tools, tools good for tweaking my vulnerable tee tees, taa taas, and other sensitive parts. I'd turn this wench into a body mechanic in no time! The possibilities were endless. Oh my God, I was getting so excited I could barely contain myself. We walked into her Bohemian-styled apartment, and I took a seat in one of the large, leopard-print beanbags she had assembled around a makeshift coffee table, which consisted of stacks of hardcover novels and a large section of plywood.

"I'll be right back, sugar. Make yourself at home."

She came back with a guitar in her hand.

"Oh, so you're a musician," I said. "That explains the rough fingertips."

"I dabble."

She sat down in the beanbag next to mine and began strumming the guitar, singing a favorite long-forgotten song of my youth.

"I, / I will be king, / and you, / you will be queen . . ."

I laid my head back, closing my eyes. Yes, I wanted to be queen just for one day, I would allow myself that today, I deserved it.

Her pink, glittery lips meshed with mine, parting slightly to explore my mouth with her tongue. She sat in my lap, feeling between the ridge of my tight satin pants, the dampness made it clear that I hungered for her. She fully undressed me, yet she remained fully clothed. She lifted me up and carried me into her boudoir, placing me gently on her bed. I tried to undress her but she stopped me, saying that there was something to be said for anticipation. Before I could answer, she was down between my legs and I wasn't going to argue with her. Her mouth encompassed the full length of my pleasure chest, simultaneously pleasing me at all angles. Right before I was about to cum, she abruptly stopped, moving behind me, spoon style. She stroked a finger along my back naughty hole.

"Are you a virgin this way?"

"Yes."

I was glad that my back was facing her, because I could feel my face begin to blush. Her fingers slithered up to my slimy frontal section, stoking backwards to my once-forbidden zone, in a gingerly, circular fashion. I felt warm with comfortable ecstasy.

"Momma Love could take you to heaven in back, if you'd like?" she whispered.

"Yes, Momma Love, show me what you know. Take me out of the Garden of Eden."

She whispered sweet nothings into my ear, while inserting a long, slender instrument up my rear. I felt cool liquid engulf my insides. She stroked my hair, simultaneously soothing the back of my neck with her safe blanket of warm breath, telling me how special I was, that I was a good girl, and that she loved me.

After she filled my virginal chamber, she stood above me lifting me up into her arms. She held me close to her chest, patting my back, and kissing the tears streaming down my face.

"There, there, baby. Momma's gunna make it all better."

Still holding me, she took me over the threshold into the bathroom, gently setting me down onto the toilet. She walked away, shutting the bathroom door behind her.

"Momma's going out for a while; I'll be back to pick you up in an hour. I love you." Her voice trailed off.

My first inclination was to run to the door screaming, Don't leave me! Don't leave me! However, just then the release began. The pressure, the pain, the buildup, it felt like decades of fluid shame, had finally been given the permission to escape out of my body. It felt so good, I felt so clean, and I felt so free.

An hour later she reappeared in the bathroom.

"Baby doll, are you ready for your bath?"

"Yes, Mommy."

She ran the bathwater with a hint of Mr. Bubble in it, and then proceeded to pick me up and place me into the tub. She lathered my hair with shampoo, singing a tender lullaby.

"Hush little baby don't say a word, / mama's going to buy you a mockingbird, /and if that mockingbird don't sing, / mama's going to buy you a diamond ring."

She towel dried me and placed me back into bed, and then turned out the lights. I heard her undressing in the darkness. She moved in beside me, turning me over, so my back was facing her again. As she pulled herself close to me, I felt a flat muscular chest up against my back, in addition to the unmistakable lean hardness of a man upon my buttocks. I gasped. A she-male. I was so incredibly aroused; I didn't have time to think. He lathered my backside with a generous amount of jelly, inserting a finger slowly in and out of my bum; then placed a butt plug inside of me, introducing me to the hidden secrets of The Tree of Knowledge. The warm and pleasurable sensation inside of my anus intensified, getting stronger from back to front. I wanted more, all of it. I wanted to know what I'd been missing.

"Give it to me. Give me all you've got!" I said. "If you're a man, fuck me like a man, goddamnit!" I dug my nails into his thigh, scratching him until he bled.

He kept me in the scissor position until my coiled rubber band expanded to accommodate him, then turned me in front of him, taking me full throttle, ass up, doggy-style. My nerve endings tingled with delight as he thrust his male organ through my tight squeeze, sending electrical waves all the way up to the front of my female paradise, where my entire body erupted into a lightning storm. This was my first man-inside-woman orgasm ever; this then proceeded into another and another and then another.

Afterward, he held me in the cradle of his arms, falling asleep. I lay awake thinking how lucky I was to have encountered this divine human being—this divine, human being.

I woke up the next morning to a standard poodle licking the insides of my nostrils, and Josephine on the other side of the bed, staring.

"Did you know all along?" he said.

I smiled and winked.

"Hey, uh, where'd the dog come from?" I asked.

"You don't remember."

He grinned at me.

I slapped the side of his arm, laughing.

The Waters of Al Adra

Thomas S. Roche

The man was thirsty. Terribly thirsty.

It was all he knew and all he had ever known; everything of the world that presented itself to him was, now, an aspect of that terrible thirst. The sun high above him, the desert wind blowing, even the mere sight of the sand swirling in dancing devils around the feet of the many camels: Everything that leached the moisture from his flesh.

He didn't know his name or where he came from or who these people were around him. He couldn't even have told you the name of the beasts on which they all rode. He couldn't have told you what country he was in, on what continent it resided, or how he had come to be on an endless desert plain with his blood like acid in his veins. But then again, no one was asking.

The man slumped in the harness, suddenly aware that the camel was swaying back and forth, that they were moving—rather quickly, it seemed to him. His limbs felt heavy; it took him some time to understand that he could move, as if the knowledge of motion had bled from him with the water. He reached out awkwardly, his arm tangled in tattered brown robes, and touched the man in front of him, the man driving the camel.

The camel driver turned and looked, his face swathed in a brown veil.

Trying to speak was impossible. His lips were parched, his tongue swollen. He gestured toward his mouth, making a strangling sound deep in his throat.

The camel driver called something out ahead of him; the caravan ground to a halt. The lead driver, a man with very dark skin and a big bushy moustache, came riding back and the two drivers began arguing in a strange language.

Arabic, thought the man. The language was called Arabic. He felt sure he should have understood it, should have known what they were saying. A flash of memory came to him: Weeks, months spent in language class, wearing a stiff uniform. The wool had felt prickly on his flesh, as the robes did now. He had learned this language from another man in a different uniform. He was sure the uniform had been different than his own. He was sure the man teaching him had not carried a gun, but at some point, the man remembered, he himself had fired one.

The lead driver finally shrugged, gestured toward the man, and spat on the ground.

The driver bent down, produced a skin bag and uncapped the nozzle. The man became aware of hands on his face, pulling away the rough cotton. He became aware of a nozzle against his lips, and in an instant he remembered another image from another life: suckling at another skin bag, this one female and giving him sustenance. He let out a desperate moan and felt his hands coming out of his tangled robes, grasping the skin bag, yanking it out of the driver's hands. The driver struggled with him, tried to take it back. The man pushed him, and the driver lost his balance and went falling out of the saddle, uttering what sounded like curses.

Water. The word came to him in a rush as he sucked it from the bag, as it streamed into his mouth. Salvation. Memories began to flood back to him: Planes overhead, dropping bombs; artillery shells and shouts of "Incoming!" Laughter coming from the lead driver. How beautiful his sister looked in her wedding dress, dancing with their father on the balcony of their home overlooking the Tennessee River. The driver standing beside him, trying to grab the bag away. The touch of a woman's lips in the back seat of a Packard, smelling cigarettes and her perfume as he unbuttoned her blouse. Two veiled women, no, three, opening their robes, placing his hands on their breasts, kissing him, the wives of a man he loved like a brother, and they were as sisters. Kicking the driver in the face. An Arab man in his arms, the Arab's head a jigsaw puzzle of brain and bone as the German soldier desperately sought to reload and he, the man, raised his revolver, screaming.

Then the convulsions began, the man's body jerking so violently he slipped from the harness and fell, one foot still in the stirrup. As he fell, the bag of water came out of his grasp and he reached for it, desperately, unable to hold on; then his eyes went snapping shut as a new round of spasms wracked his twisting body in midair. He heard himself screaming, felt his stomach contracting, felt the rush of the ground and the pain of impact as water streamed from his lips and he began coughing uncontrollably.

He vomited all the water until the parched sand had drunk it all. He watched it disappear into air and earth, his eyes wide in disbelief as the horrible thirst returned to him. He began to cry suddenly, tears flooding from his eyes as his nose began to run and he felt his bladder voiding, causing a stabbing pain in his loins. His ears, too, felt liquid, the world swirling around him as he lost his balance. He found himself on hands and knees, his stomach heaving though there was no more water for it to give up. His tears poured to the ground.

The driver stood over the man, still cursing. The driver took out his revolver.

Dr. Thornhill was napping upstairs when the merchants brought the American into the lobby, so it was Mrs. Thornhill who first recognized the signs of water fever. The man was far too weak to walk; the innkeeper told the merchants to lay him on the wicker couch. He looked like he was at death's door.

Elise's Arabic was weak, but she overheard and understood the symptoms: The American was unable to take water into his body even as he purged it, and he had experienced gradual but total loss of memory as the water left his body. Now he did not even know his own name.

She felt a stab of panic; while water fever was one of the least contagious of this country's many maladies, there was still the slim chance of transmission through direct transfer of what little fluid remained in his body. She heard the Arabic word for "bath" and felt she had to speak, even though she knew she was unlikely to be taken seriously, especially without her husband there.

"Do you speak French? *Alingli'zia, Hal Tatakalm Alingli'zia?*" The men ignored her and continued their discussion of how they would bathe the man. "I'm a nurse, I was trained as a nurse," she said, "*Infirmière, Krankenschwester,*" seeking desperately for the Arabic word and not finding it. "Doctor," she finally said. "I'm a doctor."

The innkeeper continued to ignore her, as he'd done since they first stopped in this outpost, but one of the merchants stopped and looked at her. He was an Arab with very dark skin and a thick moustache in that style some colonial Englishmen favored.

"You say you're a doctor?" he asked, and she was surprised to hear him speaking in English.

"A nurse, actually. I was trained as a nurse. I haven't worked since . . . since the war. But I've read about water fever. You must not bathe him."

The innkeeper waved his hand dismissively at her and started speaking in a different dialect, one she didn't understand at all. But the dark-skinned man was listening. "Why not?" he asked her.

"If you bathe him, his body will absorb the water through his flesh. He'll die immediately. If you give him any water, you could kill him."

"But he hasn't taken water in four days. He couldn't drink anything, or even eat any food. Each time he tried he purged it. We've been in the desert. He'll die soon anyway."

She nodded. There was a great sadness in the dark man's eyes.

"Then how do we save him?" he asked. His voice faltered, cracked. He grabbed her shoulders. "Tell me how to save him!"

She stood, mute, unable to say it, destroyed by the sadness in the dark man's eyes. It terrified her to see men cry, and Arab men sometimes scared her even after months in this country.

It had been many years since she'd seen men die. "It's almost always fatal."

He looked like he was going to hit her. "There must be something we can do!"

She shook her head. "My husband's a doctor. He'll tell you the same."

The dark man released her and started speaking very quickly to the innkeeper in what sounded like two or three different dialects. Elise watched as they took away the shroud that covered the man's face.

Her hand came to her mouth. She made a strangled noise.

The three men looked at her.

"It's Perry," she said, her voice cracking.

The dark man stared blankly. "You know my friend?"

She stared at him, her eyes following every crevasse that had been etched in Perry's face since she'd seen him ten years before. Perry's lips began moving wordlessly, faint gasping sounds coming from them as he tried to speak. "I knew him in the war," she said. "He was at El Alamein. I was a nurse."

"Did you know him well?"

"No," she lied. "He was just a patient. He had a head wound. Shrapnel from an artillery shell. He had lost his memories for a time. He got them back."

The dark man nodded, a dour expression on his face.

"Well, it appears he has lost them again."

The burning had increased; it coursed through his body. He could feel his loins inflamed; he had not urinated successfully since that time he'd tried to drink water. Sometimes the inflammation caused him to become hard; in those moments, all he was aware of was his sexual need, as if that was all that had ever been or ever would be. He welcomed those moments because it took his mind off the pain in the rest of his body. His lips were blistered and cracked; his tongue so filled his mouth that when he saw the woman's face and tried to speak, all that came out were strange hissing noises.

He felt sure that he knew her, but he did not know from where. Since he didn't know anything else about himself, about her, or about the men who carried him down the hall, this did not seem out of the ordinary. He felt them cutting away his robes, which were crusted to his body with filth.

"No water," he heard the woman's voice. "You can wipe, but only with alcohol. No, that alcohol's not pure enough. My husband has the pure kind in his bag."

"Don't try to speak," he heard someone say, distantly, a male voice, familiar, with an accent like one mixed from two places he had called home at two very different times. He realized that his lips had been moving, that he had been trying to ask the woman how he knew her.

"Dying?" he heard himself ask, unaware of what it might mean.

"You will be fine, my friend. The English woman has gone to fetch her husband. He is a doctor. The English have the best doctors; that's what everyone says. She's a friend of yours, eh?"

Perry heard men arguing in Arabic. There were boot steps as two of them stormed off. The dark man sat next to him, holding his hand.

"There is a cure, my friend. We will find you a cure. If the French doctor does not have one for you, we will take you to the baths at Al Adra. There, anything can be cured. And you mustn't worry about the price."

Al Adra. The words had meaning, he was sure, but he could not find it in his mind. He felt the touch of lips, the taste of liquor and *kif,* the scratch of beard and the moist, slick feel of a tongue against his. His tongue twitched at the intrusion and he remembered that the man's name was Majid. Then a new wave of convulsions went through his body and he began to black out. He heard himself screaming. Majid held him down to keep him from rolling off of the bed.

"Even a kiss will kill you, my friend," he heard a voice dimly, distantly. "My tongue's a serpent to you now. Not so different from the usual state of affairs, I suppose. Love has always been poisonous in the desert. Your English girlfriend seems to remember that."

"Your wife said it couldn't be cured."

Thornhill paused, his stethoscope pressed against Perry's bare chest.

"Water fever is ninety percent fatal, yes."

"Then my friend will die."

"I'm afraid that's one possibility."

"Spoken like a true Englishman," said Majid. "We will take him to Al Adra. There he will die, or be cured." There was a profound sadness in his voice, and when Elise looked at him she felt a catch in her chest, and she heard herself crying, as if it were on a phonograph record. She tried to tell herself she wasn't crying. "He will bathe in the waters of Al Adra."

"I told you, water will kill him. Inside or outside his body."

"Al Adra's waters are different."

"You're not going to tell me some Arab fairy story about a magic oasis filled with naked harem girls, are you? That story was invented for a Tijuana Bible."

Majid shrugged and left the room.

A single tear fell from Elise's cheek as she leaned over to adjust Perry's pillow. She watched it splash across his lips, and his whole body convulsed with agony.

"Elise," he said. "Your name's Elise," and the rest was lost in a siren song of plaintive wailing as he shook all over, and would have rolled onto the floor if Elise and hadn't held him down.

"How the devil did he know your name?"

She lied in a whisper. "I introduced myself to his friend. He must have overheard."

"So now you're on a first-name basis with the Arabs?" said Thornhill.

Elise turned away.

He realized that he was naked, that his clothes had been removed somehow. He couldn't imagine how; perhaps he had always been naked, always. He smelled something and remembered that it was called alcohol. He remembered smelling it long ago while he groped after his memories. That recollection came flooding back to him: His head bandaged, and this same woman's face looking down at him, telling him it was going to be all right. Only that time, her face had not been streaked with tears.

He felt the gentle stroke of the compresses all over his body: face, arms, hands, feet, legs, body. He felt cold hands, and on his loins he felt the sting in the head of his penis, felt a sudden stabbing pain as he grew.

Through the pain he felt her touch, and something told him it should be familiar even though it was not. It was a businesslike touch, as if she were doing something disgusting. The pain in his loins grew more intense as she finished wiping him; his sex throbbed in agony that didn't diminish.

"Let's turn him over."

He heard himself crying out as his erection pressed against the clean linens. The man ignored it, but the woman reached under and adjusted him, making it slightly less painful. He felt her hands again, softer this time, on his back, his shoulders, his buttocks.

"It's true, you know." It was the woman's voice.

"What's true?"

"About Al Adra," she said. "I read a journal article about three cases of paralysis."

"So now you're reading my medical journals? I thought you liked detective novels."

"It was just after the war. They couldn't explain it, but it was well documented. Two Egyptian women who had been injured in accidents. Paraplegics. And one man paralyzed in the war."

"What happened?"

"They bathed in Al Adra. The two women regained use of their legs."

"And the man?"

"He died."

"Well there you have it. Pure coincidence, I'm sure. I'd like to see a more thorough study, but this is hardly the time for it."

"Roger, the American's going to die," said the woman. "You lied to his friend."

"It's not *always* fatal."

"Much more than ninety percent, though."

"You think we should take this American to some legendary Shangri-la off in the desert that probably doesn't even exist?"

"I talked to the innkeeper. He's been there."

"Oh, was he paraplegic once, too?"

"No, he didn't go into the baths, just saw what's left of the town. He says it's only a few hours by car."

"Elise, be serious! We are not letting them take our car!"

"We'll go with them. There's room. We can lay him out on the backseat."

"It's a fairy story, Elise. Don't be ridiculous. Don't let your Irish heritage get the best of you."

He heard heavy footsteps stomping away. The door of the hotel room slammed shut. With some difficulty, the woman turned him over again.

He felt her face against his, heard her soft sobbing. She placed her head on his chest, cheek to flesh, and cried for a long while.

"I don't love him like I loved you, Alec," she said softly, and it seemed like the first time he had ever heard that word. Did it mean something? He felt sure that it did, but he couldn't imagine what. "He's an arrogant prig. I hate the English. He makes love to me like it's a distasteful act, when he bothers to do it at all. He touches as little of me as possible." She cried for a long while, her face still on his chest. "I thought I loved him for a while after you left me. I would have loved any man who was there to help me forget you. How I envy you, Alec. You've really lost everything, haven't you?"

He became aware that he was still naked. The dry air felt good on his flesh. He was no longer in pain; in fact, he felt nothing but the warmth of her face on his chest.

"Have you had many women since me? Pretty harem girls, dressed up in veils and finger cymbals for you?" She sobbed softly for a time. "I guess you don't even know, do you? Probably best that way. Don't think I hate you, Alec. I know why you left. I knew many soldiers. I heard about the things you saw. I would have left, too. It would take an incredible man to be able to love after seeing those things. And you're incredible, but maybe you're not *that* incredible."

He felt her hand on his cock; he felt a sudden surge of feeling, a brief flash of pain, the warmth of her breath brushing his lips as her hand moved up and down, stroking him. He heard her breathing quicken, felt her grip tighten on his cock.

"You were my first," she whispered. "I never told you that."

He arched his back, cried out softly. Her lips touched his, her tongue grazing his own, and everything flooded back to him in a wave of pleasure. Memories of her lips, that hand, her body against his. His name was Perry. His name was Alec Perry and he was from Knoxville, Tennessee. Her name was Elise and she was twenty-three when they'd known each other, and he had remembered nothing. The doctors told him he had a wife in Tennessee, but he couldn't even recall the woman's name until after the news had come from home that she had died giving birth to a son. Her name was Emily. The child died as well.

Elise kissed him harder, her spit dampening his thirsty tongue, and a pain began to course through him as his memories of Emily mingled with those of Elise. The curve of Emily's body where Elise's was flat. The weight of Emily's hip where Elise's was spare. Elise's kiss left his lips, descended his body like a spiral staircase, the trail of a tongue moistening his flesh.

Then her warm mouth was on his cock, her tongue swirling still, around the head, her lips around his base, again, again while her hand rested lower, stroking between his legs, a brief respite and the words from her lips: "Make me forget, Alec. Make me forget you," her breath desert hot on his sex as she hovered for an instant, before he felt her mouth on him again, her fingers curving around his shaft.

He remembered her doing this to him on a barren hill overlooking a rocky plain beneath an endless, endless sky. And, stranger still, he remembered saying those same words to her: "Make me forget, Elise, make me forget you," knowing his flight left the next day. He could feel his flesh leaching the spit from her mouth as his back arched, as he reached his climax with her mouth locked around his cock and felt a moment of ecstatic release as the vision came upon him: Elise illuminated in the slanted African light of an Algiers hotel room, a breathtaking Monet becoming a Kandinsky as it came apart violently in his mind, the flesh of his cock beginning to sizzle as he purged explosively into her mouth, his own mouth popping wide open and his eyes suddenly spurting tears in the very instant he heard her say, ten years before and yesterday in the echoes of El Alamein: "You've already forgotten me, Alec."

He began to scream. She sat bolt upright, her mouth dripping, and clamped her hand over his mouth. Her hands shook as she drew cool starched linens over his body. His eyes poured water like faucets and his cock still spouted semen, soaking the sheets. He felt more sheets as his eyes came open blurry with the tears and he wondered what he was doing here, who this woman was, and why she looked so familiar. He heard the heavy footsteps, heard a cry of alarm.

"He wet himself," he heard the woman saying hoarsely, sounding as if her mouth had been burned.

"You've been crying," he heard the Englishman's voice.

"Crying? Don't be ridiculous. The alcohol stung my eyes. He's having an attack. He wet himself."

Perry felt the Englishman's hands on his wrists, pressing hard. He saw the Englishman's face through a sea of tears. Elise bent over him and dabbed the tears from his cheeks.

"He's very far along. He's going to die."

"I think we should drive him to Al Adra."

"Leprechauns," said the Englishman. "Fairies and leprechauns."

"It's worth a try."

"All right," he said. "If it'll make you happy. But the Arab has to pay for the petrol. It's gotten bloody expensive lately. We'll leave in the morning."

"Roger, this man will be dead in the morning."

"I am *not* driving this man out to some fairy oasis in the middle of the night."

"The heat will kill him if we take him during the day. Even if he survives the night, and you know he won't."

The Englishman grumbled.

He looked up at her as she wiped his face with an alcohol swab. She had a name, he was sure of it. He opened his mouth to say it, thinking it would come to him before he spoke, but it did not. All that came out was a strangled gasp.

"You're sure you weren't crying?" The doctor again, grabbing his wife's wrist.

"Roger, don't be ridiculous. Let go."

"This is the turn, right here."

"How can you recognize it? Looks like one big flat plain of hard-baked nothing, to me."

"To me, too," said Majid. "That's how I can recognize the turn."

"How's our friend doing?" said Thornhill, puffing on a thin Egyptian cigar.

"Worse," said Elise. "How much farther is it?"

"It's impossible to know," said Majid. "It varies."

"Well isn't that just the cat's pajamas," said Thornhill spitefully. "What's supposed to be special about this place, anyway?"

"Once there were three sisters there, married to three brothers who were very wealthy and powerful merchants. Their husbands were cruel to them. The husbands went off to trade with the French—"

"Always a bad idea," said Thornhill.

"—and they did not come back for many years. The sisters were happy, and learned to live happily without men."

"This sounds like one of those Tijuana Bibles again," grumbled Thornhill.

"Roger!" spat Elise. "He's telling a story!"

"Al Adra had been an outpost for many years before the French came. There was water there, an oasis, very important on the trade routes north, which is why the brothers were so powerful. Beautiful baths were created from the natural waters. While the brothers were gone, the sisters became leaders of their village, and slowly the men became less and less important and the women began to run things. The three sisters became the leaders of the village."

"Sounds like America," said Thornhill, and Elise frowned bitterly at the back of his head.

"When the three brothers came back from trading with the French, they were furious that their wives were now in charge. All at once, they pulled out their knives and stabbed the sisters, who bled to death in the waters of Al Adra."

Elise looked into Perry's eyes and began to cry again. She wanted to kiss him very badly, and would have done so even with Thornhill and Majid there, if she hadn't been terrified that the kiss might kill him.

"That's what happens when you piss off an Arab," said Thornhill.

"Instantly the town was swallowed by a sandstorm," said Majid. "My English friend, *that* is what happens when you piss off a woman."

Thornhill swallowed and fell silent. Majid began to laugh heartily.

"Ever since then, the baths have been known for their healing properties. But only for women: men are not allowed to bathe in the waters of Al Adra."

"Then why the hell did we bring your friend here?" Thornhill spat testily.

Majid was silent for a long time.

"There are consequences to everything that is done," he said.

"Speaking of which," said Thornhill. He stopped the car in the middle of what passed for a road, got out and stumbled over to the side a bit, as if annoyed that it was improper to urinate in front of his wife.

"You and Perry were lovers," said Majid. "He cared for you very much."

Elise felt a stab of fear, as if her secrets had been wrested from her. "How . . . how did you know?"

"He talked of you often. He loved you very much. He looked for you in Algiers after the war, but he could not find you."

"I . . . I'd changed my name," she said, her voice hoarse. She looked down at the unmoving Perry, whose breathing had slowed to an alarming rate.

"I now gather. Your husband and you are not well-suited for each other."

Elise began to cry, unable to hold back the tears any longer. "Alec left me."

"He was very sorry he did that. He never forgave himself."

Elise sobbed, her face sinking to Perry's chest. "You pig," she whispered. "You fucking pig."

"That's the spirit," said Majid, laughing. "That is the spirit of Al Adra."

Thornhill got back in the car and started the engine.

"My friend would like your wife very much," said Majid enigmatically. "He only liked spunky women. My wives would have been perfect for him if they hadn't already been married to me. But then, that is not as much of a challenge in my home as it is in yours."

Elise felt her anger flaring still more; she sat up and stared at Majid.

"What's that supposed to mean? That you two had a harem together? That you like spunky women too, you pig?"

Majid laughed, harder than ever.

"Contrary to what your 'Tijuana Bibles' might say, Mrs. Thornhill, No man ever *has* a harem. If he's selected his wives properly, the harem has him."

"Well, that's all very titillating," said Thornhill. "Who lives at this place, anyway?"

"The town is gone, but the baths remain. As do the three sisters, more beautiful than ever."

"Oh, for God's sake," said Thornhill. "I should turn this car around right now."

"Don't you dare!" snapped Elise.

"There's no need," said Majid. "We are here."

What was left of the town had the look of a colonial outpost, which made Elise wonder about the truth of Majid's story. Perhaps he had just been making something up to pass the time. There were just a few scattered buildings looking weathered and worn, and there was no one on the streets—if you could even call them streets. It was all deserted.

The sun was just coming up as Majid and Thornhill carried Perry's unconscious body into a large building. It had a sign in a script that didn't appear to be Arabic. There was no door on the building, but inside it was strangely dark and smelled of spices.

"Through here," said Majid, jerking his head to indicate a hallway. Elise followed. She could smell a wet kind of scent, one that awakened her senses and made her a little frightened.

"I say," muttered Thornhill. "I wouldn't mind having my revolver."

Majid laughed. "No bandits would ever think of coming here."

"Seems likely to me. We could end up dead in those fairy tale baths of yours."

The building was furnished with broken-down tables and corroded cushions and tapestries, like it had all been abandoned in an instant. It looked like a cross between one of those Old West towns and a fortune-teller's tent. Deep inside, they found a big wooden door. Majid motioned and he and Thornhill set Perry on the ground.

"You and I cannot go any further," said Majid.

"What? Are you crazy?"

"I should have mentioned it before. Beyond this door are the baths. It is dangerous for us to continue." He looked at Elise. "Can you carry him?"

"I . . . I don't think so." Perry easily had seventy-five pounds on Elise.

"Then you'll have to drag him. If we go in, it will be very dangerous. It's risky enough taking Perry himself. Men are not allowed."

"See here, I'm not letting you send my wife into some bandit stronghold where she's going to get raped and—"

"Roger, please!" shouted Elise, feeling her anger flare again. "Don't make this more difficult than it is."

Thornhill fumed. "If you're going in alone, then I'm getting my revolver." He stormed back down the hall.

"Why didn't you tell us this before?" asked Elise, looking at Majid.

"Because your husband never would have let us come."

"Spoken like a true liar."

"Please. I swear, this is not an elaborate trick. You know Perry. You know he is a good man. Would he allow himself to be used like this? And to what end?"

"You promise me I won't be hurt?"

"I promise you that since the day the three sisters died, no one has ever been hurt at Al Adra."

"Except that paraplegic man who died," said Elise angrily.

Majid laughed. "Ah, yes. That's an interesting story. Remind me to tell it to you some day."

They heard Thornhill's footsteps down the corridor. Majid leaned close to Elise and grabbed her arm.

"You need to know something," he said. "Al Adra means 'the virgin.'"

"Why do I need to know that?"

"Each person who bathes in the waters becomes a virgin."

Elise started to laugh, hysterically, like she had finally cracked. She grabbed Majid's wrist and pushed him away.

"Just because I'm more open to your culture than my pigheaded husband is, that doesn't mean I'm a complete idiot."

Majid shrugged. "Suit yourself. If you do this you will most certainly save my friend's life, but there are always consequences to things that are done."

"Like what?"

"If he recovers, will you go away with him? Leave your husband?"

"That's none of your business," snapped Elise.

"But it is. Alec Perry is much more than a friend to me. It would kill him to remember you again and then lose you . . . again."

"In the first place, he didn't lose me last time; he left me. In the second place, I'm married, Majid. Married. That's a sacred pledge I've made, and it's 'till death us do part.'"

"You don't believe that any more than I do. Go into the waters, Elise. Perhaps you will save your lover's life for a third time."

"Christ, it took me forever to find those cartridges," said Thornhill as he appeared around the corner holding his ancient service revolver. "All right, now Majid, if this is a trick, you're in serious trouble."

"If it is a trick," said Majid, looking pointedly at Elise, "it is our friend Perry who is in trouble."

Perry looked in such a shambles that it terrified Elise to move him, much less to drag him down the rough-hewn stone stairs into the basement of the building. He was wrapped in a white cotton robe stained with his filth. His skin was dry; where her fingers dug into the flesh at the top of his arm, there remained four deep imprints, as if his skin could not rebound from its previous trauma.

But Perry was not a heavy man to begin with. Elise managed to get him down the stairs a few at a time, her body aching with the effort and hurting in sympathy with his. She made it halfway down. She was getting tired. Below, she could smell the baths, wet and earthy. Three more steps. She had to sit down and rest. She sat on the stairs, her back against the wall of the stairwell, her hand brushing softly through Alec's hair. She could hear voices below, softly whispering as if in prayer. She felt her heart pounding. She realized that she was terrified, and that she felt hot.

"Oh God," she whispered. "What have I done?"

She fought a sudden urge to run back upstairs, until she realized that she was equally terrified of going there. She tried to stand, felt herself swaying, looked down at the man's face. She wondered who he was.

"Alec," she said. "Is your name Alec?"

His eyes came open and he stared at her, dully, recognizing nothing.

"Christ, what have I done?" she heard herself whispering, wondering almost as soon as it was said why she had said it. She knew all of a sudden that she must get this man, whoever he was, downstairs, that she must bathe him in the waters of Al Adra. But when she bent over to take hold of his shoulders, she felt her entire body convulse. The world spun around her.

Her stomach seized and a torrent of vomit and water poured over the nameless man's feet and down the stairs. She could hear his flesh sizzling, burning. Then all she was aware of was the overwhelming pain throughout her body. Her tear ducts began to work violently, pumping tears into her eyes so they spilled over her cheeks and onto his flesh, sizzling, sizzling, steam rising everywhere as she felt her bladder voiding, hot urine running down her legs.

"Elise? What the devil is going on down there? I'm coming down!"

She did not know whose voice it was, but she knew it was very important that he did not come down here. She spat, turned toward the sound, speaking with a voice that came from another life. "No, no, darling, don't. Don't come down, you'll spoil it. Everything is fine. I'm doing fine."

"Are you sure? It sounds like a cholera ward down there!"

"Everything is fine. Please don't come down."

Then her whole body seized again, and she voided once more, and she fell across the man's body and felt his skin burning hers. She looked down at her soiled khakis and shirt, and knew she must get rid of them.

Her muscles felt paralyzed, tortured. She pulled at the buttons, managing to get the pants and her blouse undone, her body purging water still as she wriggled out of her clothes and, then, out of her undergarments. She began to slide down the stairs, knowing that she must fight down the screams that rose in her throat. More water came pouring out of her eyes, and she could feel her body slick with sweat.

She remembered, all of a sudden. *The first phase consists of violent purging of all excess water in the body,* she heard in her head. She remembered reading the words in a medical journal as she sat in a café in Algiers, an annoying Englishman speaking extemporaneously on Russian politics. *This occurs only eighteen hours after exposure. As unpleasant as the first phase is, phase two is even more dramatic: The patient's cells themselves begin to give up their water.*

Then the words were gone, and she knew only that she lay naked at the foot of a long flight of stairs, the damp air burning her lungs as she tried to remember how she had come to be there. And then, inexplicably, she stopped trying.

He could feel her memories soaking into his flesh as it sizzled; the water her body had purged sent spasms of pain through him even as the visions hit. Him in that same Algiers hotel room, beautiful in a way he'd never seen himself. A hard cock filling her mouth—his own, and his hand gripping hers. His body atop hers, deep inside her, telling Elise he loved her and always would. Then the pain began, and he felt himself purging. Water flowed from his tear ducts; his skin gave off sweat that instantly became steam, boiling into the moist air of Al Adra. It was only then that he realized he couldn't see. With the purging, the visions had gone, too: Now he was alone in his darkness.

He felt arms around his shoulders, dragging him down the stairs until he felt a hard, flat surface under him. He felt them unwrapping the robes that covered him. Their hands touched him, inspecting his genitals. He heard them speaking, arguing in Arabic: Three voices, and for an instant he knew that they were higher than his own, that these were things called women, that the being whose memories had echoed through him a moment ago was also called that, though he could not remember what those memories were. He also knew that he was thirsty—terribly thirsty—and that when one was thirsty one drank something called water. Then he didn't even remember that, only that he was nude and being dragged, and that suddenly he felt something warm all over his body and that a high voice was crying out.

He could feel them against him—two creatures, holding him. Their flesh brought pleasure; he could feel their curves surrounding him as they guided him into the middle of the pool. His eyes came open and he saw murky strands of sunlight filtering down from far overhead, illuminating two beautiful faces, close to his.

First one, then the other, pressed her lips to his. He tasted their tongues as they repeated the ritual, moistening his mouth with theirs, naked bodies against his own. He remembered experiencing this before, with many of these creatures, their bodies bleeding ecstasy into his own as he touched them. These women had dark skin and dark hair and were by far more beautiful than most he had touched. They were speaking a language he didn't recognize at first; then, all of a sudden, he knew it was called Arabic and that at one time he had known it well. He felt the women's hands on his face, brushing him with water, and then between his legs, caressing him under the surface. He felt himself getting hard.

In the shafts of sunlight he could see two more women, both naked, one with hair the color of desert sunlight, one with skin and hair the color of the others. The pale one was being bathed by the dark-haired one. She was gasping, sobbing uncontrollably. The two women kissed and the sobbing stopped. The pale woman silently descended and disappeared.

He felt himself sinking too, falling beneath the surface.

He opened his mouth and it flooded. He gulped. He felt himself shuddering. He sank to the bottom of the pool, realizing that this was the thing called water, that it was surrounding him, that he existed only as part of it. Then, as he drew the water into his lungs, he knew that he no longer existed at all—if he ever had.

She was first aware of the pain in her loins; she tried to recall what it signified, but she couldn't. Then the pain subsumed itself into plea- sure as she felt a mouth down there, hungry, seeking. A tongue against her sex, something she'd never experienced. A body against hers, a female body: also unknown to her. Then, suddenly, gently, in- sistently, she felt another mouth on hers, kissing, tongue pressing in. Another woman. Small, tight breasts upon her belly, smooth, hairless thighs closing softly around her face, her own mouth pressing to an- other woman's body and tasting salt and tangy musk. Hearing the softness of moans as her tongue explored the woman's body. This was a younger woman atop her, she knew, a virgin. From the young woman's sex, she began to drink, thirst rushing over her as she tried to recall her own name, and the woman's.

Her hands found the young woman's curves, from the delicate slope of her shoulders to the curve of her waist, settling finally on the swell of the woman's hips and ass, bringing the woman's sex more firmly against her face as her tongue desperately worked, seeking nourishment. The woman moaned, her hips bucking; there was a cry, a gentle sob, and then a swift exhalation of breath as it came on her, the sudden knowledge: She was Elise, and this woman . . . this woman was familiar to her. Had they made love before? That was impossible, for Elise knew with absolute certainty that she, herself, was a virgin.

The woman's mouth did not stop after she reached her peak; if any- thing, it increased its voraciousness. Elise felt surrounded, deliciously overpowered by the press of the younger woman's naked body atop hers, the swell of her breasts, the iron strength of her arms. It was as she realized that she was mounting toward something beautiful, something terrifying, that she felt the woman's fingers inside her, stretching, pressing against her hymen. Elise realized that she should not be a virgin: Neither she nor the girl should be, and all the laws of God and man had been broken by their becoming virgins again. As the girl's fingers penetrated her, Elise came with a brief gasp of surprise. It was as if she couldn't believe it was happening, as if she didn't know what to call it—and she realized, all of a sudden, that she didn't. Nor did she need to.

She felt the woman's mouth on her own, tasted her own sex. Sharp, strong, overwhelming. They kissed, embracing on the wet earth.

"Elise! What's going on down there? Damn it all, Elise, answer me or I'm coming down there!" She had the sense that the voice should be familiar to her, and that it was somehow very wrong that it wasn't. But she also had the sense that she shouldn't worry about it.

Elise saw three women, also naked, surrounding them, holding out clean, ephemeral white robes.

"Call her Adara," said one of the women softly, and Elise understood it perfectly. "It means 'virgin,' and that's what your lover has become. Don't lose her a second time." It took her a moment to realize the woman was speaking Arabic.

"Elise, I'm going to count to three!"

Elise watched, transfixed, as the three women descended beneath the waters of Al Adra, and she was left alone with her virgin lover.

"I don't understand why we couldn't bring his body back," Thornhill was saying. "There could be trouble with the authorities."

"That is not how it is done here," said Majid, his eyes riveted on the girl, who slept, white robed, in the dazed woman's arms as the car rocked softly back and forth. "The waters of Al Adra will see to him."

Thornhill laughed.

"That's not much comfort, given that my wife came out of there with her clothes long gone and some underage tart in her arms that I now have to look after. Is this some kind of scam to pass off orphaned girls, Majid?"

"You do not need to look after her, Dr. Thornhill. I will look after the girl."

Slowly, sleepily, the girl's eyes came open, and she looked into Majid's face. She lifted her hand and placed it on his cheek, and slowly shook her head back and forth. Tears formed and rolled down Majid's cheeks. The girl closed her eyes and went back to sleep, the woman's arms curved casually around her.

"I'm leaving," said Elise, not sure why she was saying it or why it was necessary, only knowing that it was.

"Great idea," said Thornhill. "Let's head back to Tangier. Things were less confusing there."

"No," said the woman. "I'm leaving you."

"Don't be ridiculous."

"I'm not."

"Where would you go if you left me, Elise?"

"Who says I need to go anywhere?"

He was struck speechless for a moment. Then, "We'll talk about this later," said Thornhill.

"I'm sure we will," said Elise, and softly kissed the girl. She ran her hand though her lover's hair, still wet with the waters of Al Adra. The girl opened her eyes and dreamily stared into Elise's. Her full lips moved and Elise heard the words "I've forgotten." Faintly, the girl smiled.

Elise could not remember who Thornhill was or why it was important that she say she was leaving him—nor did she remember who this virgin had been. She had the sense that she had been, at one time, important, and that now they would be together in a way they could not have been before—but that was merely a suspicion, and a vague one. For certain, Elise knew only that for it to be the beginning, it must sometimes be the end.

How Queer?

Simon Sheppard

He's playing with your dick.

The two of you are on the sofa, you've been together nearly two years, you long ago discovered you liked to chat while you jack each other off, and he's playing with your dick.

"You're not a Kinsey six."

"Yes I am."

His hand grips down a little harder. He's sweet, he's cute, you love each other, but he doesn't like to be contradicted.

You've been talking about being queer in the twenty-first century. What the hell does "queer" mean, anyway? You've brought up your usual complaint—that sure, you're a queer man in the postmodern, deconstructionesque, sexual-identity-is-all-just-a-recent-invention sense of "queer," the hip sense of "queer." Sure you are; you're fairly young, fairly cutting edge, fairly smart. But you're also "gay," a gay man, a Kinsey six on orientation's sliding scale, a man whose attractions and sexual contacts are solely directed to other guys. You want to be both. Queer and gay.

"You're not a Kinsey six," he repeats. "Not anymore. Not since Kyle." He takes his hand off your dick, spits on it, and goes to work again, right on the sensitive head. You're jacking him off, too—that's what "mutual masturbation" means—but you stop stroking his cock for a second.

"Because Kyle's a tranny?"

"Of course."

"Don't start in again. Kyle's a guy. Totally a guy." Your hand slides down his cock, that cock you love to feel in your palm, thick and warm, veiny, just right.

"Not totally. Not *totally* a guy." Here we go again. Your hand moves all the way down to the base of his beautiful dick, encircles it like a cock ring, like a cock ring made of flesh, loving flesh.

"Because he has a vagina?" You know that the word "vagina" isn't one Kyle would use, not one that most men who used to be women, females-to-males, FTMs, would use. Kyle had settled on "pussy," since queer biomales called their assholes "pussies," too. But he told you of one transman friend of his who liked to call his genitals a "hoo-hoo." You'd giggled. "Hoo-hoo," you'd said. "I love that. *Oh, baby, I just can't wait to fuck that hoo-hoo of yours.*" Kyle had smiled back, grabbed at his crotch, and said, "Well, come here and do it, big boy."

"God, you can be so old-fashioned sometimes. You're telling me that Kyle's not a real man?"

"Not entirely, no." He bends over, engulfs your hard-on in his mouth, gets it good and wet, then sits up again and continues stroking. You wonder if anyone else has sex like this, all dressed up with discourse. You're *sure* most discussions of Queer Theory aren't like this. Maybe academia would be a more interesting place if they were.

"But I'm a Kinsey six, Kyle turned me on, I fucked him, I'm gay, I only have sex with men, therefore Kyle must be a man. Case closed."

"Closed, my ass. Did *he* fuck you?"

"No, but he could have."

"With a strap-on."

"Yeah, with a strap-on. So what?"

"So who uses strap-ons? Women, that's who." His fingers are diddling with that tender spot right beneath the dick head, the "frenum" it's called, something you would never have known if not for the boom in genital piercings. Whatever it's called, his fiddling with it feels great. Like Kyle's hoo-hoo did.

"Well, some transmen do have cocks, you know," you say. "So you think that's what makes them men? Surgery? Jesus, you can be awfully . . . old-fashioned." No question of whether *his* cock is original equipment. You can feel the blood pulsing against your palm.

"Still, from what I hear, the constructed phallus ain't much of a phallus at all," he says. "That's why so few female-to-males get 'em, right? The other way 'round, faux vaginas, at least those are, well, closer. Taken as a whole. Badum-bum."

You refrain from groaning. "So you think biology is destiny, huh?" The discussion is getting heated now. Maybe most people would find that a turnoff, sexwise. For him and you, it's an aphrodisiac. You put your mouth on him, return the blow-job favor, feeling his cock-head nudge the back of your throat.

"No, sweetie. I think facts are facts."

And the fact is that when you first saw Kyle at that Provincetown bar, he looked like nothing but a cute guy, maybe on the short side, but a cute youngish guy with a darling goatee and a sparkling smile. His voice sounded a little reedy when he shouted to be heard over the nonstop neodisco on the sound system, but who knew? And so when he told you what was what, after your tongue had already been down his throat and his down yours, after your cock was already hard, you figured *Why would I turn down such a sexy boy?* and went back to his place. When Kyle took his clothes off, it was kind of a surprise, though you'd tried to mentally prepare yourself. He had a good body, beautiful even, muscular, nice hairy legs, but down there where a cock should have been, there was just a bush. Okay, so what? You took Kyle at his word. He was a man. You were a Kinsey six. Your dick was hard, that was what counted. And he was so at home in his body, so much into yours, that what might have been awkward was just plain hot.

"Nothing to say to that, huh?" he taunts.

You take your mouth off his dick. "How could I say anything with your cock in my mouth?" You flick your forefinger against his balls and he gives a satisfying little jump.

"Okay, I'm not stupid. I know the difference between sex and gender, right? And I'm not some stupid reactionary with a Humvee and membership in the Log Cabin Republicans. People can say they are whatever they want to say they are. But that doesn't make it so. Kyle might be a guy, but he's not a man like you and I are, not by me. And you're not a Kinsey six, not anymore."

You think back to the argument about transsexuals you had with your own father, a member of PFLAG, proqueer, but Dad was having none of it. Wrong genes, he said: Men have XY chromosomes, women XX. The Russian athlete criterion. The Michigan Women's Music Festival criterion. As if you had sex with genes, not a person.

He doesn't relent. His hand on your cock, his rhetorical position— they're both relentless. It makes you smile. It makes you want to come. Relentless.

"So what is Kyle, then?" you ask. "A woman?"

"Of course not. He's, um, a 'none of the above.'" He really knows how to stroke your cock, knows all the right places. It's bliss. But he sure is being a prick.

You have, of course, heard that "The opposite sex is neither" thesis: Trannies don't conform to the whole binary gender thing, and that's what makes them so fascinating to the straight world, and so threatening. Threatening not just to breeders, really, but to a lot of gay men and lesbians who've staked their identities on desiring the "wrong" gender. Maybe even a little bit threatening to you. But what if there's no "wrong" at all, what if gender is less a two-sided fried egg than something scrambled? Which is probably even more problematical to straights, so many of whom, even now, are trapped inside their genitals, inside the "productivity" model of sex. God invented sex for the purpose of making babies, stuff like that. Like He couldn't have come up with a reproductive device less fraught, less freighted with pleasure, pleasure like you're feeling right now.

"You distracted?" he asks. You realize that you haven't moved your hand now for minutes, are just holding onto his cock like it was the gearshift of love. You give it an affectionate squeeze.

"Sorry."

"Apology accepted. So did his cunt feel as good as an asshole?" That's certainly blunt. By "an asshole," he means *his* asshole, of course.

"Nope." And it didn't, not to you. But it was . . . interesting. Such a crappy word, really, "interesting." Like Kyle was an experiment, a tourist attraction, just another thing Provincetown had to offer, along with antique shops and overpriced restaurants. Actually, Kyle was more than interesting. Much. He was great. "But he sure did suck cock well. And enthusiastically."

"As well as I do?"

Well, what can you say? "Not *that* well. But then, you suck dick better than almost anyone." Which is actually more diplomacy than the very strict truth.

"Maybe it takes one to blow one."

"Stop that!"

"So can we go back to the Kinsey thing?" God, he doesn't give up. That's one of the things you like about him, really, his tenacity. That tenacity is why there's a big, clear drop of precum oozing from your piss slit.

"The Kinsey thing." You sigh. Enough's enough. Why should one way of being be better, more authentic? Everyone is at least *kind of* okay. Except, of course, for homophobes—they're scum. Oh well, maybe you should just go ahead and make him shoot his load so you can wash up and go make dinner. "Okay. Did I ever tell you what Kyle told me about bisexual men?"

"Yeah, maybe, but tell me again." He's accelerated his stroking now. Maybe he wants things to climax, as well.

"Kyle had put an ad on the Internet, and some of the guys who'd answered were bisexuals, mostly tending strongly toward the straight side. Bi-curious, as the phrase goes. They thought of him as some kind of an in-between, a way to have sex with a man without actually having sex with a man. The flip side of the chicks-with-dicks shtick. He said the get-togethers were, almost without exception . . . um, 'unsatisfactory' is the word he used, I think." You smile, both at the memory of Kyle's face when he told you the story, and at your impending orgasm.

"Yeah, you've told me that story. And I told you the one about Marty." Marty is a straight friend of his who found himself in a threeway with Eve and her female-to-male friend, Devon. The only way, Marty said, that he could go through with it was to try and think of Devon as a woman. Since Devon had a testosterone-bestowed full beard and a hairy chest, that must have been quite a stretch.

"He reduced all of Devon to his crotch," you say. Should you sound outraged or not? You have, after all, sucked dicks through glory holes, the dicks of otherwise-irrelevant men. And enjoyed it. A lot.

"Yeah, but in his mind, Marty kept his straight credentials intact. Just like, if you had sex with Devon . . . hey, you haven't, have you?"

Well, no, but you've thought of it. Devon is, after all, something of a hunk, wide hips and all. And now that you know how to diddle a clit . . .

". . . with Devon," he's saying, "then you would ignore his plumbing, overlook where you dipped your wick, so you could keep your gay card, right?"

"You're missing the point," you say, gently but assertively. "The point is that Marty really *is* straight, which I, God knows, am not."

"Whatever," he says, his hand moving down to cup your balls. He cradles them, squeezes gently. Sometimes he just does not fight fair.

"Okay, does any of this matter? I mean, I thought Kyle was sexy. I had sex with him, good sex. More than once. More than a few times. We both got off. So what's the problem?" Your hand is really working away on his hard-on now, the foreskin darting back and forth over damp cockhead. You love his piss slit. But you're also suddenly thinking about how hot it was to play with Kyle, how sweet he was, how great he looked while you were fucking, that big smile lighting up his face.

"Are you okay?" Kyle had asked, when you'd paused to take a breath.

"Yeah," you'd replied. "It's just that this is, um, kind of an adventure."

"Nothing wrong with adventures," Kyle had replied. That smile again. "After all, you're kind of an adventure for me, too." And he'd slipped the tip of his finger gently up your ass, your pussy, just right.

You're suddenly thinking that maybe you'll call Kyle later, see what he's up to.

You look up from your boyfriend's cock, up to his face. Could be you have a strange expression on yours, because he says, "Don't get upset. I'm just asking questions." Which he's not, of course, not really. Maybe he's just playing devil's advocate? You hope so.

So you say, more heatedly than you'd planned, "You tell me, sweetie. How gay is gay enough? How queer is too queer?"

"Jesus, it serves me right for having a teaching assistant at some too-trendy university for a boyfriend." He grins and squeezes your balls just hard enough to make you wince. Maybe it's not a totally friendly squeeze.

"Okay, then, Mr. Smartass," you shoot back. "Here's what I'm telling you. From what he told me, I'd say Kyle's a Kinsey six, and—not that it's any big deal—so am I and if you don't like it, you can get some other hot, hung cutie to jack you off." You're on the brink now, he's kept you on the brink ever since you talked about cunts versus assholes. That's one of the things, the many things, you like about him; he seems to know, telepathically, just how your penis feels to you. Knows what to do. But then, he's learned about dicks firsthand. As it were.

"Tell you what," he says, his breath coming in gasps now. "If Kyle is a real man, you can be a Kinsey six. Deal?"

You suddenly feel like slapping him, at least metaphorically. He's being so hierarchical, so stubbornly old-fashioned, as if he's learned nothing at all from that Queer Theory stuff he claims to love to hear you talk about. But at this particular nontheoretical, preorgasmic moment, there's just so much arguing you're going to do. "Deal," you say. "Now make me come."

And he does, you thrusting your hips upward, ass muscles tense, cum like a fountain pouring out onto and into the hand of the man you love. And, almost frantic with lust, you keep jacking his cock until, just endless seconds later, he shoots his load, spurting onto his chest, jizz pouring down his belly, a bounty of sperm as he curses and calls out God's name. You liked Kyle's orgasm, the diddling of the clit till his eyes rolled back and he cried out sharply, again and again and again. Just not quite as much as this, you didn't. Nothing to apologize for, not really. Dick, that's what it's about. Except when it's not. Fuck Queer Theory. One man's meat is another man's pussy. And . . . and . . . and . . . you reach for a Kleenex. Nothing's ever simple. Thank goodness.

"Okay, hungry?" he asks, and you kiss.

Wolf in Sheep's Clothing

M. Christian

Midnight, and I howl—a throaty bellow that echoes down the windowed canyons, refracts, distorts, bounces, coming back from the city sounding like a thousand dogs, a billion beasts, all calling back to me. I am not alone in this city, not alone in my celebration. And I am celebrating. Dancing in my wildness, screaming in my feral joy, I am beast, I am hunter. My balls are big, swollen with burning seed, with potential fucks. My teeth are sharp and long, animal daggers I flash in the brilliant moonlight, sending reflections of light rather than sound down the crystal gullies, the mountains of offices, retail, residential.

I and my ghostly animal kin smile flashes of moonlight. No, not alone—as their shining smiles attest. I am a man, and though I run by myself through the dark city, my images and my joyous bellow run alongside: no, not alone. Me and my kind, the rough and the brutal, the swift and the keen, we are this world. Its fields whisper our names as we sprint through their grains, the waters quench our thirsts, the hills break up the monotony, the deserts warm us, the snows cool us, and the game . . . the game run from us, flees in terror from our pursuit, and in this give us the greatest gift there is: the treasure of the hunt. I hunt, this night, but my belly is full. I hunt for the other prey—the wiliest, the most clever. I hunt the sun to my shining moon—I hunt that which has the sweetest taste, which is the most passionate pursuit.

I howl and I smile my dagger smile and I run, panting, into the cool night, smelling her, following her, hunting her. Her. The chase is rich, royal, sublime. She leads me on a good, ferocious wander through the cool canyons, past the shimmering monoliths of downtown—her evasive skill musically, artistically matching the beating tempo of my own furred legs on the unforgiving street. At first she is imagination, potential, a musky aroma carried on the cool wind of my acceleration, a trail of desire, a path of fertility that I climb with my nose, follow with my run, but then a different kind of light illuminates this simple world.

Maybe there? A pale burst of luminescence that's gone almost before it is perceived. There? A white instant of a possibility. Then—there! Yes, white; yes, pale; a flank, a limb, a foot, a sliver of back that is there and then is not as she rounds yet another corner, vanishes for an instant, during my pursuit, her flight, our chase. Fullness, an enticing swelling to her. Fertile, a pocket sprite, a devilish nymph. She works her magic, casts her spells. Her existence is an invitation for the sowing of seed, the filling with firm passion.

A vessel to be filled. She might deny this, seek other reasons, other justifications, but I know my prey, understand who I run after through the cool city night. She might run from me, but her goal is my goal: sometime this evening, there will be a capture, a conquering, a reception, a penetration, a mating. Too soon, the sky glows—a yellow brilliance that crawls too fast across the jagged teeth of the city. The dancing lights of the moon burn away with the hard dawn, making the canyons of glass and refined metals scorch into steel clarity, casting long shadows in front of me, fading strips of night. Too soon, the chase becomes hot. Too soon, the city changes around me: details replace cool darkness, a nocturnal preserve.

My eyes ache from the overabundance of . . . abundance: too many fine elements of the previous darkness thrown into my squinting eyesight. Changes, but others as well. At first just a glow on my body's edge, just a hint, a suggestion but then with crawling, looming details. My prideful teeth, my renders, my cutters, my sabers, my knives . . . are they smaller now, smoother of edge? My shagged coat that holds the odors of my assertive presence—is it softening as it vanishes? And that presence, the hard tang of my statement, my marking of my territory—do I dream, a linger of the night, that it, too, is less, is of a different nature?

But as the sun grows in the sky, crawling from its hiding on the other side of the world, suspicions are illuminated, shown to have basis in truth, in fact. My coat barely remains; my hide of scars from many kills has smoothed; my knives are less, their edges indeed gone; my hard forefront, where muscles previously had made armor of my chest, swells now, sways now, undulates now; and where had been just dots, now spring sensitive points that wrinkle in the cool dawn. And my pride, my self, my purpose, my true weapon, my true reason—details there as well, though I might deny them with another kind of bellow, another kind of scream into the echoing columns of the city, a voicing not of challenge and of joy, but of fear, terror. My knives are dull, and my glorious saber is gone. Where it was, only the cleft of a sheath resides. Where once—in the hard illumination of a climbing sun—was straining purpose, fertilization, and penetration, now is an absence, a void, a gap, a hole.

With the sun, I have gone from giver, to taker. Again my call, again my howl. I cannot fight its release, and as the sound climbs and refracts, I hear that this, too, has been taken, made wrong, made un-me. As it goes, it cracks and breaks, climbing in octaves and tones. My saber, now my call. I am not myself today. But if I am not beast, hunter—then what am I? Denial again, and again it holds no safety in the burning dawn. Their world is but two, separated by dawn, dusk. You are one, in this world, my world, or you are other. Hunter, pursuer, penetrator or . . . yes, penetrated. I stand on the hard street, a changed man. A new woman. The dawn meets my eyes, and I see it differently. I deny it at first, try to turn away, to shield my understanding, but like the light that brings me a view of the city around me, perception comes. I do not run. These are not hunter's legs. They are supple and full, the skin soft and delicate. No scars on these legs, no tension to spring, to pursue. These are walking legs, and so I let them take me along at a stately, slow pace. These eyes see differently. Oh, I see the world around me, the structures, the streets, the windows that reflect light—though sun rather than moon. The elements remain, that does not change.

There. I had not noticed it before. It would have been beneath his notice, something passed and not perceived. But she sees it, pushing through the firmament that he has laid over the soil. It is small, but its strength is noble and persistent. Its bloom is yellow, not a brilliant shade like he would spray to torture the eye—no, it is a natural shade, a real shade. A healthy shade. There, wheeling through the bluing sky, darting to and fro in its constant cycle: maybe worms in its beak, food for chicks; maybe twigs for nesting; maybe simply the joy of flight, the freedom of life. There, the cool majesty, the sparkling of sunlight through dappled leaves, of a tree. The royalty, the stately dignity of roots, trunk, and branches. Living, taking part, taking in and giving out, part of the great wheel, the turning cycle. Maybe it feeds on kin of the birds, fallen and decomposed, maybe it has its leaves nibbled by squirming caterpillars; maybe its twigs are stolen for nests.

Whatever it does, it exists as part of the turning world. As do I, walking through the garden—though he might try to tame it, hide it, behind glass and steel—I rest a calm hand on my belly, feel the glow of potential. Cells within, dividing and growing, dying and being consumed. The wheel turns without me, within me. Potential. I receive, perhaps, but as does all life. And, as does life, I grow. I am part of the turning, part of the whole. I walk, and as I put one foot down on the firmness of the ground, the warmth of the street, I feel myself and the world around me—all fertile, all part of the process, the turning of life. I am not a sheath. No, that was his description, his feelings. I am not a receptacle, whose life is to be filled. I am a part of the whole: I take what he gives, and within me it grows, it receives hope and safety, warmth and security. It emerges, after a time, to join the dance, to take a turn on the wheel. Hole? No. Prey? No.

I am walking down the road, feeling life spinning around me, inside me. I am not taken—for nothing can leave life, everything has its part. Ahead of me, the sun sinks, impaling itself on his works of metal and glass—yet with the setting I also see the outline, the flicking of leaves on firm branches, and know that while he approaches, while he builds and tames, hunts and kills, I walk . . . and leave sprouts and shoots in my wake.

One comes, one goes. Dusk brings soft shadows, the world turning as it always does. I do not notice the change yet, if it is to come, my own turning back to that now strange world of scents and knives, sabers and the hunt—but if it does, if this new identity will fall away as it fell on me one cycle before, I will try and hold some of this, capture the feeling, the revelations . . . so my howl might be touched, toned with acceptance, with knowledge.

About the Editor

M. Christian is the author of the critically acclaimed and best-selling collections *Dirty Words, Speaking Parts,* and *The Bachelor Machine.* He is the editor of *The Burning Pen, Guilty Pleasures,* the *Best S/M Erotica* series, *The Mammoth Book of Future Cops* and *The Mammoth Book of Tales of the Road* (with Maxim Jakubowski), *The Best of Both Worlds: Bisexual Erotica* (from Haworth, with Sage Vivant), *Love Under Foot* (from Haworth, with Greg Wharton), and over fourteen other anthologies. His short fiction has appeared in more than 200 publications, including *Best American Erotica, Best Gay Erotica, Best Lesbian Erotica, Best Transgendered Erotica, Best Fetish Erotica, Best Bondage Erotica,* and . . . well, you get the idea. He lives in San Francisco and is only some of what that implies. Visit his Web site at www.mchristian.com.

Contributors

Kai Bayley is a pseudonym for a pseudowriter mired in the Midwest with two nail-polished lesbian enablers, an exceptionally intelligent pooch, a special-needs mutt, and a feline retired from the French Foreign Legion. "Overboard" is a work of pseudofiction, based on a calamitous interval spent in Florida.

Barbara Brown's erotic writing has been published in *Hot & Bothered 3 & 4, Recreations,* and *The Journal for Lesbian Studies.* She is the editor of *My Breasts, My Choice: Journeys Through Surgery* (Sumach Press), which explores people's experiences of breast and chest surgery through photography and storytelling.

Cait is forty years old, and has been published before in *Wilma Loves Betty.* She's also The Luckiest Woman in the World, having the very most wonderfulest (sic) partner ever, Janelle, and three delightful kids, all of whom enjoy their dog and life in Kitchener, Canada.

Patrick Califia is a fifty-year-old transgendered, bisexual leatherman who has been redefining queer sex and politics in his twenty-five-year career as a freelance writer. He also works as a therapist in Northern California, where he lives with his cat and many, many books.

Bree Coven originated the "Baby Dyke" column for *Curve* magazine, where she was a regular columnist for three years. Her writing has also appeared in *On Our Backs, Erotic New York, Best of the Best Lesbian Erotica, The Best of Both Worlds: Bisexual Erotica, Up All Night: Adventures in Lesbian Sex,* and *Generation Q,* among many others. Her first book was titled *Shecky's NYC Apartment Guide.*

William Dean is associate editor for *Clean Sheets* magazine and special features editor for the Erotica Readers & Writers Association. His fiction also appears on Nightcharm, Velvet Mafia, Suspect Thoughts, and on other Web sites. His work is available in print, including *Love Under Foot: An Erotic Celebration of Feet* and *The Wildest Ones*.

R. Gay is a writer leading a double life in the Midwest. Her work can be found in *Best American Erotica 2004, Best Lesbian Erotica 2002* and *2003, Sweet Life, Shameless: Women's Intimate Erotica,* and many others.

Raven Gildea is a tranny fag and a butch dyke, both at the same time. So there. Raven lives in Seattle and has been writing for a long time. His work has appeared in *Best Bisexual Erotica, Best Transgendered Erotica, Wire, Deneuve, PUSH, Art Speak, Hel's Kitchen, Nannygoat Trannygoat, Scars Tell Stories,* and on the Roughriders, Pervgrrl, Playbutch, and Feminist Art Dialog Web sites.

Ralph Greco Jr. is a forty-two-year-old short story writer, published worldwide in the erotic fiction field. His credits include Penthouse Publications, Circlet Press, Marquis, and many others. He is also an ASCAP-licensed songwriter and has played all over the world. He began his writing career penning 800- and 900-number phone scripts. He makes his home in northern New Jersey.

Chris Jones, a librarian in upstate New York, has other ruminations on gender in issue four of Verisimilitude, an online 'zine about alternative masculinities. You can find it by following the links at www. bearhistory.com. You can read some of Chris's transgendered erotica in *Best S/M Erotica 2* and *Wet*.

Raven Kaldera is a pansexual polyamorous FTM transgendered intersexual activist, as well as a farmer, homesteader, astrologer, and shaman. He is the author of *Hermaphrodeities: The Transgender Spirituality Workbook, Lies and Scars;* co-editor of *Best Transgender Erotica,* the co-author of *Urban Primitive,* and others too numerous to mention. 'Tis an ill wind that blows no minds.

Shaun Levin's novella with recipes, *Seven Sweet Things,* was published in 2003. His stories appear in anthologies as diverse as *Boyfriends from*

Hell, Modern South African Stories, Best Gay Erotica 2004, and *The Slow Mirror: New Fiction by Jewish Writers.* He is the editor of *Chroma,* a new queer literary journal. Having lived in Israel for over fifteen years, he now lives in London. You can find him on www.shaunlevin.com.

Ann Regentin has written everything from reading comprehension tests and reference material to poetry and music. Her work has appeared in such diverse places as *The International Journal of Erotica, The Albion Review,* and *Slow Trains,* and she is a contributing editor for *Clean Sheets.* She lives in the Midwest.

Jean Roberta was born in the United States and moved to Canada as a teenager with her family in the 1960s; she now has dual citizenship but only one gender. She teaches English at a Canadian university. Her erotic fiction has appeared widely in collections such as the *Best Lesbian Erotica* and *Wicked Words* series.

Many of **Thomas S. Roche**'s hundreds of published erotic stories have addressed gender in some way. He is a largely monogendered San Franciscan who lectures on sexuality and teaches at San Francisco Sex Information. Roche is also the marketing manager at San Francisco's Good Vibrations. His books include three volumes of the *Noirotica* series, *Sons of Darkness, Brothers of the Night, In the Shadow of the Gargoyle, Graven Images, His,* and *Hers.* His Web site projects include his personal Web site at www.skidroche.com, a weblog at http://thomasroche.livejournal.com, and a forthcoming Web site based on the *Noirotica* series. Roche has recently taken up erotic and sex-radical photography, and is working on both an art show and an online erotic comic book.

Linda Rosenkrans is a writer residing in Los Angeles. Her writing depicts everything she wanted to say verbally but couldn't due to the fact that a cat got her tongue, slipped on it, and then accidentally ate it. Her short stories and poetry have appeared in hard copy as well as online magazines, such as Abby's Realm, Any Dream Will Do Review, Babel Magazine, Cherry Bleeds, Darklives.com, EIDOS Magazine, Erosha, FreeSexStory.com, Get Underground.com, Girlphoria, KungFu Online, Megaera, Muse Apprentice Guild, The Nocturnal

Lyric, Poetry Superhighway, Prometheus, Scriberazone, Fighting Chance Magazine, Thunder Sandwich, Undershorts, Unlikely Stories, 63channels, and many others.

Jason Rubis lives in Washington, DC, which has a far more vital drag scene than you might imagine. His fiction has appeared in the anthologies *Desires, Erotic Fantastic, Guilty Pleasures, Love Under Foot: An Erotic Celebration of Feet, Sacred Exchange,* and *Leather, Lace and Lust,* and a number of Web 'zines. He has been called a tranny-chaser. He has been called a lot of things.

Helena Settimana's stories have appeared on the Web and in several anthologies including the *Best Women's Erotica* and the *Hot & Bothered* series, *The Mammoth Book of Best New Erotica Vol. 2,* and *Penthouse.* Once, she stayed in a room at the Hotel Vancouver, with a smashing view of the Art Gallery. Who'd have thought? She is features editor at the Erotica Readers and Writers Association (http://www.erotica-readers.com).

Simon Sheppard's books include *Kinkorama: Dispatches from the Front Lines of Perversion,* and the short-story collections *In Deep* and *Hotter Than Hell.* He's also co-editor of *Rough Stuff* and *Roughed Up,* and his work appears in over 100 anthologies. For the sleazy details, check out www.simonsheppard.com. Thanks to Patrick for his help.

Annie Sprinkle has been an enthusiastic lover and supporter of trans folk since 1979. For three years, she cohosted an F2M social group in her Manhattan apartment. She produced and costarred in the first F2M trans love story and sex film in 1989 titled *Linda/Les and Annie,* to great controversy and acclaim. To contact Annie go to anniesprinkle. org.

Susan St. Aubin's most recent stories are in *Dyke the Halls, Best Women's Erotica 2004, Best American Erotica 2003,* and *The Best of Both Worlds: Bisexual Erotica* (Sage Vivant, M. Christian, Eds.). New work is forthcoming in *Seduce Me* (Michele Slung, Ed.) and *Blowing Kisses* (Mary Anne Mohanraj, Ed.).

Greg Wharton is the author of the collection *Johnny Was & Other Tall Tales*. He is the publisher of Suspect Thoughts Press, co-coordinator for Project:QueerLit, and an editor for two Web magazines titled SuspectThoughts.com and VelvetMafia.com. He is also the editor of numerous anthologies including the Lambda Literary Award Finalist for *The Love That Dare Not Speak Its Name*. He lives in San Francisco with his husband Ian, a cat named Chloe, and a lot of books.

James Williams is the author of . . . *But I Know What You Want* (Greenery Press, 2002). His stories have appeared widely in print and online publications and anthologies, including *Best American Erotica of 1995, Best American Erotica of 2001, American Erotica of 2003,* all edited by Susie Bright (Simon & Schuster); *Best Gay Erotica 2002,* edited by Richard Labonté (Cleis); *Best Gay Erotica 2004,* edited by Richard Labonté (Cleis); and *Best S/M Erotica,* edited by M. Christian (Black Books). He was the subject of profile interviews in *Different Loving* by Gloria Brame, Will Brame, and Jon Jacobs (Villard), and *Sex: An Oral History* by Harry Maurer (Viking). He can be found in the ether at http://www.jaswilliams.com.

Copyright Acknowledgments

"Coming Soon to a Theater Near Me," by Bree Coven, first appeared in *On Our Backs* magazine (April/May issue) and *Up All Night: Real Life Lesbian Sex Stories* (Alyson Books, February 2004).

"Shoes," by Shaun Levin, first appeared in *The Everglade Chronicles* (Winter), and in *The Slow Mirror: New Fiction by Jewish Writers* (Five Leaves Press).

"Twist," by Helena Settimana, first appeared in ERWA (http://www.erotica-readers.com).

"My First Female-to-Male Lover," by Annie Sprinkle, first appeared in *Hustler Magazine,* 1989.

"Finger," by Greg Wharton, first appeared in *Johnny Was & Other Tall Tales* by Greg Wharton (Suspect Thoughts Press).

"Bridges," by James Williams, first appeared in *. . . But I Know What You Want: 25 Sex Tales for the Different* (San Francisco: Greenery Press).

Order a copy of this book with this form or online at:
http://www.haworthpress.com/store/product.asp?sku=5508

TRANSGENDER EROTICA
Trans Figures

_____in softbound at $14.95 (ISBN-13: 978-1-56023-491-3; ISBN-10: 1-56023-491-1)

Or order online and use special offer code HEC25 in the shopping cart.

COST OF BOOKS_____

POSTAGE & HANDLING_____
(US: $4.00 for first book & $1.50
for each additional book)
(Outside US: $5.00 for first book
& $2.00 for each additional book)

SUBTOTAL_____

IN CANADA: ADD 7% GST_____

STATE TAX_____
(NJ, NY, OH, MN, CA, IL, IN, PA, & SD
residents, add appropriate local sales tax)

FINAL TOTAL_____
(If paying in Canadian funds,
convert using the current
exchange rate, UNESCO
coupons welcome)

☐ **BILL ME LATER:** (Bill-me option is good on
US/Canada/Mexico orders only; not good to
jobbers, wholesalers, or subscription agencies.)
☐ Check here if billing address is different from
shipping address and attach purchase order and
billing address information.

Signature_____

☐ **PAYMENT ENCLOSED: $**_____

☐ **PLEASE CHARGE TO MY CREDIT CARD.**

☐ Visa ☐ MasterCard ☐ AmEx ☐ Discover
☐ Diner's Club ☐ Eurocard ☐ JCB

Account # _____

Exp. Date_____

Signature_____

Prices in US dollars and subject to change without notice.

NAME_____

INSTITUTION_____

ADDRESS_____

CITY_____

STATE/ZIP_____

COUNTRY_____ COUNTY (NY residents only)_____

TEL_____ FAX_____

E-MAIL_____

May we use your e-mail address for confirmations and other types of information? ☐ Yes ☐ No
We appreciate receiving your e-mail address and fax number. Haworth would like to e-mail or fax special
discount offers to you, as a preferred customer. **We will never share, rent, or exchange your e-mail address
or fax number.** We regard such actions as an invasion of your privacy.

Order From Your Local Bookstore or Directly From
The Haworth Press, Inc.
10 Alice Street, Binghamton, New York 13904-1580 • USA
TELEPHONE: 1-800-HAWORTH (1-800-429-6784) / Outside US/Canada: (607) 722-5857
FAX: 1-800-895-0582 / Outside US/Canada: (607) 771-0012
E-mail to: orders@haworthpress.com

For orders outside US and Canada, you may wish to order through your local
sales representative, distributor, or bookseller.
For information, see http://haworthpress.com/distributors

(Discounts are available for individual orders in US and Canada only, not booksellers/distributors.)

PLEASE PHOTOCOPY THIS FORM FOR YOUR PERSONAL USE.
http://www.HaworthPress.com   BOF04